Sweet Temptation

"Charity . . ." Lord Alistair savored the name. "Charity means love, does it not?" And I have a feeling you would love very sweetly. . . ."

His mouth came down on hers, searching, insistent in its gentle probing—and she, who had long since abandoned all hope that anyone would find her desirable, felt an exultant tremor run through her. Time lost all meaning, but at last he lifted his head, leaving her mouth bruised and tingling and longing for more. He said softly, "Ah, yes. Sweet Charity indeed. I have been wanting to do that for some considerable time."

Now was Charity's chance. She could break free of Lord Alistair's insidious spell. She could escape his avid embrace. If only she wanted to . . .

SHEILA WALSH lives with her husband in Southport, Lancashire, England, and is the mother of two daughters. She began to think seriously about writing when a local writers' club was formed. After experimenting with short stories and plays, she completed her first Regency novel, *The Golden Songbird*, which subsequently won her an award presented by the Romantic Novelists Association in 1974.

SIGNET REGENCY ROMANCE
COMING IN SEPTEMBER 1990

Elizabeth Hewitt
Airs and Graces

Amanda Scott
Lord Lyford's Secret

Emily Hendrickson
Miss Wyndham's Escapade

The Arrogant Lord Alistair

by

Sheila Walsh

A SIGNET BOOK

Published by the Penguin Group Penguin Books USA Inc., 375 Hudson Street,
New York, New York 10014, U.S.A.
Penguin Books Ltd, 37 Wrights Lane, London W8 5TZ, England
Penguin Books Australia Ltd, Ringwood, Victoria, Australia
Penguin Books Canada, Ltd, 2801 John Street, Markham, Ontario, Canada L3R 1B4
Penguin Books (N.Z.) Ltd., 182-190 Wairau Road, Auckland 10, New Zealand

Penguin Books Ltd, Registered Offices:
Harmondsworth, Middlesex, England

First published by Signet, an imprint of Penguin Books USA Inc.

First Printing, August, 1990
10 9 8 7 6 5 4 3 2 1

REGISTERED TRADEMARK—MARCA REGISTRADA

Printed in the United States of America

1

Brussels, June 1815

Even with the window open, the room was hot and airless. For the second day running, black cumulus rolled around overhead, and from a long way off came an ominous rumbling, but there was no way of knowing whether it was thunder or guns. Charity Wynyate's muslins clung damply to her slim figure as she leaned out, suppressing the now familiar feeling of panic as yet another stream of carriages clattered past heading for the Antwerp road, carrying the last terrified remnants of the pleasure-seekers who but a short time ago had been rejoicing in the prospect of witnessing a great Allied victory. It was yet another reminder that they, too, might have left days ago had her sister not dismissed the idea as absurd.

"I refuse to be coerced into flight in such a scrambling way," Arianne had said "and besides, it would mean missing the Duchess of Richmond's ball, which, you may depend on't, she would not be holding if there were the slightest danger. Ned told me that she consulted the Duke of Wellington and he had assured her that all was well, and that he would in fact attend himself with all the important Allied officers." Arianne, still full of pride that her husband, Lord Edward Ashbourne, had been appointed to Wellington's staff with the rank of colonel, had been quite immoveable. "He calls them his family, you know. It will be Ned's first official social function, and I simply must be there!"

Charity had listened with something approaching despair. No one but Arianne would account a ball, however prestigious, above the danger to life and limb—her own or anyone else's—of remaining in Brussels; in fact, no one but Arianne would even contemplate attending such a ball in her present condition, though it had to be admitted that even a figure thickened by advancing pregnancy could not detract from her sister's looks—if anything, approaching motherhood lent an added luminous quality to her loveliness. Every feature was perfection and only those closest to her knew how swiftly the deliciously curving mouth could take on an obstinate pout when things did not go her way, as it had threatened to do at that moment.

Yet Charity persisted in her attempt to persuade—not out of fear for her own safety, for she placed no credence in the rumors, doubtless put about by French sympathizers, that Napoleon had promised his army the sacking of Brussels when they had triumphed. It was rather the worry that her sister's delicate condition would make a last-minute decision more difficult, which might in turn jeopardize the safety of her young son.

"I am quite sure that Ned would be much happier to know you and Harry were safe," she had ventured persuasively, though with little hope of being heeded.

"That is very well for you to say, but then you are not married, and cannot possibly know the agony of being torn away from a loved one at such a time!"

It was a thoughtless remark, but then Arianne so often spoke without stopping to wonder whether her words might cause hurt. Even now, at four and twenty—a year older than Charity, and already the mother of a five-year-old boy—she continued to be what she had always been, a delightful willful creature, light-minded and irresponsible. Small wonder that she was frequently taken to be the younger of the two sisters. And yet the quieter Charity, with her more practical disposition, had grown up loving her light-minded sister and wanting only to protect her from every wind that blew.

Arianne's husband was almost as irresponsible as his wife. He had a charming but reckless disposition, excellent qualities in a soldier, no doubt, but he had also a penchant for gambling which frequently reduced his funds to nil and made any settled way of life well nigh impossible. He and Arianne had met several years earlier at the house of a mutual friend while Ned was home from Spain having had a musket ball extracted from his leg. The romantic appeal of this handsome invalid with the merry eyes and intriguing limp, to say nothing of a fine set of regimentals, had enslaved Arienna's susceptible young heart from the first, and before one could blink, they had fallen head over ears in love. Charity, much troubled by Ned's apparent lack of thought for the future, begged her sister to stop and think, but her pleas went unheeded.

Ned had joined the army against the express wishes of his father, the Duke of Orme, whose heir he was. And the duke, a difficult man at best, had retaliated by cutting off his allowance. When his son further defied him by announcing that he was to marry a nobody, his grace's rage knew no bounds and, though powerless to disinherit Ned, he had refused to recognize him thenceforth during his lifetime.

Whereupon Ned, in a gesture of sheer bravado, had taken his dwindling funds to the faro table at White's and with the devil's own luck, had come away handsomely in pocket. Thus, he was able to acquire a small house on the outer fringe of fashionable London, where he and his bride spent two blissful extravagant months, at the end of which he was pronounced fit and was recalled to the Peninsular, leaving the distraught Arianne, already with child, in Charity's care.

By then, the bulk of the lightly acquired fortune, together with Arianne's modest dowry provided by their father, had been as lightly frittered away. Charity had carefully husbanded the remainder, having little faith in her brother-in-law's promises to send a draft very soon, and being unwilling to have further recourse to her parent, who had recently remarried himself. She therefore resigned herself to the expectation that life in the future would be anything but predictable, though it was little consolation to her in the years that followed to find herself proved right.

A sound from within the stuffy room drew Charity's attention away from the window and useless recollection, and into the more agonizing present. How dark it had grown—she would be obliged to light some of her precious stock of candles. And yet the day had seemed unending.

"Charity?" Her sister's fretful voice came again. "Can you not open the window? I can scarce breathe!"

"It is as wide as it will go, my love—but soon it must rain, and then we shall all feel better."

Arianne lay on the crumpled bed, her lovely face flushed and ravaged with pain. Charity, unable to sleep, had been at the window in the early hours of the morning listening to the distant sounds of the trumpets and drums beating to arms, when her sister had come home from the Duke of Richmond's ball in a state of near collapse, having clung to her beloved Ned until the very moment he left for the battlefield. "He was s-still in his ball dress!" she sobbed. "S-so handsome he looked! I hope it does not get s-spoiled . . ."

Charity had given her laudanum and put her to bed. And within hours the first labor pains had begun, growing worse as the day wore relentlessly on into another night, but still the baby did not come. Any hope of finding a doctor had long since been abandoned, and now, well into the second day, as Arianne again arched her back and screamed, it needed no doctor to tell Charity that something was badly wrong, for she had been present at Harry's birth five years ago, and the difference was quite marked. Her glance flew to the laudanum bottle on the mantelshelf. There were but a few drops left, and Arianne might have more urgent need of it later. In the small sitting room beyond, a large skillet of hot water still straddled the few coals, making the air more stifling than ever.

"Hold on, dearest," she said calmly, sitting close and smoothing back the damp, tangled hair that was usually so bright and silver-fair. If only Madame Bertholt would come! Madame had been recommended to her by the landlord of their rather cramped first-floor apartment when in desperation she had gone down to ask his advice. The landlord had been less than pleased to hear of Lady Ashbourne's condition—a small boy was trouble enough, he grumbled, but a squalling infant would not be at all to his liking; it had not been part of the agreement and furthermore, the rent had not been paid for two weeks.

"Well, my sister certainly cannot be moved at this stage, so you will have to resign yourself, monsieur," she had retorted with more confidence than she felt. "I am sure his lordship will recompense you the moment he returns."

"*If* he returns," Leclerc muttered as he gave in with ill grace. Charity refused to contemplate such a possibility and at once dismissed the landlord from her mind. On her way back to Arianne, she had put her head around the door of the tiny room which she shared with Harry, and was relieved to find him in a sleep of sheer exhaustion, the small heap of blankets unmoving. Pray God he would remain that way for some time yet.

Arianne's condition showed little change, and with every moment that passed, Charity steeled herself, coaxing and cajoling her sister through the last agonizing moments with mingled love and fear, in the knowledge that she might yet be called upon to deliver the baby. When the knock finally came, she scrambled to her feet and ran to open the door.

Madame Bertholt was large and comfortable and overflowing with sympathy, and Charity had never been so relieved to see anyone in all her life. "You have done well, mademoiselle," she wheezed as she keenly assessed Arianne's condition. "but now we must move swiftly, for unless I am mistaken the cord is wrapped around the infant and is thus preventing the delivery."

Another piercing scream from Arianne seemed to confirm her words, and Charity, striving to hold her sister's writhing form, felt utterly helpless. "Can nothing be done? Oh, if we could but get a doctor . . ."

"Gently, mademoislle. It would not be the first time I have saved such a child, but first I shall require you to provide me with more light—and the hot water you already have, that is good." Her eyes strayed to the bottle on the mantelshelf. "Ah, do I see laudanum? Then I think we must now make use of it."

For all her bulk, Madame Bertholt was surprisingly deft

in her movements. In no time, it seemed, her fingers had
released the cord and a tiny bewizened creature was between
her hands. For one terrible moment there was no sound, but
already a plump finger was clearing the mouth and a few
judicious slaps brought forth a faint, protesting cry.

"A girl!" Charity watched as quick fingers tied and cut
the cord. Then she held out a blanket to receive the slippery
wriggling infant and began to clean her up while madame
devoted herself to Arianne, who lay still as death.

"By the good God's grace, the cord was not around the
child's neck," she wheezed as she completed her ministrations. "But, ah, the *pauvre maman*."

"My sister will be all right?"

"That is not in our hands, mademoiselle, but I must tell
you that the portents are not good. Too much blood has been
lost." Madame clambered to her feet, her bulk swaying. "Do
you have no friends to be with you at this time?"

Charity shook her head. "Many have already left and those
who remain are much preoccupied with their own affairs."
She did not add that they were mostly Arianne's friends rather
than hers, and about as uselss in an emergency; to make such
comparisons, even in her mind, at the present time seemed
like a betrayal. "Ned, my sister's husband, is with the
army . . . and the landlord . . ." She made a helpless
gesture, and to hide her feeling, lifted the wriggling, mewling
bundle that was her niece, seeing the crumpled face and spiky
hair through a blur of tears. "Poor mite. She has been thrust
into the world weeks before her time, and what a world! I
don't even know how I am to feed her."

Madame made a soft clucking noise. "Well that, let me
tell you, is not a big problem." Her plump fingers drew aside
the blanket. "She is of a certainty very frail and undersized,
but with care we shall contrive. My Marie has not long since
borne a fine son, and she has milk enough for two. I will
go at once and send her to you . . ."

"Oh, madame!"

"It is nothing. And later I shall myself return to see how
your poor sister goes on."

Only then did Charity realize that the threatening storm

had come at last. She glanced around quickly—Arianne had
not moved. She popped the infant into a drawer, hastily
contrived to serve as a cradle. "I'll slip downstairs with you,
Madame," she said. "There is a cloak of Ned's in the hall
that will serve to keep the worst of the rain off you."

As Madame Bertholt gathered the cloak about her and disappeared into the wall of water which seemed as if it were
being poured from heaven from barrels, a flash of lightning
showed it streaming from the gables and already running in
rivers along the gutters. Charity shivered and turned to
retrace her steps when she heard her name called. A horse
had appeared out of nowhere and stood, pawing the cobbles,
its rider soaked to the skin.

"Fitz! Is it you?"

Captain Fitzallan, Ned's closest friend, grinned wryly.
"Devilish, ain't it? Can't stop, m'dear. Dispatches to deliver.
Thought Arianne would like to know Ned was fine when last
I saw him—dashing about in the thick of things with orders
from his lordship!"

"I'm glad." She said nothing of their present plight. He
had enough to think about. "How does it go?"

"Been a close call, but we'll soon have Boney on the run
now." He gathered up his reins. "Must go." He lifted a
hand and disappeared from view.

Charity heard Leclerc's door creak, and dashed upstairs
before he could accost her.

In the bedchamber, she sat rocking the baby, her eyes
never leaving the gray face of her sister as she watched for
some sign of returning consciousness. A part of her longed
for sleep—oblivion. She had almost forgotten what it was
like to sleep. There were so many things to be done, but she
lacked the energy to begin. Outside storm still raged, but
the room remained fetid, as if the aura of death were already
about it.

A sound behind her made her start. She turned to see Harry
standing uncertainly in the doorway, the sleep not yet out
of his eyes, his cotton nightshirt clinging damply about his
sturdy legs—and looking so like his father that her heart
squeezed within her.

"Aunt Charity?"

She swallowed painfully and rose to go to him. "See," she whispered, crouching down to his level with her feather-weight burden. "You have a new little sister."

Harry, who had very much wanted a brother, strove to master his disappointment as he peered dubiously into the blanket. "She's *very* small and wrinkly," he said. And then, unable to resist the question uppermost in his bright five-year-old mind, "I s'ppose we couldn't change her?"

Charity uttered a choked laugh. "No, darling, I don't think we can. She will soon look much prettier, I promise you."

But Harry had already lost interest, for his gaze had been drawn beyond her to where his mother lay so still and lifeless. "Is Mama going to die?" he asked in a small voice.

"I . . . I don't know, Harry. We must pray very hard that she will not." She laid the baby down very carefully in the drawer and took his hand to lead him into the sitting room. "Would you like some supper?"

He shook his head. "I'm too hot." And after a moment's hesitation, "The thunder is very loud. Is it as loud as the guns?"

"I don't really know, Harry." She felt his forehead, which was damp with perspiration, and said with forced cheerful-ness, "Perhaps you could manage a glass of that nice cordial I made this morning?"

"Yes, I think I'd like that."

While he drank thirstily she sat talking to him in a quiet reassuring way, telling him what Captain Fitzallan had said, and soon he began to droop again. "I'll ask Papa about the thunder when he comes," he muttered as he drifted into sleep again, and Charity found herself praying as she had never prayed before that Ned's incredible luck would hold and that he would come back to them unscathed.

She went again to Arianne, bending close and calling her name, desperate for some sign of life. At the third try, the eyelids fluttered open. Eyes, once bright blue and full of fun, stared dully up at her, faded now and almost empty of life. But she recognized Charity and tried to smile. "My dear, you have a lovely little sister for Harry. Would you like to see her?''

There was an almost imperceptible shake of the head.

''Well, later perhaps,'' Charity said huskily, giving her also the news about Ned as she managed to coax a few drops of cordial between her lips. ''Also, we have a new friend—a very nice lady who brought your daughter into the world. What is more, she also has a daughter who is to nurse her for you.''

Again Arianne tried to smile, but her eyes were already closing again. Something that was little more than a breath of sound issued from her cracked lips. ''Call her Emily . . . after Mama.''

Madame Berthold's Marie was a younger version of her mama. She crooned over little Emily and having suckled her, suggested diffidently that it would be preferable if she were to take the *pauvre petite* back with her so that mademoiselle would be at liberty to spend more time with her sister. And perhaps the little boy might also like to join them. ''I have also a son of a similar age and Maman suggested it might perhaps be good for him to have a companion.'' Also, she said to pay Monsieur Leclerc no heed. ''If he becomes too tiresome, we have three rooms doing nothing now that so many people have left Brussels.''

Such kindness was almost too much to bear. But, both then and in the days that followed, Charity was to find Madame's bounteous good nature a constant source of strength. Harry had at first been reluctant to leave in case his father returned, but when she promised faithfully to send for him at once, he offered no real resistance.

It almost broke Charity's heart to see him go, but she was sure he would be better away from the apartment. And so it proved, for Arianne slipped quietly away the following day while through the open window came the sound of the people of Brussels rejoicing in a great victory.

2

London, January 1816

The hack turned down Grosvenor Street and pulled up outside
Ashbourne House. The driver watched with renewed curiosity as his fare descended and turned to help the child down.
Shabby genteel, he decided, taking in the slight, too-thin
figure wearing an unfashionable bonnet and a gray pelisse
that had seen better days.

London was full of 'em since last summer when Boney
had been routed once and for all—poor widow women
struggling to keep body and soul together, bringing up a
family. Though what such a one as this would be wantin'
wiv the Duke of Orme—as crusty an old curmudgeon as
you'd find anywheres about, so he'd heard tell—was a bit
of a puzzle. Get short shrift, like as not, though she wasn't
a light-skirt, that much he'd swear to.

"Want me to wait, missus?" he asked, as she took a small
purse from her reticule. She hesitated as though weighing
the cost and then ruefully shook her head.

"Thank you, but I have no idea how long we may be,"
she said with a smile that made the dismal January day seem
brighter.

As she reached up to pay him, he noticed her eyes—right
pretty they were, a sort of bluey-gray like her dress, with
dark curling lashes. "Good luck," he found himself saying
gruffly. For an instant, apprehension clouded those speaking
eyes, and then the smile returned more brightly than before
as she nodded her thanks yet again.

Charity felt a momentary rush of panic as the hack

departed. The imposing facade of the house gave no hint of welcome, and not for the first time she questioned the wisdom of what she was about to do.

And then a small hand crept into hers, and tugged insistently.

"Aunt Charity, does my grandfather really and truly live here?"

The tremor of apprehension in the childish treble smote Charity afresh, but she stifled her own nervousness to say as cheerfully as she could manage, "Really and truly. Isn't it a fine house? I can't wait to see inside it, can you?"

"I think p'raps I could wait a few more days," Harry said hopefully.

I know exactly how you feel, my boy, Charity thought wryly, wishing the next hour over and done with, but what couldn't be cured must be endured, so her old nurse was used to say. She straightened Harry's warm woolen coat that had rucked up in the carriage, noting with a sigh that he was already growing out of it. As for the streak of dirt that disfigured one leg of his clean nankeen trousers, all she could do was hope that it would pass unnoticed. At least his face was clean.

"Well, now that we're here," she said, giving his hand a sympathetic squeeze, "it would be silly to waste the opportunity, don't you think?"

Harry nodded, but with a distinct lack of enthusiasm.

Poor Harry—he was not much above five, and had already been subjected to more upheavals in his young life than any child his age should be expected to endure. From infancy he had known no settled home. His father had not been above a few days in Paris at the end of the war, in 1814, when he had sent for them—and she and Harry had been swept up and carried off by his impetuous mama.

It would be wonderful fun, Ned had assured them. And so it had been, for the English aristocracy, so long deprived of visiting Paris, were descending upon the city in great numbers. As for Arianne and Ned, they were irresponsible as ever, very much in love and seeing life as one long adventure, and their light-heartedness was infectious. The encumbrance of a small child troubled them little, for was not Charity there to watch over him as she had been from the first? Not that she had any complaints on that score, for Harry was her joy. And had she not always wished to travel? Then, when Bonaparte escaped from Elba and seemed certain to make for the Low Countries, nothing would satisfy Arianne but that they should follow Ned to Brussels, for that too would be fun; that she was by then *enceinte* again was but a tiresome detail.

Brussels attracted the cream of the aristocracy in much the same way as Paris had done. Uniforms of every hue abounded, setting the ladies' hearts a'flutter; an atmosphere of gaiety prevailed, and balls and picnics became the order of the day. But as rumors concerning the imminence of a battle hardened into certainty, Charity began to sense a curiously frenetic unreality about the revelries. Also, she worried about Arianne, who was by then well into her pregnancy. Arianne dismissed her fears. Ned had introduced her to many of his acquaintances and she seemed determined to throw herself into the giddy social round. There was something akin to desperation about her gaiety—almost as though she had a premonition of tragedy to come and was wringing the last drop of pleasure out of the time remaining. Inevitably, her recklessness began to take its toll on her health.

Charity could only watch and worry, doing her best to give Harry's life the kind of quiet stability that his parents, for all their love of him, were incapable of providing. Fortunately for Harry, the Ashbourne blood flowed strongly in his veins, and when the worst happened, he had shown an astonishing resilience in the face of the double tragedy that changed his life forever. Baby Emily too, so frail at the start that they had feared for her life, had with Charity's care, and the good offices of Madame Berthold's Marie, clung stubbornly to life. It had been some months, however, before Emily was strong enough to be weaned so they could make the journey back to England.

She had taken the children first to her father's house in

Upper Wimpole Street, but Mr. Wynyate's second wife was not welcoming, and an uncomfortable atmosphere had prevailed from the moment they arrived.

If anything could serve to convince Charity that she was doing the right thing, it was the conviction that if all went well, the children would henceforth enjoy a more ordered existence and, more important still, their future would be secure. It was this consideration which had caused her to persevere when her initial communication had vouchsafed no answer from the duke; having ascertained that he was in residence, she dispatched a second note advising him of the time at which she intended to call.

The porter on the door at Ashbourne House viewed Charity and her charge with deep suspicion, for she was not the first to attempt to install her come-by-chance within these hallowed portals. "Not so fast, if you please. On what business was you wishful to see his grace?" he demanded in tones of lofty disdain.

But Charity had not come thus far to be so easily intimidated. She said pleasantly, but with a calm authority that brooked no argument, that her *business* was with his grace and not to be confided to mere underlings. There was a steely light in her eyes that discouraged him from taking further issue, and indeed, why should he trouble himself when the formidable Hamlyn would see her off soon enough.

Harry, with a child's capacity for sudden and total absorption, was immediately captivated by the entrance hall, which was of noble proportions, with four marble pillars supporting a molded ceiling and two extraordinary ebony figures, half man, half beast, standing guard at the foot of the staircase and brandishing the most gruesome-looking weapons.

"They look jolly fierce," he whispered with obvious relish.

Charity's reply was a trifle abstracted for already the butler was moving majestically toward her, flanked by two footmen.

They took one another's measure in silence. Then: "Pray be so good as to inform his grace," she said in her clear, unaffected way, "that Miss Wynyate has brought his grandson to meet him."

Hamlyn was seldom discomposed, but just for an instant as his glance encompassed the diminutive figure pressed close against her skirts, his face uplifted in rapt contemplation of the statues, the memory of just such another little boy was so vivid to him that his own face quivered. "Lord Edward's boy," he murmured. It was a statement rather than a question.

"Yes, indeed," Charity said, her manner softening. "Lord Edward's boy. And you must be Hamlyn. His lordship often spoke kindly of you."

"A rare scamp he was when just such an age," the butler so far unbent as to confide with a shake of the head, "but as sound as you could wish at bottom." And then, as if conscious of having overstepped the bounds of what was proper by confiding his thoughts so freely, he pokered up and beckoned to one of the footmen. "I will apprise his grace of your coming—" he hesitated, a note almost of apology creeping into his sonorous voice, "though I cannot vouchsafe that he will consent to see you."

"Oh, but he must! For all that he and Lord Edward were estranged, the duke would surely not be so mean-spirited as to vent his spleen upon innocent children?"

But this was going too far. Her plain speaking put Hamlyn very much on his dignity. If those who had served his grace through thick and thin occasionally so far forgot themselves as to criticize his grace's conduct, that was one thing, but to have this slip of a young woman making free of his grace's character was quite unacceptable. It needed only a glance at the goggle-eyed footman to confirm the damaging nature of opinions so freely expressed.

"William," he said with an awesome frown, "show Miss Wynyate and Master Harry into the Blue Saloon, if you please." Then, with an infinitessimal inclination of his head in Charity's direction, he turned to mount the graceful curving staircase with stately tread.

The young footman, aware of Charity's rueful grimace, murmured reassuringly, "You don't want to take no notice of Mr. Hamlyn, miss. It's just his way." And as he led them across the fine marble tiled floor he grinned to see how the small boy succumbed to irresistible temptation, hopping nimbly from one square to another.

They were on the point of entering the Blue Saloon when the front door opened again and a gentleman strode in, stripping off his gauntlets and handing them, with his hat and cane, to the second footman. Harry stared in awe as he shrugged his way out of a long drab driving coat with any number of capes. The exceeding elegance of dress thus revealed was enough to make anyone stare, but it was his face that drew Charity's attention—a long vivid face with uncomfortably alert eyes, not entirely masked by weary eyelids, and a scar faintly discernible along one cheekbone. Her immediate impression was of an intelligent man disenchanted with life.

As if aware of being assessed, he looked up. Slowly, he raised the quizzing glass which hung from a plain black riband around his neck, and subjected the unprepossessing visitors in turn to an unhurried and comprehensive scrutiny, which took particular note of Harry before coming to rest on Charity in a manner clearly intended to demolish any pretensions she might entertain.

In Charity, however, his insolence provoked quite the opposite reaction. Having grown up in the shadow of Arianne's beauty, she had few such pretensions; Arianne's silvery blond hair was in her diffused to a soft light brown, and the eyes were decidedly more gray than blue, and of a frankness that, as now, could be disconcerting. Also, there was a decided obduracy in the lift of her chin as she gave him back that clear-eyed stare which showed no hint of wavering. He frowned awesomely, and a moment later walked past her and up the stair as though she had suddenly ceased to exist.

Well! she thought. And then, "Who was that?" she asked William as curiosity overcome prudence.

"Lord Alistair Ashbourne, his grace's youngest son, ma'am—the only son left to him now, as you'll perhaps

know." William threw open the door and ushered them into
a pleasant room with two long windows looking out upon
the street. "I reckon this house has known a fair deal of
unhappiness, one way and another," he continued in a sudden
burst of candor. "What with her grace choosing to live in
the country until she was took, and then his grace's eldest,
breaking his neck not above half a dozen years since—over-
turned his curricle in some madcap race, so I've heard tell.
And then, well, you'll know the rest, I've no doubt."
William's brow furrowed as he shot an embarrassed glance
in Harry's direction before concluding lamely, "Lord Alistair, now—well, he's not so bad if you takes his top-lofty
manner in good part. Reckoned to be something of a Corinthian, is his lordship."

"Does he live here?" Charity asked.

"Lord bless you, no. Got a fine house of his own in St.
James's Square." And then, aware that he ought not to be
so free with his confidences, he said, "Well now, you just
make yourself comfortable, ma'am, and I'll see if I can't
find some cordial." He gave Harry a conspiratorial wink.
"You'd like that, I daresay, young shaver?"

"Yes, please."

"Thought as much. I've got several brothers like you at
home."

"You are very kind," Charity told him. "Thank you. If
you are sure it wouldn't be any trouble." As the door closed
behind the footman she made her way to a velvet-covered
sofa and sat down. "Come, Harry," she said, patting the
place beside her. Harry came dutifully to do as he was bid,
swinging his legs disconsolately as together they studied the
room in more detail—the walls hung with blue brocade, a
patterned carpet that was soft to the feet, and cabinets and
tables of gleaming rosewood.

"Aunt Charity?" Harry's voice was subdued. "I won't
have to live here, will I?"

"Why do you ask?" She stifled her unease. "This is a
charming room. Don't you like it?"

"I'd rather have Madame Bertholt's rooms in Brussels,"

he confessed, looking around at the formal furniture. "Jacques and I could run about there and not worry about knocking a few cushions on the floor."

Oh dear! She saw exactly what he meant. Madame Bertholt was such a comfortable, motherly person, and her home reflected her personality. What she would have done without her and Marie during those long, trying months following the double tragedy, Charity dared not think.

How different was Ashbourne House. And yet what choice had she? This was, after all, Harry's birthright—with Ned's death, he was now heir to the dukedom, and she had given her word to her brother-in-law that should anything happen to him, she would bring his little family safely home whence they rightfully belonged. "For we both know Arianne ain't too clever about such things, and the way things were between us, I never did get 'round to notifying Papa of Harry's existence . . ." he had confessed with that charm which endeared him to all who knew him. "Daresay he might cut up rough at first, but he'll come about when he sees the little fellow." Ned seemed to see nothing amiss in leaving her to face what he had so blatantly shirked, merely adding cheerfully that it wouldn't be necessary, of course—he had every expectation of coming through, as ever, without a scratch.

He could not have known that his luck was about to run out, or that his wife would fare no better.

Charity sighed. It was not a happy situation, to be left with the delicate task of interpreting Ned's last wishes to the best of her ability, and just for a moment she quailed at the thought of facing the duke, though he could not in all conscience deny his heir. What she had not envisaged, however, was the added complication of Lord Alistair. Ned had mentioned him often enough, of course, but the gentleman who had subjected her to such a raking inspection bore little resemblance to the brother described with careless affection by Ned.

Striving to be fair, she acknowledged with some sympathy the situation with which he was about to be faced. He must by now have grown used to the idea of one day becoming duke. It would take a generous man indeed to relinquish his position with grace—and to a child whose existence, until that moment, had been unknown to him. Charity would not blame Ned's younger brother if he felt aggrieved, but it was a complication she would as lief have done without.

At this gloomy point in her reflections the door opened to admit William with a tray, and hard on his heels came that same Lord Alistair. She studied him anew, seeking to find something of his brother in him. He was taller by several inches, and his eyes were a deep slate gray where Ned's had been blue. His lordship's shirt points were starched, his cravat a miracle of complexity, and his hair, rather darker than his brother's, was fashioned in the style she had heard referred to by Ned and his friends as windswept. But his figure was well-proportioned, and his close-fitting, biscuit-colored pantaloons gave a hint of well-muscled thighs beneath their unwrinkled perfection, confirming him as something more than a mere dandy. Yet nowhere in Lord Alistair's face could she find a trace of the merry nature that had made his brother so approachable.

"Ma'am—" he addressed her with exquisite formality, "my father has, with considerable reluctance, consented to spare you precisely five minutes of his time." His tone conveyed that he considered the offer more than generous, and as her glance flew instinctively to Harry, "I repeat, his grace will see *you.* The boy is to remain here with William."

"Oh, but surely . . ." Charity began, and then, sensing his rising impatience and noting with a pang the relief on Harry's face at being thus reprieved, she concluded hurriedly, "Yes, perhaps that would be best for now," and gathered up her reticule. "Be good, Harry. I won't be long."

"Oh, that's all right," he said. "I'd much liefer stay with William."

As she turned to go with Lord Alistair, she noticed the faint curl of his lip, and her own mouth tightened. No doubt he considered their rightful place to be with the servants. She mounted the staircase in his wake, very conscious of the uneasy silence, which was broken when he came to a halt upon reaching the wide first landing and turned to face her.

"A moment, Miss Wynyate. Before you meet my father, perhaps we should get one or two things clear."

"I am hardly in a position to prevent you, my lord, though I cannot vouchsafe to be cooperative. It is the duke I have come to see, and only to him will I say what I have come to say."

A faint line of color ran up under his skin, making the scar on his cheek more marked. "Fine words, ma'am," he observed with a decided drawl, "but I advise you not to build up hopes of feathering your nest at my late brother's expense. His grace is a difficult, nay impossible, man to shift when his mind is made up. And since my brother could not bring him to recognize his marriage—if indeed there ever was a marriage—and he was ever his favorite for all their differences, no amount of flummery on your part is like to succeed. In fact"—there was unconcealed cynicism in Lord Alistair's dark eyes as they encompassed her slight figure—"you would probably be well advised to cut line now, and save yourself an exceedingly unpleasant five minutes."

Charity felt the anger rising in her. How dare he cast doubt on the validity of his brother's marriage to Arianne, let alone infer that she would resort to anything short of straightforward dealing! "I daresay it would suit you very well if I were to abandon my mission," she retorted, feeling a moment of triumph as his flush became more obvious. Well, he had asked for it! "However, I am not that easily dismissed. Harry is only a child, too young to fight his own battles, but I mean to ensure that he is not sold short and you will not find me squeamish when I see my duty plain."

His mouth twisted. "Duty. Is that what you call it?" And then, seeming suddenly to tire of the argument, "Very well. But never say you weren't warned." He turned and led the way across the landing, not troubling to see whether she followed, and finally flung open a door.

The room Charity entered was vast by comparison with the Blue Saloon, and nothing like so light and airy—very much a gentleman's room, with wine-colored hangings and a great many books lining the walls. She stood uncertainly by the door, not immediately perceiving any sign of life. But

Lord Alistair was already moving in the direction of the fireplace where flames leaping hungrily around a cluster of huge logs sent light flickering over a large wing chair with its back half-turned to the room. She remained irresolute until Lord Alistair, with one arm negligently stretched along the mantelshelf and one gleaming, hessian-booted foot resting on the wide fender, addressed the chair's unseen occupant.

"Father, Miss Wynyate is here."

There was a kind of subdued rumbling which did little to bolster Charity's confidence, and made her thankful that Harry had remained below. And then a voice bellowed irascibly, "Well, tell the encroaching creature to come over here where I can see her."

Indignation almost robbed Charity of her resolve to argue her case with cool reason. She had always known that this interview with the Duke of Orme would not be easy. His grace had been much angered when Lord Edward had so comprehensively defied him, and father and son had not communicated since that day. Yet because Ned had continued to hold the duke in some rough kind of affection in spite of their estrangement, she had supposed that there must be an element of good in him somewhere. Now, as she moved stiffly forward, it seemed that this optimism was grossly unfounded, and only Lord Alistair's expressively quirked eyebrow, which came dangerously close to saying "I told you so," enabled her to hold apprehension at bay.

"Your grace." She curtsied and then stood erect, looking with some curiosity at Harry's grandfather. He was not at all the crabby, white-haired tyrant of her imaginings. The Duke of Orme was in fact almost as fine a figure of a man as the son who stood close by, although she could only hazard a guess as to his height as he made no attempt to rise. She had no way of knowing whether he would have done so but for the heavily bandaged right foot at present resting on a footstool, but she very much doubted it. He was a lean-featured man, with the aquiline nose inherited by his children, and a long arrogant chin less marked in Ned than in his brother. The duke's hair, though sprinkled with silver, appeared at first glance to be almost black, but it was the eyes that dominated his face, dark deep-set eyes that glittered angrily as she continued to meet his stare.

"Well, so you're the highty-tighty miss who is seeking to pass off y'r brat as my orphaned grandchild—a Banbury tale if I ever heard one!"

"No, indeed, sir," she retorted through gritted teeth. "Harry is Lord Edward's son, born to my sister, Arianne, who was his lawful wife."

"So that's your story, miss. And why, pray, does this sister not come to do her own begging?"

The insensitivity of the question made Charity wince. She closed her eyes for a moment in order to compose herself, for even now the events of that time were distressing to relate. She said simply, "Arianne died giving birth prematurely to Emily, their second child, without knowing that Ned, too, had lost his life."

There was a moment of silence during which she was made very much aware of Lord Alistair's intense scrutiny, while she in turn was trying to read the duke's expression. Surely there had been a flicker of emotion, but it was gone before she could define its nature.

"You have proof of all this, I suppose?" The duke's voice was almost painfully harsh.

"There is my word, of course," she said with scrupulous politeness. "But I doubt that will suffice." Charity removed the papers from her reticule and held them out, "I have here my sister's marriage lines, also a record of Harry's birth. I have no official confirmation of Emily's birth." She stumbled over the growing ache in her throat. "There was so much confusion in Brussels at the time . . . so many dead and wounded, and news of Ned's death came about the same time . . ." Memory, searingly vivid, brought the narrative to a temporary halt, but after drawing several deep breaths she continued, "The children have been in my charge ever since. I brought them to England as soon as Emily was able to sustain the journey. We are presently staying with my father, but . . ." she looked from one to the other, her eyes overbright, "their place is rightfully with you."

"You think so, do you, madam?"

The harsh voice jangled Charity's nerves, but she did not flinch. "I do. Harry is your heir, and it was Ned's wish that he should not suffer as a result of your estrangement. Your son had faults, as have we all, but he acquitted himself most nobly at the last." She hesitated, and then, meeting no immediate objection, continued, "I'm not sure if you are aware that Lord Wellington thought so well of your son that he promoted him to his staff only days before his death, and made a point of commending him for his bravery and fearlessness during the final battle."

It seemed a long time before the duke answered. He sat forward a little, staring into the fire, and finally, without looking up, said with a chill and terrible implacability, "How very typical. Ever impetuous, ever throwing himself headfirst into danger—just like his brother before him! And neither exhibited the least interest in obedience where simple filial duty was concerned. Only my youngest son pays me any heed, and, God help him, he's little more than a fashionable fribble! Had Edward been less cavalier in his duty to me, he would be alive to this day."

Charity could not believe the evidence of her ears. She looked to Lord Alistair, but his eyes were masked by those heavy lids, their expression unreadable; only a faint angry flush betrayed his reaction to the implied insult. The duke, for his part, made no further attempt to communicate beyond thrusting the unread papers into his son's hand before turning to stare into the fire.

"Do you have any other documents?" Lord Alistair said at last.

"No. At least, I have this which your brother wrote on the battlefield, on the eve of his death, and which his servant brough to me afterward. He wished it to be delivered to his grace in the event of his death." Charity withdrew a letter from her reticule and extended it toward the duke, who maintained a stony indifference, refusing even to glance at it. Reluctantly, she relinquished it to his lordship together with the receipts. Thereafter there was silence, until finally she looked helplessly at Lord Alistair and then at the duke, who still sat as though graven in stone, and was driven to say impulsively, "My lord duke, whatever your differences, Ned's love and respect for you continued to the end, and Harry is so very like him. Hamlyn marked the likeness at once, as, I am persuaded, did Lord Alistair. If you would but consent to see him . . ."

"*Have done, woman!*" The anguished bellow halted her in mid-sentence. "Understand this—I am not interested. Alistair, do you have Edward's letter?"

"I do, sir," he drawled.

"Burn it."

But this was going too far, even for his lordship. "You ask too much, sir!"

"My lord duke, you cannot!" Charity exclaimed at the same moment.

"*Cannot?*" His grace swung around at last to face her. "You dare to tell me, madam, in my own house, what I can or cannot do? Your insolence is insupportable!" The wide unflinching disbelief in her clear gray eyes seemed to fuel his anger to a new pitch. It was as if he had to use physical force to drag his gaze away from her to fix it instead upon his son. "Alistair, do as I say. I want that letter burned— now!"

The younger man hesitated, then he shrugged and dropped the letter into the flames. "As you will, sir."

Charity could hardly bear to watch as it flared into life and in a matter of seconds curled to become a charred wisp before disintegrating finally into ash. But the duke seemed not to experience any such difficulty; only when the destruction was complete did he turn to face her again, his piercingly defiant eyes daring her to comment.

On her part there was nothing left to say. But he, having established the extent of his power, suddenly became less reticent.

"So—I must recognize these children, must I? Must make provision for them, and if my lawyers consider his case is proven, even acknowledge the boy as my heir?" He glanced at his son, and as swiftly away again. "Well, so be it. But I will not see them. There is a house in Surrey where they may be accommodated. Alistair, I leave the arrangements to you. The housekeeper at Ashbourne Grange may engage such staff as she sees fit. I make only one stipulation—'' A hint of pure malevolence crept into his voice. "You, madam, will relinquish any hold upon them. You will not visit or in any way communicate with them."

Charity felt the blood draining from her face. "But . . . that is impossible! I have as good as raised Harry from birth . . . Emily, too! Think what it will do to them if we are separated now!"

"Children are surprisingly resilient."

"How would you know?" she cried, no longer caring what she said. "Above all, children need to be sure that they are loved and cherished. My constancy is the one thing that has enabled Harry to remain a normal happy child through all that has happened, and I won't allow his life to be so cruelly destroyed now. If this is the best you can offer, I am more than willing to assume full responsibility for Harry and Emily, and you may forget their existence, as you so clearly wish to do. Ned wouldn't have tolerated your terms for an instant, and no more will I!"

He remained implacable. "You have no say in the matter, Miss Wynyate. Either the children are Edward's, in which case I am their rightful guardian and have total control over the company they keep, or they are imposters, in which case you are welcome to them and may do with them what you will. Either way, it is for the lawyers to decide."

"But that isn't fair! Isn't right!" Charity cried passionately. She swung around to seek the support of Lord Alistair, but he showed little evidence of willingness to come to her aid. His father smiled thinly.

"It is the law, madam—that same law which I have no doubt you meant to invoke had I proved reluctant in my duties." He inclined his head. "And now, you have taken up considerably more than the five minutes allotted to you. If you will be so good as to leave your direction with my son, he will arrange matters once the lawyers are satisfied that all is in order. Until then, you may keep the children. Good day to you."

She realized the futility of further argument; all that

remained to her now was to gather the remnants of her pride, determined that he should not have the satisfaction of seeing her brought down. Her curtsy was impeccable, but she made no attempt to conceal the contempt in which she held him, and as Lord Alistair accompanied her from the room, her back was straight, her head high.

Out on the landing, however, she sagged momentarily, leaning against the wall, her eyes tight closed.

"Are you all right, Miss Wynyate?" Lord Alistair's voice sounded little more than politely concerned.

She nodded, not trusting herself to speak.

"I did warn you."

That brought her back to life, her answer forced through stiff lips. "So you did, my lord. That must give you a great deal of satisfaction. But I mean to oppose your father, just the same. He is quite mad, you know. Any man so callous as to order the destruction of his son's last letter to him without even reading it is capable of anything! How could he do such a thing?" She glared at him accusingly. "And how could *you* collude with him in its destruction?"

His eyes narrowed angrily. "I had no choice. I have learned from hard experience never to provoke my father when he is in one of his moods—a lesson you have just learned to your cost." For a moment he seemed about to say more on the matter, but his next words followed a different tack. "As for opposing him, I don't advise it. You cannot hope to win—he is too strong for you, and the law will be on his side." The look he bent upon her was piercingly direct. "A short time ago you spoke to me of duty. A powerfully emotive word—duty. But duty toward whom? Your charges?" His drawl became more pronounced. "Or did you perhaps think to profit by it also?"

"No!" Charity was shocked. "Oh, how could you suppose any such thing?"

Lord Alistair's glance flicked over her. "Quite easily, ma'am, for unless I mistake your situation, you do not presently have the wherewithal to support yourself in any degree of comfort, let alone hold yourself responsible for two children."

He was right, of course. She had not even considered how it was to be done—only that anything was preferable to the duke's ultimatum. But to suggest that she should wish to benefit from the situation?

"Therefore," his relentless voice concluded, "unless your primary concern all along has been to attempt to further your own ambitions at their expense, your *duty*—or so it would seem to me—is plain," the inexorable voice concluded.

"I have only ever wanted what is best for them," Charity cried. "Which is more than can be said for his grace! However, for the moment it seems I am powerless to help them." She stumbled over the words, the back of her hand pressed hard against her mouth. "But—oh, how am I going to tell Harry?"

3

In the Blue Saloon an air of total absorption prevailed so that the opening of the door went unnoticed.

Harry lay sprawled on the carpet beside his new friend, who was endeavoring to explain to him the principle involved in flipping a coin into a dish by clipping it with another coin. That the carpet was priceless Aubusson and the dish in question was of the finest chased silver, bearing the ducal crest, seemed of little consequence to Harry, whose small pink tongue protruded with the effort of concentrating his aim.

Charity's heart lay like a stone in her breast as she watched the little boy she loved more than anyone else in the world. Lord Alistair had at least granted her the courtesy of permitting her to tell Harry in her own way and in her own time, but seeing him now, playing so light-heartedly, she found it impossible to contemplate a life in which he was to be allowed no part.

Lord Alistair, meanwhile, had raised his quizzing glass to survey the happy pair, and as he did so Harry's exultant "I did it! I did it!" rang out. In the same moment William perceived that they were no longer alone. He scrambled to his feet, his face scarlet with embarrassment, hands shaking as they surreptitiously moved to adjust his disordered livery. "Beg pardon, m'lord. I was attempting to keep the little lad amused as instructed, m'lord!"

"Quite so," murmured Lord Alistair with gentle irony. "A task which you would appear to have discharged admirably. However, we need not detain you further." There was an infinitessimal pause. "Before you depart perhaps you would be so kind as to return the little comfit dish to its accustomed place.''

William hurriedly obeyed and, bowing low, backed speedily from the room, thankful to be let off so lightly.

"You've forgotten your pennies!" Harry cried, running after him.

"That's all right, young 'un. You keep them," the footman muttered as he closed the door.

Harry watching his abrupt departure with mixed feelings, not the least of which was disappointment at having his game so speedily brought to an end. "We were having such a splendid time," he said wistfully. "And I was winning."

"Yes, dear," Charity said with determined lightness. "But William has his work to do, you know, and we must go home."

Harry's eyes sought hers. She looked a bit serious, but the mention of home reassured him. Perhaps, after all, his grandfather didn't want him to come and live here. Happy in this thought, he turned with candid interest to the gentleman beside Aunt Charity. "I 'spect you must be my Uncle Alistair?"

His lordship admitted with no more than a faint lift of the brow that he believed he was.

"Papa used to talk a lot about you. He said you were a most complete hand and could drive to an inch." Harry repeated the words with a certain relish and continued ingenuously, "I s'ppose that's your carriage the groom is walking up and down outside the window—the one with the big yellow wheels and the splendid black horses?"

Again Lord Alistair replied in the affirmative.

"I bet they are real prime goers!"

"Harry!" Charity was pink with mortification. "Lord Alistair cannot possibly wish to be pestered with your questions."

"I wasn't pestering," he explained. "Papa did say those things . . .''

"Yes, I know, dear, but now is not the time." She transferred her embarrassed gaze to his uncle. "I'm sorry, my lord. Harry is, by nature, inquisitive—incorrigibly so for his age.''

"Like father, like son, it would seem," Lord Alistair murmured, frowning down into the eager, uplifted face. "What else did your papa tell you?"

"That you sometimes fought with swords for sport," Harry said, warming to his theme. "And that once he lost the button off the tip of his sword and almost killed you . . ." He regarded Lord Alistair's face with awed interest. "Is that why you have a scar?"

"Harry!"

Charity's warning went unheeded as his lordship brushed the faint line with one slim finger. "It is," he admitted ruefully. "He was a fine swordsman—a trifle impetuous at times, but tenacious to the end."

"Yes." Harry wasn't sure what tenacious meant, but the word end brought an uncomfortable reminder of his papa's death. However, the hurt was outweighed by the lure of being able to talk to someone who had known him for years and years. "Papa could do lots of things, couldn't he? He taught me to ride . . . once, he even let me ride his big bay, Romulus. Only we haven't got him anymore, or Remus." His voice was suddenly subdued as he concluded, "Aunt Charity said they were cavalry horses and would be happier with Major Walters, who bought them off her."

Lord Alistair shot Charity a piercing look and she, fearing that at any moment Harry would say more than he ought, took her nephew firmly by the hand and bade him make his farewells, which he accomplished with a politeness that did not shame her. She thought his lordship looked relieved.

"You will be hearing from me in due course, Miss Wynyate. And now, I believe my father's town carriage will be waiting to take you home."

Surprise made Charity brusque. "Thank you, my lord, but I would as lief not accept any favors from his grace."

"Then you are more foolish than I take you for," he said coolly. "It is coming on to mizzle, and, for the boy's sake if not for your own, I would account it the height of foolish-

ness should you spurn a comfortable ride home merely out
of pique.'' She thought he took a certain satisfaction from
observing the tide of color that mounted in her cheeks.
''However, you must do as you will. I can keep my own
horses standing no longer.'' His lordship bowed with studied
formality and turned to the door, where he paused to look
back, a deeply sardonic gleam in his eyes. ''Should it be of
any assistance to you in making up your mind, my father
is entirely unaware of his generosity.'' And then he was gone.

So it was that Charity returned with Harry to her father's
house in a coach bearing the ducal crest, a circumstance
which set many a muslin curtain in Upper Wimpole Street
twitching and brought her stepmother hurrying from the
drawing room.

Charity had never quite forgiven her father for putting
Maria Sedgely in place of their beautiful, intelligent mama—
and within so short a time of her death. To be sure, Papa's
disposition was such that he was at a loss with no one to tell
him what he must do, and Charity occasionally felt that some
of the blame must be hers—if she had been more caring of
his needs, had not attached herself so wholeheartedly to
Arianne, Papa might not have fallen prey to the first
encroaching female who came along. But at the time, and
with a baby on the way, Arianne's need of her had seemed
the greater, and in any case, no good ever came of repining.

Maria was pretty in a plump, rather coarse fashion and
could, when she set her mind to it, exert a certain coquettish
charm, though why such a young woman of no more than
eight and twenty—a mere five years older than Charity
herself—should wish to marry a gentleman of moderate
means with two grown daughters, one of them still to be
established, was not immediately obvious. There was no
evidence of any genuine affection in her manner toward Papa,
and it was some time before Charity perceived that Arianne's
marriage to the Duke of Orme's heir was the key, presenting
as it did the alluring prospect, destined to remain unfulfilled,
of being admitted to the *haut ton*. That her ambitions might
yet achieve fruition was reflected in her rouged face, in the

naked triumph evident in her china-blue eyes as she waited at the head of the stair.

"My dear Charity! Your interview with the duke has gone as you hoped, then? Well, one must suppose it to be so, else his grace would not have sent you home in his own coach. And such an equipage! The duke's coat of arms is quite unmistakable. I declare, I never saw anything so fine! Everyone will know about it before the day is out . . . Mrs. Allan across the street will be quite beside herself with jealousy!"

Charity's disgust was such that she could not bring herself to answer, busying herself instead with removing Harry's coat. "Run along, now, and find Meggie," she said quietly. "She will be wanting to know all that you've been doing. I shall come to you presently."

Harry needed no persuading and was off up the next flight of stairs as fast as his legs would carry him. He did not care for Mrs. Wynyate, who was forever shouting at him—and if not at him, then at Emily. He could hear her shrill voice complaining even now.

"Well, for all that one does one's poor best to be patient, I shall not be sorry when the children leave, I can tell you! That baby has grisled from the time you left here this morning. I never knew a child to cry so much! One can hear it all over the house! It is more than enough to give one the headache. How Meg puts up with her, I cannot imagine."

"Emily has had a very unsettling time. Meg understands that and doesn't mind in the least. She is extremely fond of the children," Charity countered, unwisely driven to defend her charges.

"Well, *I* mind" Maria said spitefully. "Meg is not employed to act as nursemaid, and I cannot see why we should employ extra staff to oblige you. You brought the children here without so much as a by-your-leave, twisting your poor papa around your finger, appealing to his sentiments in the most ingratiating way, with never a care that we should be put to a great deal of extra expense and inconvenience while you shilly-shallied about confronting the duke with his responsibilities."

Anger rose up so violently in Charity's breast that she could not trust herself to retort that they were Papa's grandchildren, too. As for accusing *her* of twisting Papa around her finger—small chance there was of that when it was blatantly evident that *she* had him so much under her thumb that he had become little more than a cypher! She turned blindly toward the staircase, dragging at her bonnet ribbons as if they would choke her.

"And where are you going now, pray?" Maria's voice sharpened further. "Am I to know nothing of this morning's events? You may think yourself vastly superior, but as your father's wife, I believe I may expect to be treated with at least a modicum of courtesy!"

She was right, of course, but for the life of her, Charity could not bring herself to apologize. Without turning, she said, "I have no wish to come to cuffs with you, ma'am. As for the outcome of my visit to Ashbourne House, you may be easy, for you will very soon be relieved of our presence."

4

Lady Tufnell was renowned as a hostess without equal, a reputation unreservedly endorsed by all who were privileged to count her among their friends. She was both witty and wise, and wore her years with a grace envied by many a younger woman.

"I wish I had the knack of it," sighed her long-time companion, Miss Berridge, standing a little to one side and watching as her ladyship welcomed yet another small group of guests to her reception. "She seems completely ageless, and in all the years I have known her, not one single malicious remark has, to my knowledge, passed her lips."

"A veritable paragon, in fact," murmured Sir Rupert Darian, a slim exquisite whose handsome features were marred by an air of ennui. "So much goodness in one person—it don't bear thinking of."

"Oh, Sir Rupert!" Miss Berridge cried, all a'flutter in defense of her dear friend. "How can you say any such thing?"

"Quite easily, my dear ma'am," he drawled. "I pray you, only conceive of the sense of inferiority it must afford one to be confronted with such perfection day after day across the dinner table. Ruinous to one's appetite."

"Take no notice, ma'am," said Colonel Masters in his bluff, kindly way. "Darian's roasting you, ain't you, sir?" he added, fixing Sir Rupert with a choleric eye.

"Oh, assuredly, ma'am," came the smooth reply. "I am at her ladyship's feet, I assure you. How could anyone suppose otherwise?"

She gave a little titter of relief. "How, indeed! Though

I declare that for a moment I almost believed you.''

Darian, finding Miss Berridge poor sport, looked around for a more enlivening prey. A fresh stirring in the doorway brought his quizzing glass into play. ''Ah, I see Lady Vane arriving with the delectable Melissa. I wonder if they have heard yet about Ashbourne?''

It was so casually said that for a moment the full import was not appreciated. Then, imperceptibly, the group about him drew closer. Sir Rupert had at times a viperish tongue, but there was no denying that he was always first with any hint of scandal—and even the most fair-minded of people relished a little scandal now and then, especially when it concerned one who was in general thought to be above reproach.

''Why, what is this, then?'' grunted the colonel.

Sir Rupert waited, eyeglass raised to mark the graceful advance of a beautiful brunette, savoring the moment until he was reasonably sure that his reply would reach the ears of the Honorable Melissa Vane. ''Rumor has it that he no longer ranks as Orme's heir,'' he drawled. ''He has been supplanted by Edward's son, a mere babe. Diverting, is it not? One wonders if he will show his face this evening.''

''That was not kind in you, Darian,'' murmured a quiet voice.

Without troubling to turn his head toward the fashionable young gentleman at his shoulder, he replied, ''But I am seldom kind, my dear Trowbridge. It does not amuse me.''

Mr. Theodore Trowbridge was well used to parrying Sir Rupert's barbed thrusts and, having made his point, knew better than to pursue the argument. Instead, he bowed to his companions and moved hurriedly to Miss Vane's side, greeting her in his amiable, unruffled way.

Melissa Vane carried her nineteen years with assurance, in the certain knowledge that her beauty was without rival. Her figure was slender, her face an exquisite oval with which every feature was perfection, the whole dominated by the brilliance of thickly lashed blue eyes. But for once those much vaunted sapphire eyes were clouded.

"Is it true, Theo?" she asked in tones of suppressed agitation. "About Alistair?"

"My dear ma'am, I am as much in the dark as you. Been out of town for several days, d'you see, visiting the parents. Don't care much for the country, in the general way of things, but one occasionally feels a sense of duty . . ." He sensed a certain impatience in her. "Forgive me . . . prattling on like that."

But Melissa hardly heard him. Her mind was racing with a confusion of thoughts. She had been besieged by suitors last year, during her first Season, but she had kept them all dangling. Only when her papa had read in the paper of the death in battle of the Duke of Orme's heir did her destiny become clear: Lord Alistair Ashbourne should be the fortunate recipient of her heart and her hand. Already he was one of the greatest prizes on the Marriage Mart, his wealth prodigious, his looks sighed after by many of her friends, though she had always found them rather austere. However, she was more than ready to think him the most handsome man in the world in the light of his latest and most alluring asset—namely that he had become overnight, as it were, the heir to the Duke of Orme. And likewise her ambition was instantly fixed upon becoming, in the fullness of time, a duchess.

Her mind made up, and her choice approved by her mama, there had been the trifling matter of engaging Lord Alistair's interest, for he had never been at her feet along with the rest, though she had occasionally seen him glancing at her in a way guaranteed to put most young ladies to the blush. She had never doubted her ability to win his affections and her confidence had not been misplaced.

Now, if one were to believe that tiresome creature, Darian, Fate in the unlikely guise of a small boy was set to rob her of her much prized destiny. If it should prove to be true, something must be done about it, and if Alistair was as mad for her as he professed to be, he must be made aware of her feelings, must appreciate how deeply she revered his family's noble lineage, and find some way to discredit the child's claim. They had been betrothed for several months, her mama being firmly of the opinion that one did not vulgarly rush into marriage, and in any case, his lordship's bereavement would inevitably have cast a cloud over the ceremony. But Melissa had been content to wait, preening herself with the thought that her wedding, arranged for the end of May, would undoubtedly be one of the highlights of the coming Season. And so it would be. Her chin lifted stubbornly. Nothing must be allowed to dim the magnificence of that occasion.

"But surely," she said, "the duke must have known if Edward had a son. It seems very odd to me, his coming out of the blue like that."

"Oh, I don't know . . . circumstances being what they were . . . family squabbles and the like. Ned was a hothead, y'know, though everyone liked him. And then, the suddenness of his end . . . Bad business." Mr. Trowbridge shook his head. "As for Orme—close as wax when he chooses. No reason why he should let on if he did know. Wouldn't give you the time of day if it didn't suit him."

But Melissa was no longer listening. Her gaze had gone past him, drawn to the doorway where a familiar figure was presently exchanging politenesses with their large, amiable hostess. Something he said to her made her ample bosom shake, and she tapped him with her fan. A moment later, Lord Alistair was making his unhurried way down the room, seemingly unaware that many pairs of eyes were upon him.

"My dear." He was taking her hand, raising it to his lips, smiling into her eyes. "So this is the new gown." His finger brushed the ivory silk with an easy familiarity. "Vastly becoming. I vow, there is scarcely a gentleman in the room who will not be envying me."

Such compliments seldom failed to divert her, but his seeming ignorance of the interest being accorded him overshadowed all else. "Alistair . . ." she began urgently.

"Not now, my love, and certainly not here," he said, and although his eyes still smiled, there was a note in his voice which warned her not to proceed. He lifted his gaze to encompass Mr. Trowbridge, who had discreetly stepped back several paces. His smile took on a hint of mockery. "Theo, I believe I stand in your debt."

"Do you?" His friend, mistrusting him in his present mood, was wary. "Damned if I know why."

"Why, for looking after Melissa so well, my boy. What else?" The bland reply disguised a more serious message.

"Ah. Quite so." It was downright unnerving, Mr. Trowbridge reflected, not for the first time—the way Alistair had of knowing things almost before one knew them oneself. "Think nothing of it, Stair. Happy to be of service."

"I would have been here earlier but for the most extraordinary circumstance." Lord Alistair raised his voice to ensure that his words would be heard by all close enough to hear. "You will scarce believe this, my dear Melissa—Ned's children have descended upon my father from Brussels in their aunt's charge without a word of warning. His house has been like Bedlam all day, with so many arrangements to be made." Over Miss Vane's head, his eyes met Darian's. "Diverting, is it not?"

The slight pressure of his lordship's fingers on hers constrained Melissa to make some reply. She knew not what she said, nor was she aware that the fury in her breast at this cruel turn of fate gave an added brilliance to her smile, at which Sir Rupert's eyebrow lifted eloquently.

Meeting Lord Alistair later in the card room, Sir Rupert was at him most urbane. "My felicitations, Ashbourne. Though I confess the mind balks somewhat at the prospect of our noted Nonpareil as the family man."

"It does indeed," Lord Alistair returned with equal civility. "However, you may be easy. The children are not my responsibility, thank God. I have merely engaged to assist my father in setting a few arrangements in train."

"You take it all remarkably well, I must say," drawled Sir Rupert, adding with a touch of spitefulness, "Let us hope that your prospective father-in-law will receive the tidings with equal felicity."

Lord Alistair's mouth tightened, but he would not be drawn. The baronet realized this, and having reached the faro table, he bowed mockingly and begged to be excused. Mr.

Trowbridge, watching the finicky exquisite settle himself, murmured softly, "I wonder no one has drawn Darian's cork before now, except that he's not a man that anyone but a fool would care to cross. Even so, I don't how you manage to keep your hands from his throat."

Lord Alistair turned him gently in the direction of the door. "But then, I suspect that was exactly what he wished me to do, my dear Theo, and you would not have me gratify his whim?"

"Rather not! But you'll allow he will delight in making things devilish uncomfortable for you with his infernal innuendos . . . for Melissa, too." By now they were crossing the hall, and for the moment alone. He ventured tentatively, "I fear Darian was right about Vane. I have no wish to be uncharitable about your future father-in-law, but I never knew a name to fit anyone so admirably—as pretentious a man as I ever met. Daresay he won't be best pleased to learn that his daughter's prospects of one day becoming a duchess have suffered a reverse."

Mr. Trowbridge was about to recall the scandal involving Melissa's only brother, a vicious young man whose habits had led to his being hastily shipped off to India under a cloud lest he sully the family name, but a swift glance at Alistair's face caused wiser counsels to prevail. In fact, his friend was silent for so long that he wondered if he had touched a raw nerve. Only a real concern made him persevere, albeit tentatively. "I suppose there ain't any doubt of the child being Ned's?"

His lordship had a sudden vision of young Harry, and, quite unbidden, of the young woman who seemed to love him so fiercely. "None at all, I should think," he said.

"And you don't mind?"

At this, Lord Alistair stopped in his tracks and turned, his eyes slate hard. "Mind? Well of course I mind. The whole affair is damnable from beginning to end, with my father behaving like the devil incarnate! But what would you have me do about it?"

His young friend looked taken aback. "Me? Lord, Stair,

it's not for me to say!" And tentatively, "This ain't like you
at all."

"No—no, you're right, it isn't." Alistair shrugged, and
a faint wry smile made his face less austere. "My apologies.
Unforgivable to vent one's spleen on friends. It isn't the
child's doing, either. The possibility was always there. It
is, as ever, his grace who has set me all on end! As for
Darian, let him but try to harm me or mine and I shall deal
with him."

There was a note in his voice that caused Mr. Trowbridge
to shudder inwardly. It had been obvious to him for years
that something more than mutual dislike existed between
Alistair and the baronet—and knowing the two of 'em,
there'd be a woman in it somewhere; in Mr. Trowbridge's
experience, there was always a woman at the root of such
matters. In an attempt to restore equanimity he observed
prosaically that it would probably all blow over in no time,
and no harm done.

"I hope you may be right," said Lord Alistair.

It was quite late into the evening when he managed to get
Melissa to himself, and ignoring her protests, drew her into
a vacant anteroom and closed the door.

"Alistair, you must not . . . this is most unwise. Mama
would have a fit if she should learn of it!"

"Oh, surely not? Lady Vane is made of sterner stuff."
He took her chin masterfully between long slim fingers,
tilting her lovely face toward him. "Besides, what am I to
do when you prove so elusive? You have been avoiding me,
I think?"

"No . . . no, of course I haven't. What a ridiculous thing
to say!" But her voice was a trifle haughty and lacked
conviction. He let her words hang unchallenged in the air,
until finally she exclaimed, "Well, can you blame me?
Everyone is talking!"

"Yes, I have no doubt they are, beloved. But what is that
to us?"

He felt her stiffen, and there was an angry sparkle in her
eyes. "I should have thought that was quite plain! How do

you suppose I felt—hearing *that man* gloating over your misfortune and knowing full well that he meant it for my ears? I believe I am not out in thinking that you might have had more consideration for my feelings!"

Lord Alistair released her at once, and stepped away, his manner suddenly cool. "Are you not being a trifle over-sensitive, my dear? My misfortune, as you are pleased to call it, is hardly the stuff of high drama. Had you not been promised to Lady Jersey this afternoon, I daresay I may have called upon you to tell you what had happened, but I could hardly be expected to know that Darian and his like would learn of it so soon."

This was not at all the reaction she had expected. He had been an indulgent suitor thus far, and so accustomed was she to having her own way in all things that she had never doubted her ability to manipulate him. But worry had made her careless, and she saw at once that if Alistair was to be brought around her finger, as she intended he should be, she would need to use guile. For all that Mama was incensed by what had happened, he was still highly eligible, and she had no wish to lose him. And in any case, although the arrival upon the scene of his brother's child was tiresome, time was on their side. The boy was young, anything could happen. It was a known fact that young children were a prey to any number of ailments!

Thus reassured, she regarded her beloved through veiled lashes and uttered a tiny sob.

It had exactly the effect she desired, making Alistair uncomfortably aware of how hurtful his sharpness had been. Suppressing his irritation, he took her in his arms again. One glistening tear rolled down her petal-soft cheek and he wiped it away with the lightest of touches. "Come now, dearest. I would not have us come to cuffs, so let us agree that I am a thoughtless clod not to have forewarned you, and have done with it. I daresay your mama is not best pleased by Darian's mischiefmaking, and has made her feelings known to you. Is that it?"

Melissa murmured something incoherent, her head turned aside submissively, affording him a tantalizing glimpse of dark curls against the slim creamy-white column of her neck.

"My dear, this is all very silly," he said huskily. "I will speak to your mama—set her mind at rest. And I promise you, the children will make no difference to our lives. They are to go to the country almost at once."

She gave a hiccuping sob and still would not look at him. "How can you pretend they w-will make no difference? Sir Rupert s-said that the boy is now your father's heir!"

He was very still suddenly, his eyes seeking her face. "And that matters so much to you?"

"Well, of course it matters!" She looked up then, dazzling him with the brilliance of her loving gaze. "I do so *feel* for you, you see! And I cannot bear that you should be denied your rightful place in such a shabby way!"

Relief made him quizzical. "My dearest girl—if that is all, you may stop worrying your pretty head." He bent to kiss her very gently. "I don't give a toss about the succession. In any case, my father could well outlive the lot of us. If he does not . . . well, we shall see. In the meantime, I had hoped you might help me to engage nursemaids and the like. I haven't the first idea how one goes about such things, but I'm sure Lady Vane will be able to give me the benefit of her own experience—and only consider how that will frustrate tattler-mongers like Darian!"

Melissa agreed, smiled prettily, and lay her head against his coat, well pleased.

5

Charity folded the last of Harry's new shirts and laid it in the portmanteau with the rest. She had been given leave to purchase everything the children might require, and to charge it to the duke's account, and because they both desperately needed new clothes she had swallowed her pride and done so, blanking out of her mind why she was doing it.

But now, too quickly, the days were passing. Telling Harry had been bad enough; she thought that nothing would ever equal, for sheer anguish, the moment when Harry had realized that she wouldn't be coming with them. At first he had been quite excited at the thought of going to the country, especially when she had assured him that the duke would not be there.

"I 'spect there'll be horses, don't you, Aunt Charity? And lots of places to explore. Just you and me at first, of course, until Emily grows enough . . ." And when she had finally made him understand that she would not be coming, he had fallen silent and then said valiantly, "Oh, well, me and Emily won't go either."

It had been a long, painful struggle to convince him, and when the truth at last sank in, he had cried as she had never seen him cry before—and worse, much worse, when she tried to comfort him, he had rounded on her in a fury of bitter accusation, stuttering between the sobs that racked his small body that she didn't truly want him any more or she wouldn't be sending him away. The whole household had heard him finally clattering up the stairs to fling himself on the bed, there to cry himself to sleep.

"What that child needs is discipline," Maria had observed

unwisely, meeting Charity just beyond the drawing room door, but her words had died before the expression in Charity's eyes.

In the room that served as a nursery, Emily lay sleeping in that trustful way babies have, one tiny hand flung up. She was still very small for her age, and was inclined to take a chill at the slightest provocation. Automatically, Charity stooped to tuck the blanket more firmly around her. She must remember to tell whoever was to look after Emily that she needed special care. Please God, she at least was still too young to feel the hurt of being abandoned to strangers.

"You mustn't tek it so hard, Miss Charity," Meg had said, finding her later sitting dry-eyed by Harry's bed, staring unwaveringly at him as he slept. She had attempted to comfort her. "Children is like corks—never down for long, no matter what. Not but what that duke ain't got a lot to answer for with his highty-tighty ways, takin' them two poor little mites away from you when it's clear as day to anyone with eyes to see that you've been better'n a mother to 'em. But what I say is, the Lord has his ways, so his grace'd better look out, for no good'll come to him out of this piece of work." Having said her piece, Meg peered at the rigid figure, not knowing if Miss Charity had heard a word she'd said. Then she sighed and concluded with false cheerfulness, "Well, you just drink that tea I brought you while it's hot. Fell out of Madam's caddy, it did! Like as not, it'll make you feel better."

That was asking too much, but the next few days had to be got through somehow. She had had another long talk with Harry, explaining to him as clearly as she could to so young a child why he had to go away; less easy, without revealing the spitefulness of an embittered old man, was the task of explaining why she was not to go with them. She hoped she had at last managed to convince him that it was not through any want of love on her part.

But although Harry accepted, he remained withdrawn, doing all that he was bid without argument but with a face of stone that worried Charity more than a display of rebellion would have done, while Emily—no doubt sensing the general

mood—protested with increased vigor. It was with a curious
kind of relief that she at last received the letter from Lord
Alistair, informing her that the children should be ready to
leave at ten o'clock on the following morning.

The last night she sat by the window with Harry. "Listen
to me, my dear. The fact that we can't be together for a while
won't mean that I love you any the less." She drew his
attention to the evening star, winking brighter than all the
rest in the early dusk. "Every evening," she said quietly,
"I shall look out at that star and say a prayer for you and
Emily—and if you will look out of your window and do the
same for me, it will be like a special kind of talking to one
another."

"But I might be too far away to see it," he said
tremulously.

"You won't be, I promise. It's a magic star—you'll be
able to see it wherever you are. So, shall we make a solemn
pact?"

"Well, all right." They joined hands and closed their eyes,
and afterward he said, a little more cheerfully, "but you will
come and see us, too?"

"The moment your grandfather will permit it," she
vowed, hugging him and hoping for a miracle.

By a quarter to the hour on the following morning they
were assembled in the downstairs parlor—Harry quiet and
unfamiliarly neat in his new clothes, while Emily was for
once on her best behavior as she crooned softly and played
with the pink ribbons on her bonnet.

Charity maintained a determinedly bright, if one-sided,
conversation, until at last she heard the unmistakable sound
of a carriage approaching and stopping outside. Harry heard
it, too, and moved a step closer to her. They listened to the
heavy tread of Higgins, her father's manservant, as he
answered the summons of the door knocker.

And then Lord Alistair was filling the tiny parlor with his
presence. He was dressed for riding, and one corner of
Charity's mind registered appreciation of the well-cut olive
green coat and close-fitting buckskin breeches beneath his
open topcoat and of riding boots whose mirrorlike sheen must

have entailed hours of polishing on the part of his lordship's valet. But overshadowing all else was the necessity to keep her composure until the last.

They exchanged formal greetings, and then he said tersely, "You are punctual, I see. Good. I dislike protracted farewells. John, you may take the boxes out to the carriage."

A burly groom came in and tipped his hat politely to Charity before hoisting the portmanteau under one arm and grasping the two shabby bags in the other. "This the lot, is it, ma'am?"

She replied in a stifled voice that it was and he departed, edging his way, crabwise, through the doorway. In his place came a slim, severe-looking young woman in a dark service-able pelisse and a neat round bonnet.

"This is Nurse Fenton, Miss Wynyate. She will be taking particular charge of the baby."

For a moment Charity clung to her niece as if she could not bear to part with her. "You will look after Emily most particularly," she said impulsively. "Her constitution has been delicate from birth, which makes her prone to illness. I fear it can also make her fractious at times."

"I am well used to dealing with fractious infants, madam," the nurse said in a cool, complacent way that filled Charity with apprehension, making her want nothing so much as to turn and run with the children—anywhere away from these cold, uncaring people. But there was nowhere to run—no choice in fact but to drop a last kiss on the baby's forehead before relinquishing her. As the nurse's arms closed firmly around her, Emily's bright eyes vanished in a mass of angry red wrinkles and her mouth began to pucker.

"Oh dear." Charity instinctively stretched out a hand, but even as the first piercing scream of indignation found voice the nurse was walking swiftly to the door and out to the waiting carriage. Lord Alistair frowned momentarily, and then, mastering his feelings, turned his attention to his nephew.

"Well now, Harry? Are you ready?"

Instant panic flashed into Harry's eyes and he moved even

closer to Charity, his hand fumbling for hers. She took it in a firm grasp and bent to say quietly and steadily, "It is time, my dear. Remember all that I have told you. Try to be a good boy and do as you are bid. And take care of Emily. As she gets a little older she will look to you, her big brother, for love and example." Her voice was threatening to let her down, so without further ado, she hugged him to her, and felt his arms come up to wind convulsively around her neck. It took every ounce of her dwindling courage to kiss him and turn him to face his uncle. "Go along now, Harry. Remember the star—and may God keep you safe."

Lord Alistair had watched the little scene in silence, impressed, in spite of himself, by the restraint with which she was handling the parting. He had steeled himself for tears and last-minute pleas, knowing that most of the women of his acquaintance would have created a scene. But this woman seemed to possess an inner strength which put any such thought to shame. Nor, to be fair, could he discern the least hint that she had attempted to poison the boy's mind against his father or himself, though he was left in little doubt that she considered his part in the whole affair to be despicable.

As a result, he was able to view the sight of Harry, dragging his feet and manfully striving to hold back his tears, with more sympathy than he would otherwise have felt. He made no comment, but laid a bracing hand on the boy's shoulder as he paused to take his leave of Miss Wynyate.

"Do you have any plans?" he found himself asking abruptly.

And because the mere thought of what her life would be was so unbearably painful, Charity's reply was equally brusque. "No. I shall probably seek some kind of teaching position." Her chin lifted. "I taught English in Brussels for a short while when funds were low."

"Did you, indeed?" He seemed about to say more, but when he spoke again it was merely to assure her that the children would be well cared for.

"My lord . . ." Her voice, forced out with difficulty, was vibrant with passion. "I mean to hold you to that undertaking.

And should I ever hear anything to the contrary, you may be certain that I will move heaven and earth to thwart his grace's will.''

He bowed, and began to guide Harry toward the door, while Harry, now that the moment had come, twisted constantly beneath his hands to look back in mute appeal.

Charity held her breath, feeling like a traitor, until she heard Higgins shut the front door and walk slowly back up the hall and through to the back regions. Only then did she move, running wildly up the stairs and slamming the door of her bedchamber behind her.

The journey was not a happy one; Lord Alistair had never thought that it would be, and with great presence of mind had elected to ride beside the coach, preferring to brave the weather, which was showing a tendency to snow, rather than be subjected to company of the formidable Nurse Fenton and the screams of his niece who, however suspect might be her constitution, had a pair of lungs that would rival the strongest pair of bellows. When he occasionally glanced in at the window, it was to see Harry miserably hunched in a corner with his eyes tight shut; from the way he occasionally rubbed at them with one clenched fist, there seemed a strong possibility that the child was crying. Not for the first time he cursed the whole business, which had so comprehensively destroyed the even tenor of his life.

When they stopped to change horses for the second time, the weather had cleared. He opened the door on Harry's side and extended a hand. ''What would you say to riding with me for a while?''

A variety of emotions struggled for supremacy in Harry's red-rimmed eyes. ''I'd as lief not, sir,'' he muttered at last; then, remembering as an afterthought Aunt Charity's exhortations on politeness, he added, ''Thank you.''

His lordship, a trifle piqued at having his generous offer thrown back at him, said roundly, ''Never mind what you'd as lief, my boy. Some fresh air will do you good.''

He had been prepared for some further token resistance, but Harry seemed too apathetic to argue and when they were ready to set off again, allowed himself to be lifted up by John to sit in front of his uncle, who closed a protective arm around him.

They rode for a while in silence, leaving the coach behind, and after a few moments Harry's natural resilience began to assert itself. He stroked the horse's creamy mane with tentative fingers and patted its neck. "He's a prime 'un, isn't he, Uncle Alistair?"

"He is indeed," his uncle said dryly. "I thought you might like him."

Harry thought this over. "Will there be horses where we're going?"

"I doubt it. But I imagine something could be arranged."

This produced a longer silence. Then Harry said diffidently, "I should think you could arrange anything if you wanted to." And when this produced no more than a faint smile, he added with more daring, "I s'ppose you couldn't arrange for Aunt Charity to be there, too?"

Damn! thought Lord Alistair. "No, Harry. That is quite beyond my powers."

Harry sighed deeply and soon began to droop again, so that his lordship was obliged to return him to the carriage. By the time Ashbourne Grange was reached, both children were disgruntled from being so long on the road, and Nurse Fenton had long since found her patience worn thin. Their welcome was tempered with a kind of bristling efficiency which hardly helped matters, although the housekeeper, Mrs. Bennett, who was a bustling sort of woman rather rounder than he remembered, greeted them pleasantly enough and did not seem to mind that her hitherto uneventful life was to be disrupted. She was a trifle in awe of Lord Alistair, not having seen him since his boyhood visits.

"It will be quite like the old days, my lord," she said, dropping him a curtsy, "having children's voices about the place again."

The children's voices at that moment however became decidedly querulous, with Emily's screams in danger of drowning out all conversation, so that she and the nurse were quickly dispatched to the nursery quarters, while Harry was taken in charge by a highly efficient governess who waited a few paces behind the housekeeper. Miss Throstle was even thinner than Nurse Fenton, and her black bombazine skirt rustled as she advanced to make her own curtsy to his lordship.

He found the whole atmosphere distasteful and was in consequence unnecessarily curt over Mrs. Bennett's tentative offer to provide dinner for him, if he should not mind simple fare—"For cook is getting old and has quite got out of the way of preparing those fancy dishes her grace was used to enjoy so much."

"Thank you," he said, not caring to be reminded of happier times, "but I came only to see the children safely delivered."

"Like a parcel!" as she later told cook indignantly.

Miss Throstle, however, saw nothing untoward in his lordship's words. Having learned something of the circumstances surrounding the children's presence here, she considered that he had done all and more than might have been expected of him and must by now be wishing his tiresome relations at Jericho. She curtsied and begged leave to take Harry to his room, and receiving his consent, bade the child thank his uncle for his great kindness and say his good-byes.

This Harry did, though grudgingly, but as the governess attempted to bustle him away, he slipped her grasp and ran back toward his uncle, who was his only link with life as he knew it and who was on the point of leaving him. "Uncle Alistair, Uncle Alistair! Will I be able to see the star from the window in my room?"

"Star?" repeated Miss Throstle, advancing on him with awesome sternness. "What nonsense is this? Your uncle has better things to do, I am sure, than to be worrying about such trivial matters."

"It isn't *trivial*," Harry insisted, mistrusting the word, "it's *very important!*"

"Bless the child," murmured Mrs. Benson, but Miss Throstle tutted, called him a wicked boy, and reiterated that his lordship must by now be quite tired of his chatter, and that he must learn obedience if he was to grow up to be a fine gentleman.

Yet something in Harry's face, in the urgency of the entreaty, made his uncle pause. Had Miss Wynyate not made some mention of a star? "What star are you talking about, Harry?"

"The evening star . . . the bright one that shines before all the others! I have to be able to see it . . ."

"Oh, really! This is really very wicked of you, Master Harry . . ." Miss Throstle began, only to flush with mortification as Lord Alistair cut her short and turned his attention again to the boy.

"And why is it so important that you should be able to see it?"

Harry explained about Aunt Charity and the pact they had made. His uncle was silent for so long that he became worried. "The thing is, I don't 'xactly know where it is in the sky, and if I don't keep my side of the promise, it won't work." He tried valiantly to keep his lip from trembling. "So you see, it is dreadfully important!"

"Yes, I do see," Lord Alistair murmured, half to himself. So, Miss Wynyate had found a way to bind the boy to her in spite of the worst his father could do, though how long so tenuous a bond would prove effective remained to be seen. He would hazard that without any personal contact, and as he adapted to his new life, the boy's attachment would begin to wane. Meanwhile, it would do no harm to humor him. "Very well," he said. "We will go up to your room together and try if we cannot work out in which direction the window faces. Miss Throstle, if you will lead the way?"

She complied, but with reluctance, her rigid back betraying that this form of indulgence did not accord with her own principles.

His lordship was not unfamiliar with Ashbourne Grange, for the house had been much favored by his mother, and his early childhood days had often been passed here rather than at the family seat in Berkshire. In later years, when she could no longer tolerate the duke's black moods, his mama had retired almost permanently to the Grange, where she had died a relatively young woman. Since that time, his father had shown no interest in the place, and his children had found other ways to pass their time. Lord Alistair, looking at it with fresh eyes, thought how charming a house it was in spite of its rather sad air of neglect—pleasantly Palladian on the outside and light and spacious within, having well-proportioned rooms which, though grown shabby, were pleasing to the eye.

The nurseries were up three pairs of stairs and, unlike the rest of the house, wore an unwelcome air of coldness. The boards echoed to the sound of their feet, and from somewhere behind closed doors the baby's screams continued unabated. His mouth tightened with distaste as the governess led the way past the schoolroom to a small, sparsely furnished bedchamber beneath the eaves.

"Did you and Papa used to live here?" Harry asked in a small voice.

"Yes—quite often when we were about your age." But surely it had never been this spartan? How quickly one forgot the privations of childhood, he reflected, eyeing his surroundings grimly. He stepped inside the room, conscious of the small, perspiring hand which curled convulsively tight within his own, his expression inscrutable as together they crossed to the tiny mullioned window. Below, rolling parkland stretched down to a small, distant lake. If he remembered aright, the lake lay roughly to the west.

"This window should give you a clear view of your star," he said. "If not," he half-turned to Miss Throstle, "Master Harry has my permission to seek one that will."

Harry swallowed over the painful lump in his throat, his relief beyond words. When his uncle turned to go, the feeling of panic returned and he found voice enough to make a final plea: "Must I stay here?"

Lord Alistair felt a kind of impotent rage rising up in him. It made him say with repressive brusqueness, "Yes, of course you must. And you will be a good, obedient child for Miss Throstle. Is that quite clear?"

"Yes, sir." It was little more than a whisper.

The coach was to remain overnight, to give the horses time

to rest, and Lord Alistair could not wait to shake the dust of Ashbourne Grange from his system. For the first few miles, he rode as if pursued by the devil himself. John, keeping pace with him, cast covert glances at the grim profile. He'd been with his lordship for many a long year and reckoned he knew all his moods, good and bad, but he'd seldom seen him in such a black humor as now. And if those kiddies weren't at the bottom of it somewhere, his name wasn't John Gage.

6

Her tears all spent. Charity splashed her face with cold water, put on her pelisse and bonnet, and prepared to leave the house, unable to bear its unnatural quietness for a moment longer. As she passed her father's library, the door opened and he stood there uncertainly, as though conscious that he had failed her, yet half afraid that Maria would pop up to prevent him from saying so.

Charity had seen very little of him during this short time at home—it was as though Maria had deliberately kept them from being alone together lest she should seek to influence him. Maria need not have worried. She wanted nothing from her father. Yet, for all that, she was distressed to observe how sadly he had deteriorated. Mama had been his rock, of course. Now, signs of weakness, of indecisiveness, were clearly evident in his face. This could perhaps explain Arianne's flightiness, for all that in looks she took after Mama. Charity reflected wryly that she could make no such claim to beauty, but at least she seemed to have inherited her mama's strength of purpose.

"Charity, my dear . . ." he began.

"It's all right, Papa," she said quickly, "I do understand."

His mouth was trembling. "I could wish to have done more. I . . . it grieves me to see you unhappy . . ."

She shrugged. "Unhappiness seems to be a condition one must needs endure from time to time. But I have overcome it before and shall do so again, no doubt, so don't, I beg of you, upset yourself."

"You are so very like your mother," he sighed, echoing

her earlier thoughts. "Quite indomitable. But I do hope . . . that is, I do not know what plans you have made . . ."

"I have made none as yet," she said, unable quite to keep the bleakness from her voice, "except to acknowledge that I must clearly seek employment of some nature." Charity ignored his faint exclamation. "Meanwhile, I shall take a walk in the Park. Perhaps the fresh air will give a clearer direction to my thoughts."

An early sprinkling of snow had kept people within doors, but she was glad to have the streets to herself. Inevitably, her thoughts turned to the children, whose journey could well be made uncomfortable by the inclement weather. However, as she turned in at the Park gates, the sun was already beginning to struggle through the grayness, melting the dusting of white that coated the grass.

Charity walked quickly at first, glad of the exercise, for it enabled her to work off the lethargy induced by her recent storm of weeping. But that was all finished—she would cry no more tears. Instead, all her energies must be directed to the future. In sending the children, as he thought, beyond her reach, the duke no doubt considered that he had won. But nothing could be further from the truth. Separated they might be, but she could no more cut Harry and Emily out of her life than she could stop breathing.

Already several half-formulated plans were swimming around in her mind. The children were in Surrey, that much she knew, and with a little determination it should be possible to discover the exact whereabouts in Surrey. Once she knew that, even his grace could not prevent her from seeking employment somewhere in the vicinity—as a lady's companion, perhaps, or even a teacher or governess? She had not made such a bad job of raising Harry. The greatest drawback to this scheme was the need to provide references, a fact which pinpointed all too closely her dismal lack of connections.

So deep in thought was Charity that she did not hear the approaching horseman, or his muffled exclamation as he wheeled his mount to bring it around alongside her.

"Miss Wynyate—Charity?"

She was jolted from these confused reflections by a voice that sounded vaguely familiar, and glanced up to see a gentleman in the act of dismounting from his horse. "Captain Fitz! Oh, what a splendid surprise!"

"Yes, indeed, ma'am." He shook her warmly by the hand. "But it ain't really Captain Fitzallan any longer, you know. Sold out last month. Didn't seem quite the same, y'know—the war at an end and so many good friends gone."

"I suppose not," Charity agreed quietly.

"And how do you go on after all your troubles?" He looked down at her. "You seem a trifle down pin, if you don't mind my saying so. Things can't have been easy. The children are well, I trust? Young Harry must be quite grown since I last saw him."

Charity scarcely knew how to reply. In her agitation she began to walk rather quickly, and he, sensing her mood, kept pace with her. "Something *is* amiss, I can tell. The children . . ."

"Oh, they are well enough . . . ," and then, because she knew her story would receive a sympathetic hearing, she told him all.

"But this is frightful news, ma'am! I guessed you must have delivered them into Orme's care—only thing to be done, his responsibility, after all. But that he should behave so shabbily! After all you have done—and young Harry so devoted to you!" Captain Fitzallan's habitually good-natured features had grown pink with outrage. "As for Alistair's part in the affair, well, I am shocked—and yes, surprised. I had thought better of him."

"To be fair," she admitted, "I believe his lordship had little choice in the matter. The duke is an obsessively overbearing man."

"Even so . . ." Captain Fitzallan shook his head. "So, what will you do now, dear ma'am? Or is it impertinent in me to ask?"

"No, indeed. One could never be in danger of mistaking your kind interest for impertinence! The truth is, I don't know what I am to do, except that I must, somehow, earn a living." His muffled exclamation brought a wry twist to her mouth.

"I confess the prospect is not a pleasing one, but I have always been something of a realist, you know, and recognized long since that it must be so. If only the rest could be as it was, I think I should not mind." Charity found to her horror that her throat was becoming constricted yet again. "Confound it!" she exclaimed. "I will not become a watering pot!

Captain Fitzallan stopped and turned to face her, his concern very real. "No one has more cause for distress than you, my dear Charity, and if there is any way that I can be of help, I beg you will not hesitate to call upon me. Ned was my friend, and I know he would wish me to do all I can."

"You are very kind. I wonder . . ." She hesitated and then told him of her plans. "But if I am to try for anything of the kind, I shall require some proof of good character."

Captain Fitzallan was shocked. "Oh, not a governess, I beg of you!" And then he bethought him of some of the dabs of women he had seen in times past, running around at the bidding of his mother's friends in the guise of companion, and wondered if such a situation would be much better. His mother! Now there was a thought. "Tell you what? I mean to travel down to Guilford within the coming weeks to see m'family. Mama's a positive fount of wisdom. If you had no objection to my telling her of your trouble, I shouldn't wonder if she might not be just the person to advise you." His face brightened suddenly. "Or, better still, you could accompany me—stay for a while."

"Oh, no! I couldn't think of imposing!" The idea was so tempting that Charity's vehement protest was addressed as much to herself as to him. "I am quite unknown to her, and besides you have been so long away that your family will want you to themselves. It is more than kind in you to suggest it, but I am persuaded that I should be very much in the way!"

"Nothing of the sort, you have my word on't," he assured her with a smile. "They are never happier than when the house is filled with friends. In fact, the more I think about it, the more certain I am that you should come." He hesitated before saying a trifle diffidently, "There is nothing to keep you here?"

"Nothing at all," she said bleakly.

"Well then? At least allow me to write to my parents, suggesting that I might bring you."

Charity was on the point of refusing when a sudden thought struck her. "Guilford? Is that not in Surrey?" And when he confirmed it, "I suppose your home would not be anywhere near the Duke of Orme's estate?"

"Not above a few miles away, ma'am." His smile widened. "By Jove, I see what you mean! Well, that rather settles the matter, wouldn't you say? I will write to them at once."

And because the opportunity seemed nothing less than heaven-sent, she agreed. "But only if you will stop *ma'aming* me, for it makes me feel a positive antidote," she said.

"Gladly, my dear," he said, a little shyly. "It will be famous to have your company for a while."

Their bargain sealed, Charity's spirits began to lift, for from that moment Captain Fitzallan went out of his way to ensure that she had no time to mope. He had been so long out of London, he declared, that he scarcely knew anyone to speak of. "Been invited out, of course—friends of Mama's mostly, doing the polite—only the thing is, I never was much of a lady's man, and I would consider it a great kindness in you if you would lend me your support."

Since Charity had never supposed him to be at a loss during their Brussels days, this was patently a device to take her out of herself. However, she allowed herself to be persuaded, for anything seemed preferable to spending more time than was necessary in Upper Wimpole Street. Maria was already beginning to question her continuing presence, though never when her father was within earshot.

But if she was to go into company, something would have to be done about clothes. Her own were few and, for the most part, practical rather than decorative. She had, however, kept several of Arianne's prettier dresses. At the time, she had no clear reason for so doing beyond sentiment, her sister having been much slighter in build than herself. But now that she had only herself to consider, Charity realized that there was nothing to stop her unpicking the dresses and reusing the material.

She had a talent for sewing, and set to with a will, spending every spare moment cutting and pinning and fitting, with Meg as a willing helpmeet whenever she could escape Maria's ever-

watchful eye. In a very short time the initial fruit of their labors
lay upon the bed for both to admire—two highly becoming
gowns, one for afternoons in sprigged muslin with a brief
bodice and frilled hem of a plain soft blue, and the other for
evening in a very pretty amber silk with an overdress of cream
gauze.

"Right elegant, they are, miss," Meg enthused, impressed
by her capacity for invention.

Charity laughed, feeling happier than she had for some
considerable time. "I'm not sure about elegant, but they will
serve. And I have material enough for at least one more."

Maria's eyebrows had lifted when Fitz first called to take
her for a drive, and she was not slow to comment waspishly
upon the speed of her recovery from grief following the
departure of the children. The barb wounded, as it was meant
to, but Charity held her tongue, resolved for her father's sake
not to exacerbate a situation which, hopefully, would soon
be resolved.

And indeed, on the very next day she received the kindest
note from Mrs. Fitzallan, expressing the pleasure it would
give them if Miss Wynyate would consent to be their guest
during Fitz's forthcoming visit to Guilford. She replied at
once, and could only hope that the good lady would not be
supposing her to have designs upon her son.

Mr. Wynyate was very quiet upon hearing her news. He
had already surprised Charity once by rousing himself to
reprove his spouse after overhearing one of her more cutting
remarks. And when he called her into his library later in the
day, he was to surprise her yet again by putting a purse into
her hands.

"If you are to stay with Captain Fitzallan's family for any
length of time, I daresay there will be some extra things you
will need. No, no. Pray do not refuse the money, my dear
girl. In these past few weeks I have become very much aware
of my deficiencies as a father—belatedly, I fear, but there,
what is done, is done." He closed her fingers around the
purse and patted her hand. "So take this to please me. It

is a trifling amount to be sure, but it will perhaps buy you a few necessities.''

More moved than she would have believed possible, Charity stammered her thanks, but he waved them away, saying rather sheepishly as she turned to leave, ''Only perhaps . . . if you could refrain from making any mention of this to Maria?''

She agreed willingly, taking the purse at once to her room where, having tipped the contents out on the bed, she found that it contained forty guineas. A veritable fortune! She would be able to purchase a new pelisse and bonnet and some new shoes and stockings, and still have plenty to hold against possible future needs.

Charity's initial ventures into society proved relatively painless, and included a musical afternoon at the home of one of Mrs. Fitzallan's closest friends. ''Music ain't really much in my line,'' Fitz confessed. ''But Lady Tufnell is a charming old bird and she was most insistent that I should come.''

There were not above thirty people present, mostly ladies of a mature age, some of whom were accompanied by their daughters, and a mere handful of gentlemen, drawn there she suspected by the said daughters rather than the entertainment. Charity took an instant liking to Lady Tufnell. She was large and jolly, and had a happy knack of making one feel instantly at home.

''Delighted to see you, m'boy,'' she wheezed, her several chins wobbling. ''And Miss Wynyate. We have not met, I think, but you are very welcome to my little soirée. Fitz tells me that you go with him shortly to make a stay with his family in the country.'' Her eyes twinkled knowingly. ''Splendid. You will enjoy it enormously. I daresay you will not know many people here, but Miss Berridge will be happy to make them known to you. Celia!'' she boomed, and a fussy little woman appeared from somewhere behind her immense girth and was introduced.

''Yes, indeed. Most happy,'' Miss Berridge echoed breathily, and proceeded to do as she was bid.

How awful, Charity thought, convinced that Lady Tufnell had formed quite the wrong impression about her relationship with Fitz! She glanced at Fitz, but he seemed not to have noticed anything amiss.

The afternoon passed pleasantly enough, with music to smooth over any awkward moments such as her introduction to a certain Lady Vane and her beautiful daughter, who were barely civil and thereafter attempted to stare her out of countenance whenever their glances chanced to meet. At one point, she saw Lady Tufnell in conversation with them, and from the look of interest which her ladyship bent upon her, she doubted it was anything to her credit.

"Nonsense," Fitz said when she told him what had occurred. "Lady T ain't one to heed any kind of tattle. You ask Miss Berridge." His eyes twinkled. "They are probably admiring that very pretty bonnet you are wearing."

Charity, well aware of the bonnet's limitations, thought this highly unlikely, but did not say so.

Shortly before they were due to leave for Guilford, Fitz persuaded her to accompany him to an altogether grander affair—a reception to be given by Lady Sefton. He dismissed her fears with assurance that the cream of the *haut ton* would still for the most part be languishing in the country, making preparations for the coming Season. "Like as not, the company will be tedious—a lot of diplomatic and government folk. Wouldn't bother going, but Lady Sefton is—"

"A friend of your mama's," she finished for him, and he grinned.

"Quite. She's sure to get wind of it if I cry off."

Charity did not believe this for a moment. In fact, she was by now certain that he had gone out of his way to cultivate some of his mother's friends for her benefit, though he would never admit the fact. This time, however, she would most assuredly be out of place, but Fitz looked so downcast when she attempted to convince him that in the end she relented, saying with a sudden flash of humor that if she disgraced him, he could always disown her.

She had not been above five minutes at Lady Sefton's before her worst fears were realized, and the utter foolishness of allowing her initial judgment to be dismissed came back to mock her. Beneath the glittering chandliers the rooms were already alive with color and movement, and the general tone of the conversation only served to confirm that Fitz had underestimated the quality of the gathering. Her sister would have felt quite at home among so many bedecked and be-jeweled ladies, thinking herself as fine as anyone present. Charity had not begrudged her this talent, for she had never felt the least inclination to move in such exalted circles. The few times she had been persuaded to do so in Paris and Brussels, had merely given credence to her own view that she lacked the ability to make the kind of empty small talk which seemed so necessary if one were to be easily accepted.

Now, as then, she felt gauche and ill at ease. Even her pretty amber gown, the brief bodice of which she had pain-stakingly embellished with tiny seed pearls, working far into the night to the near ruination of her sight, and which until this moment she had naively supposed to be reasonably stylish, looked suddenly what it was—shabby genteel! Not even Arianne's best lace-trimmed shawl could save it. Also, she was certain, from the covert glances cast her way, that she was fast becoming an object of conjecture. One saturnine gentleman, complete with eyeglass, was quizzing her in a particularly odious way. However, it was no use repining. With any luck, they would soon find other diversions.

Fitz had been drawn into conversation with a military acquaintance, leaving Charity momentarily at the mercy of the exceedingly boring gentleman to whom Lady Sefton had so very kindly introduced them. As it was unnecessary to do more than interject an occasional yes and no at appro-priate intervals, her attention soon began to wander. Beyond a sudden gap in the crowd, she glimpsed the beautiful Miss Vane, whose dark hair was exquisitely fashioned à la Sappho, a style so often favored by Arianne. Charity was about to look away when a gentleman came into view—tall, imposing, elegantly clad in black and white; she felt the blood rush into her face and then drain as quickly away, for there was no mistaking the gentleman's identity as he greeted Miss Vane with a marked air of intimacy.

It seemed an age before Fitz rejoined her, and even longer before they managed to rid themselves of the egregious Mr. Blount and she was able to whisper urgently, "Fitz, I must leave now—at once!"

He glanced at her in surprise. "Oh, come, m'dear. Blount was a bit of an oaf, I admit, for all that he's something in the Admiralty, but he ain't typical of Lady Sefton's guests."

She shook her head impatiently. "It isn't that."

"Well, then?" And, noting her agitation, "Is something amiss? You don't look quite the thing, I must say."

"I'm perfectly well," she said impatiently, "but I have just—there," she seized his arm, "do you not see—across the room, to the right of that lady wearing the hideous turban with the purple plumes?"

Captain Fitzallan looked. "Egad, it's Alistair—and with Miss Vane!"

"Precisely. Oh, Fitz, please get me out of here at once. I cannot—will not meet him! The embarrassment . . . Heaven knows what he will think, seeing me here, of all places!"

"Well, why shouldn't you be here? My dear, this ain't like you at all! You have Lady Sefton's blessing, so I'm dashed if I can see that it matters a toss what Alistair or anyone else thinks. Got a perfect right to be wherever you choose."

It was true, of course, except that Lady Sefton did not perhaps know her for a sham, and it might reflect badly upon Fitz should she be exposed as a penniless young woman flying false colors who had no place in such company. But even as Charity rationalized the argument, she knew it wasn't the real reason for her panic—that what really mattered was her discovery by Lord Alistair. But, she decided fatalistically, there was little she could do about it, since Fitz saw no reason to leave. Perhaps, among so many people, their paths might never cross.

But Fate was in a capricious mood that night, for scarcely had Charity calmed her fears when, in an irrepressible need to assure herself that she was in no danger, her glance strayed once more over the heads of the crowd—and she found herself looking straight into Lord Alistair's eyes. They widened in disbelief before hardening into something much less pleasant. Short of abject flight, there was now no way of avoiding an encounter. She looked for Fitz and found he had been claimed by yet another acquaintance. Realizing that she must face him alone, Charity became of a sudden quite calm. After all, what had she to fear? There might be much he would wish to say, but he was much too well bred to make a scene.

"Miss Wynyate." He had reached her side with a speed and purpose remarkable in one who gave a permanent impression of indolence, and now he towered over her like an elegant bird of prey in his black swallow-tailed coat. A diamond nestling in the pristine whiteness of his cravat mocked her with its brilliance. "I had not expected to see you here."

He did not add *where you so clearly do not belong*, but the criticism was implicit in the tone of his greeting. No doubt he would be comparing her apparently carefree demeanor with that of the grief-stricken woman he had seen so short a time ago, a woman who had virtually confessed to being without resources—and he would be judging her accordingly. Well, let him.

"Or I, you, my lord," she said pleasantly. "A small world, is it not?"

Charity saw his eyes flare into anger. "Little fool!" he said, so low that only she could hear him. "You are already being talked about."

Thanks to Miss Vane, she thought. "So?" she said with calculated flippancy.

"Do you not care that people are like to make you an object of ridicule?"

"Not really, my lord. Do you? Or are you perhaps afraid that your own reputation might suffer as a result?"

She looked full at him and for an instant it was as though time stopped—and they were quite alone. How intolerant was the thrust of his jaw, how intimidating the narrow glittering eyes and the scar, which assumed a sinister prominence in the tautness of his face as he stared down at her. Let him stare. Looks never killed anyone. He thought himself so clever, but very soon, and in a way he could not quarrel with, she would be within reach of the children. Not that she meant him to know of it.

How dare she stand there, he raged inwardly, in her simple homemade gown, making every other woman in the room look overdressed and laughing at social disgrace. How dare she attempt to stare him down, armed only with that infuriating air of challenge that invariably seemed determined to make him feel guilty, and to which was now added something new—a hint of defiance, perhaps even of contempt, almost as if she knew something he didn't. And he had almost made the mistake of feeling sorry for her. My God, she had better not cross him!

And then, close by, someone laughed. The mood was broken, and Fitz was hurrying toward them. She said calmly, "You are acquainted with Captain Fitzallan, I believe?"

Fitz, having rushed to her rescue, stared to see her so composed, but he quickly recovered himself. He'd told her it was all a hum.

"Of course." The two men exchanged greetings. "How are you, Fitz? Still with the Regiment?"

Captain Fitzallan explained his changed circumstances, and then, feeling that the subject could not be ignored, haltingly expressed his condolences over Ned's death. "Not the place to go into detail, I know, but if you would care to, we could speak more on it another time."

"Thank you. I appreciate the thought." His lordship's deceptively incurious gaze traveled from one to the other. "I daresay it was through my brother that you and Miss Wynyate became acquainted?"

"Yes indeed!" Fitz, eager to put in a good word for Charity, prepared to launch into a catalog of her many virtues and how much Ned and Arianne, God rest them both, owed to her selfless dedication, but she hastily cut in before he could mention the children, as she was sure he was about to do.

"Enough, Fitz, or you will put me to the blush. I am quite sure his lordship doesn't want to hear a lot of trivial domestic detail.'' Her look challenged him to deny it. There was a dangerous glint in his eyes, but he made no attempt to refute the allegation, and Charity concluded with unusual defiance, "Fitz and I met quite by chance last week in the Park.''

"Oh happy chance!'' he drawled softly. There was no mistaking his meaning and he watched as the furious color mounted into her cheeks. So, he had got under her guard at last. Well, she had been asking to have that damned composure pricked, and was well served!

Fitz, however, missed the finer nuances of his observation, and so took it at face value. "Why, so I thought. Almost the first friendly face I'd seen since arriving back in London, aside from a few dowagers! One gets dreadfully out of touch with things, y'know, being abroad for so long.''

"So I should imagine.''

"Alistair! I have been looking for you everywhere.'' Miss Vane's voice at his shoulder carried the merest hint of a reproach. He turned unhurriedly, though a certain tightness around his mouth indicated to Mr. Trowbridge, who accompanied her, that he was less than pleased to see them.

"You left me with scarcely a word, and poor Theo has been obliged to bear me company.''

"Always a pleasure, ma'am,'' Mr. Trowbridge avowed gallantly, while eyeing Alistair's companions with veiled curiosity.

"Yes, but that is hardly the point—''

"The point, my dear Melissa,'' Alistair said with rather more shortness than his beloved could wish for, "is that I had a particular reason for leaving you, and had you exercised but a small degree of patience, I would have returned in good time.''

Miss Vane bit back the indignant retort that sprang to her lips, realizing with commendable swiftness that she was not the true object of Alistair's wrath. It had taken her but a moment to recognize Miss Wynyate, and to know how furious he must be to find her flaunting herself here. She therefore accorded Miss Wynyate no more than the briefest nod as they greeted one another, and it was left to Mr. Trowbridge to invest the introductions with some warmth.

"Theo, you will remember Fitzallan? Ned's friend."

"I do, indeed." He said, proferring a hand while his curiosity remained centered upon the young lady. So this was the current thorn in Alistair's flesh! She was not in the least as he had expected, and he found himself smiling at her with genuine pleasure. She returned his smile, and although there was a light in her blue-gray eyes which gave evidence of good humor allied to intelligence, he sensed, too, a certain steely resolve. That would not sit well with Alistair; indeed, even now one could not but be aware of a certain atmosphere between them. That Alistair had cursed the whole business from the start, and had been little more than a reluctant cypher for his father, had acted upon him as an irritant. And Miss Wynyate, if his judgment was accurate, was no submissive minion to be dispatched at will, which might further exacerbate the situation. If his friend had a besetting weakness, it was that he could not bear to be thwarted. It occurred to Mr. Trowbridge that, whether or not Alistair already had Miss Wynyate's measure, she might well be the one to prove to him that he could not always call the tune. All in all, the next few months should prove interesting.

Mr. Trowbridge was not the only person to be intrigued by the situation. Sir Rupert Darian also watched from a vantage point close by. He knew who Miss Wynyate was, of course, and had witnessed the meeting of the protagonists with mounting appreciation. One could sense the antagonism, even at a distance. The lady's object in tangling with the powerful Ashbourne family was of little interest to him, except insofar as it might be used to discomfort or even discredit Lord Alistair. His glance strayed to the delectable Melissa—she too looked less than pleased.

Sir Rupert lowered his eyeglass and wondered how he might best turn the situation to his own advantage.

7

Charity could not have been more warmly received by Mrs. Fitzallan, who proved to be a motherly lady with twinkling eyes and a nature that accepted whatever came along with equanimity.

"You must not thank me, my dear Miss Wynyate," she exclaimed when Charity attempted to express her gratitude, "for there is nothing we like more than a house full of young people. What with Mary's friends and Eliza's, not to mention the young rips Joshua and Ben will forever be bringing home, we are seldom without company. I only hope that you will not find us too boisterous!"

Charity assured her that she also enjoyed the company of young people, and something in her voice must have betrayed her, for the older woman patted her hand. "Fitz has explained something of your situation, my dear. I hope you don't mind . . ."

"Indeed, no, ma'am. I am relieved that he as done so, for it saves me the difficulty of broaching it myself."

"Quite so." Mrs. Fitzallan nodded vigorously and a strand of graying blond hair escaped her tucked muslin cap. "I fear you may find it very frustrating to be so near to your loved ones and be denied access to them. However, should you feel the need to talk, you will find me very willing to listen, and if we put our heads together, who knows what might not come of it. In fact, my housekeeper, Mrs. Treadgold, is a bosom bow of Mrs. Bennett's, the housekeeper at Ashbourne Grange, and has more than once spoken to me about his grace's grandchildren."

"She has?" This was more than Charity had hoped for.

She could hardly bear to ask, and yet could not bear not to know. "Oh, ma'am, how are they faring? Has she said?"

"Oh well, as to that, it is much as you would expect." Mrs. Fitzallan, seeing the agony of longing in her young guest's eyes, rather wished she had spoken less freely. But it was not in her nature to dissemble, and in any case, Miss Wynyate was by all accounts a most sensible young woman, not given to freakish starts. "Children will often take a little time to settle, you know, when they are uprooted and thrust unaccompanied into strange surroundings in such a skimble-skamble fashion. How like Orme to behave so shabbily! But it comes as no surprise when one considers how he treated the poor dear duchess, God rest her soul!"

At any other time, Charity might have been curious enough to find out more, but for now one thought alone filled her mind—that all was not well with Harry and Emily. "They are miserable, are they not?"

"Oh, my dear Miss Wynyate, I beg you will not think the worst. Children quite often take a while to settle in a strange place, especially when they lack a familiar face to turn to, but it would not do, you know, for their sake or for yours, to go off like one of Congreve's rockets!" This brought a faint smile, and Mrs. Fitzallan continued, "Apart from anything else, only consider what might be the outcome if Mrs. Bennett were to learn of your connection with the children and let the information slip—at best it would further unsettle the children, should they hear of it, and at worst the duke might be informed and remove them to a less accessible place."

Charity said with an air of self-disgust, "You are right, ma'am. I am behaving like the veriest pea-goose."

"Understandably so. Fitz has told me of your selfless dedication to those children . . ." She saw her young guest's little moue of depreciation, "Yes, of course, I am well aware that you don't see it like that in the least, but you do care deeply for them, and as a mother, I know how I should feel in similar circumstances. So for the present, we will keep the matter between you and Fitz and myself, and if you will trust me to glean what I can from Mrs. Treadgold, between us we may perhaps see how best to go on." She beamed at Charity. "In the meantime, I trust you will make yourself at home, and we will try if we cannot put some color into your cheeks."

"Thank you. You are very kind, allowing me to impose upon you in this way," Charity said, much moved. "But you must not let me outstay my welcome. I don't know how much Fitz told you, but it is my earnest hope that I shall be able to obtain some kind of employment in the vicinity. If you should know of anyone in need of a companion, or a governess . . ."

"Oh, there is time enough for that later," Mrs. Fitzallan said vaguely. "When you are fully rested. No, no, my dear, not another word, I beg of you."

It was so long since Charity had been completely free of responsibility that at first she found idleness difficult to sustain for any length of time without an accompanying sense of guilt. But gradually, as the days went by, she discovered that her hostess had not exaggerated the degree of hospitality that reigned within the walls of the unpretentious manor house. Mr. Fitzallan was a quiet, rather studious man who seldom emerged from his study before the dinner hour. He affected to regard his family's gregarious ways with patient resignation, but Charity had occasionally caught a glimpse of something in his eyes which surely gave the lie to this, and there was no mistaking the pleasure with which he had greeted his eldest son, or his kind reception of herself.

The daughters, Mary and Eliza, were eighteen and seventeen respectively, and were pretty unaffected girls, Eliza being the more gregarious of the two. She had her mama's fairness and looked very much as Mrs. Fitzallan must have done as a girl, while Mary favored her elder brother, with her dark chestnut hair, pale complexion, and sweet gentleness of manner. Joshua and Ben completed the family. They were twins coming up to nine years old, as alike as peas and with an infinite capacity to tumble in and out of scrapes, showing a blithe disregard for the decorum which their hapless tutor, Mr. Frank, endeavored to instill in them. At times they reminded Charity so markedly of Harry that she was obliged to stifle the pangs of longing.

"Fitz told us you had been about the world a great deal, and were even in Brussels at the time of the great battle," Eliza said when the two girls had initially carried her off to the comfortable parlor which was their own private sanctum and out of bounds to small boys. "I do so envy you, for we haven't been anywhere!"

"That isn't quite true," Mary said with a reproving frown, remembering the less pleasant side of Charity's life which Fitz had hinted at. "We have been to Margate, and once to Brighton, and we are forever going to stay with Aunt Alice in Bath."

"Don't be idiotish, Mary. Bath don't hold a candle to Paris!" Eliza tossed her curls and leaned forward eagerly. "Do tell us about Paris, Charity! Was it prodigiously romantic?"

"Oh, prodigiously," Charity agreed with a faint smile. "Though I fear you will think my experiences dismally flat, for not once did I come close to being swept off my feet by a handsome French aristocrat returning to claim his inheritance."

Eliza accepted this unhappy disclosure with fortitude, while Mary maintained prosaically that such paragons must have been few and far between, there being little likelihood of there having been any fortunes left to claim.

It was quite impossible to be unhappy for long in the company of so many agreeable people, and although there was never a day when the children were not in Charity's thoughts, she gradually began to relax and enjoy the simple pleasures so freely offered. Among the happiest of these was the chance, for some time denied her, to go riding.

The Fitzallan's kept two riding horses, and ponies for the boys, as well as a fine pair of carriage horses. Fitz's own mount was still stabled in London, but since of the two girls only Eliza showed any disposition to ride, and she not often, this number more than sufficed. Most days Charity and Fitz rode out alone before breakfast, both having formed the habit of rising early.

Fitz had been a good friend to her over the past weeks. His manner toward her was both cheerful and supportive, with no suggestion that he desired more than friendship. For this Charity was grateful; had there been the least suggestion that he was beginning to cherish a tendre for her, she would have found it difficult to continue to accept the hospitality offered by his parents. And while she knew that she could not remain indefinitely, the stay not only brought her tantalizingly close to the children, but afforded her a valuable breathing space and time to think without Maria breathing down her neck.

The confrontation between Lord Alistair and herself during Lady Sefton's reception had been altogether different from their previous encounters, and somewhat to her dismay, though she would die rather than admit it, had left her senses in disarray. It had also given her much food for thought, and the knowledge that he was betrothed to Miss Vane did little to ease her general disquiet.

Several days after they had first ridden out together, Fitz took Charity in the direction of Ashbourne Grange, where, by mutual consent, they reined in.

From the imposing entrance gates the parkland stretched away, curving out of sight. Of the house there was no sign, which gave it such a sense of isolation as to make Charity despair of ever again being able to get close to the children.

As if reading her thoughts, Fitz said quietly, "The Grange is about a mile away, beyond that far clump of trees. You know, Charity, I have been thinking—there is nothing to stop me riding over here one day to do a little harmless reconnoitering. I could ask to see young Harry. After all, I was a bona-fide friend of his father's—they could hardly refuse me access to him. It wouldn't be the same as seeing him for yourself, of course, but at least I'd be able to tell you how he is. What do you think?"

She turned to him, eyes alight. "Oh, Fitz, do you suppose it might be possible? He would be so pleased to see you!

But he must not know that I am here.'' She hesitated, ''Perhaps we should consult your mama before doing anything which might jeopardize her own delicate inquiries.''

Mrs. Fitzallan, when her son broached the idea to her, thought there could be no possible harm in her son's visit, ''as long as you don't give the boy the slightest hint that his aunt is in the vicinity.''

''Not you, too, Mama,'' he said disgustedly. ''As if I'd be such a clunch!''

Her eyes twinkled. ''I have no doubt you will be the very soul of discretion, my dear. I never for one moment supposed otherwise.'' Her smile faded. ''To be honest with you, and I would not tell Charity for the world without more confirmation of the facts, I would not be at all sorry if you were to go, for I am less than easy in my mind about the happenings at Ashbourne Grange. If Mrs. Bennett is to be believed, and I see no reason to doubt her word, all is not as it should be. Oh, I am not suggesting for one moment that the children are being ill-treated,'' she hastened to add, seeing alarm spring into his eyes. ''In fact, I am sure they are not. But it does not seem to be a very happy place at present.''

If anything had been needed to spur Fitz on, this was it. He resolved to go the very next day. ''And you will tell me the truth when you return?'' Charity urged him as he was about to set off. ''Even if it is not good?''

Fitz gathered up his reins and gave her what he hoped was a reassuring smile. ''You shall have my honest assessment,'' he promised.

But that was to be easier said than done. He almost did not get to see Harry at all, and when he did, it was only through the kind offices of Mrs. Bennett, who prevailed upon Miss Throstle to relax her rigid routine.

''She is bringing him down in just a moment, Captain Fitz,'' she said, sounding not a little aggrieved as she showed him into the small saloon and poured him a glass of her best elderberry wine. ''It isn't that Miss Throstle is deliberately unkind—just a bit of a high-stickler. But I told her, oh, yes! 'Captain Fitzallan was a good friend of Harry's father,' I said. 'Many's the time he's played here when he was no bigger than young Master Harry, and I'll not have him or his parents slighted now to suit any staid old routine!''

"Oh, well said, Mrs. Bennett." Fitz nodded, and sensing that she was in a garrulous mood, he pressed his advantage. "While we are waiting, perhaps you wouldn't mind telling me how the children are faring. It cannot have been easy for them, adjusting to such a different way of life."

"Well, of course, sir, it's not for me to say, though there's plenty I *could* say, and that's a fact." The housekeeper lowered her voice. "The baby's a sickly wee thing. Many's the time I'd have had Dr. Thomas to her, myself, but that tight-faced nurse thinks she knows best . . ."

"And Harry?" he said, for although the baby's welfare was important, he wished to learn all he could about Harry before they were interrupted.

"Ah, well, that's altogether a different kettle of fish, sir. I mean, I'm all for discipline, but boys need an outlet for their high spirits now and again. The duchess, God rest her, understood that." Her round face grew melancholy as old memories stirred. "Well, you'll remember right enough how it was with you and Lord Edward. High old times you had! Only it isn't that easy if you've no one to play with. Still and all, it's not good enough! I tell you, it grieves me to see that child moping about all on his own . . ."

There was a sound beyond the door and she stopped in midsentence as it opened to admit a thin gorgon in black, and, one step behind her, Harry. His face lit up. "Captain Fitzallan!" he cried, and seemed about to run forward when, without a word from the governess, he stopped abruptly, the light dying out of his eyes.

Indignation moved strongly in Fitz, but for the child's sake he contained it, holding out his hand instead. "Hello Harry. My word, how you've grown! I would scarcely have known you." And that was true enough. His eyes moved to Miss Throstle. "I wonder, ma'am, if I might walk for a few moments in the garden with my young friend?"

He might have been asking for the moon. The governess bristled. "I cannot countenance any disruption of our studies. Children's minds are so easily distracted."

"Oh, come, ma'am." Fitz longed to bark the words at her, but sensed that charm might well succeed where short shrift would not. "I have not seen Harry since last year, and I may not be in the district for long." He forced a smile. "Surely a little fresh air can only be beneficial?"

"Very well." It was a grudging assent. "Five minutes. I shall wait here." She sat rigid, immoveable. "Master Harry, see that you behave."

"Yes, Miss Throstle."

Fitz could not believe that the meek voice belonged to the Harry he remembered. Even when they were out of reach of the house, he remained subdued. "Well, now, this is better, isn't it?" he said, sounding overhearty in his efforts to break the barrier. "Suppose we cut across here—I believe it leads to a small gazebo."

"A gazebo?" At last a flicker of interest brought Harry to life. "That's a funny sounding word."

"Yes, isn't it? It's a kind of small ornamental building. Your father and I used to pretend it was a fort surrounded by enemy soldiers . . ." He chuckled. "We were army-mad, even then."

It was as though they both held their breath, and then Harry said with some of his old spirit, "I want to be a soldier, too, when I grow up. Then I can have a horse and gallop for miles, chasing the enemy. Uncle Alistair said he *might* arrange for there to be some horses here, but they haven't come." He sighed. "Anyway, if they did, I don't suppose Miss Throstle would let me ride them."

Fitz held his anger in check with an effort. "Well, suppose we ask her, and then, perhaps the next time I come . . ."

Harry stopped still, as if he hardly dared to believe. "Are you coming again?"

"Certainly I am. I can't promise quite when, but soon."

"Gosh!"

"Look, there is the gazebo," Fitz said, pointing ahead. "Tell you what, I'll race you to it. First one there gets to raise the flag."

Harry laughed aloud and set off, with Fitz trying desperately not to catch up with him until they reached the small ornate building with its little balconies all around. "Well done!" he cried, and produced from his pocket a large spotted red handkerchief. He presented it to Harry with a flourish, and lifted him to stand on one of the rails, showing him the place where he and his father had secured the flag by tucking it into a crack.

Harry chattered most of the way back, much of what he said being more illuminating than he could possibly know. Only as they approached the entrance to the house once more did he fall silent. At the last minute, before they went back inside, he asked, almost out of desperation, "Have you seen Aunt Charity?"

Fitz chose his words with care. "Yes, I have seen her. She is very well, though she misses you greatly. Would you like me to give her a message when next I see her?"

"I . . ." Harry was struggling not to cry. "Tell her I remember the star every night . . . and that Emily coughs a lot . . . And tell her that I love her." He ran up the steps without waiting for Fitz, and vanished into the house.

Charity was waiting impatiently for Fitz when he returned home. He had ridden long and hard to get the anger out of his system, but even so there was no escaping her inquisition. She took one look at his face and said, "I knew it! Tell me at once what is wrong, for I had much rather know the worst."

Fitz dismounted and handed the reins to the groom. "Now, don't go leaping to conclusions, m'dear," he said, striving to appear less concerned than he felt as they turned in the direction of the house. "The children are in good health—at least Harry is," he added, judiciously amending the facts. "He did mention that little Emily had a bit of a cough, but you will know yourself how frequently small children pick up such things. Ben, as I recall, was forever snuffling and sneezing when he was in the nursery."

"You need not humor me!" she snapped, and was immediately contrite.

"Lord, don't apologize." Fitz grinned. "Skin as thick as a plank, so Eliza tells me! Anyway, I have persuaded the governess to let me take Harry out riding for an hour or so tomorrow when his lessons are at an end. We should be able to fix him up with one of the ponies.''

''Oh, he would enjoy that. How kind of you, dear Fitz!'' On impulse Charity hugged him, and laughed to see how he blushed. ''If only I could see Harry!'' she exclaimed. ''To be so near and yet—''

''Yes, I know, but it wouldn't do—unsettle him badly, d'you see, as well as upsetting yourself to no good purpose.''

She sighed. ''You are right, of course. I must be sensible. Oh, Fitz, will it ever come right, do you think?''

''Sure to, given time,'' he said confidently. But with his mother he was much more outspoken. ''That nurse seems to have a fixation about small boys—men, too, probably, that sort usually do! Mrs. Bennett reckons she never lets him near his sister. And the governess ain't much better—frightened the life out of me, I can tell you! Though, to be fair, I'd say she's strict rather than deliberately unkind, and seemingly she don't get on with the nurse at all, and don't scruple to tell the woman her business.''

''Oh dear,'' sighed Mrs. Fitzallan. ''Then it is every bit as bad as I feared.''

''Worse, I'd say. Oh, Mama! If you could but see that boy—the spirit almost crushed out of him. It would break Charity's heart! Tell you what,'' he said with sudden resolution, ''I've a mind to go up to London to give Alistair a piece of my mind.''

Mrs. Fitzallan was less convinced of the wisdom of this; also, she was beginning to be a little concerned at the way her son was becoming embroiled in Charity's affairs. And, not an hour since, she had seen them practically embracing! No doubt it was all quite innocent—Charity Wynyate was a delightful young woman, generous, warm-hearted, and not in the least conniving, a woman who would make a wonderful wife for some lucky man. But, even so, surely it was not impossibly selfish in her to wish that might be some other man. Family connections *were* important, whether one liked it or not, and Charity's connections were patently negligible, if indeed she had any at all, for one could hardly place the Duke of Orme in that category. And because she was genuinely fond of Charity, these feelings warred with the more benign side of her nature, so that guilt made her speak a little more sharply than was her wont.

"I know how you feel, Fitz, but I really cannot see that it is our place to interfere. Apart from anything else, Charity is no fool. Any action on your part must surely lead her to suspect that you have not told her the whole."

Fitz looked surprised, and a little puzzled. "I thought you would approve, Mama. Something has to be done about those children—and soon. As for my visit to London, there is no need to invent an excuse. I do have some unfinished business at Horse Guards, which should suffice. No reason for Charity to suspect any ulterior motive."

"Even so. She is already beginning to grow a trifle restive about accepting our hospitality indefinitely. Suppose she should decide to return to London with you?"

"And move out of reach of the children? Never, Mama. Especially now. And even if she did, there is no reason on earth why she should twig my real reason for going."

"Well, you must do as you think best, my dear," said his mother, realizing suddenly that a visit to London would be no bad thing—if nothing else, it would part him from Charity for a while. Again, a small part of her felt shame at the thought.

"Tell you what," Fitz said, suddenly inspired. "Pa has been going on for years about getting his library catalogued. Why should he not ask Charity to undertake it for him? I'm sure such a task would be well within her capabilities."

"Employ her, you mean? Oh, I hardly think your father would agree to that. And besides, we shall be going to London ourselves in a matter of weeks. You surely cannot have forgotten Mary's come-out?"

It would be difficult to forget something which was already threatening to turn the house upside down, with fashion magazines strewn across every available surface and endless discussions as to the rival merits of this design and that. The girls spent long hours closeted in their back parlor going through the swatches of material recently delivered by the local dressmaker, Miss Croll.

"Well, I know what I shall have next year," Eliza announced with a great deal of decision. She riffled through the pages of *The Ladies' Companion.* "Here it is. A gown of the utmost elegance," she quoted aloud, "the Russian bodice discreetly embellished with diamonds . . ."

"Well, you won't get it," Mary said. "I doubt Miss Croll has ever heard of a Russian bodice, and as for diamonds— well, setting aside the expense, it is not good *ton* for *jeunes filles* to wear anything so . . . so showy. It will be pale muslins and silks for you, sister dear, and if you are lucky, a modest string of pearls, the same as for me."

"Then I shall take a rich husband as soon as possible, and wear what I please!" declared Eliza, not one whit discouraged.

Charity, listening to their chatter, was reminded of happier days when she and Arianne had many similar arguments. Arianne had always wanted to shine, while she—but this was treading on dangerous ground. She must not allow herself to dwell on the past, for it would inevitably lead to the more painful present.

Over the last day or two, more noticeably since Fitz had left for London, she fancied that she had discerned a hint of strain in his mother's manner toward her. It was difficult to define, for Mrs. Fitzallan could never be anything other than kindly. But nor was it imagination. Which led her to the dismal but inescapable conclusion that she was in danger of outstaying her welcome, and must take positive steps to find employment. Each day, when Mr. Fitzallan had discarded his newspaper, she secretly scanned the advertising columns in the hope of finding a relatively local vacancy. But there was nothing. And each day she became increasingly aware that, in spite of the company of the girls, she had never felt so alone in all her life.

The sudden indisposition of Miss Croll offered Charity a temporary respite; for a short while, at least, she was able to be of some use. It was when she was in the middle of pinning a flounce on a pretty muslin day dress, that Mrs. Fitzallan put her head around the parlor door and beckoned to her urgently. In the drawing room she begged Charity to be seated, and did so herself, puffing from her exertions.

"I have no wish to worry you, my dear," she began in some agitation, "but I thought you should know at once . . ."

Her opening words had already set Charity's pulse racing with alarm. "Something is wrong at Ashbourne Grange. Is it Harry?"

"No, no indeed! I'm sorry, I am being very clumsy about this, am I not? But the thing is, Mrs. Treadgold has just returned from her weekly visit to Mrs. Bennett, and she tells me that Nurse Fenton has walked out—she and Miss Throstle have been at odds from the first, of course, and this morning she simply packed her bag and left without so much as a moment's notice, declaring that she could not stand Miss Throstle's constant interference one moment longer!" She paused for breath. "What do you think of that? I was never so surprised, for in the circumstances she will find it very difficult to obtain another position!"

Charity couldn't have been less interested in the petty squabbles of the two women. "But what will happen to Emily?" she demanded, her mind racing ahead.

"Quite! My very thought. That was what decided me that you ought to be told, especially in the light of events. For it seems that the poor child has been ailing for weeks, and her cough has not improved as it ought. Nurse insisted that it was nothing more than an attention-seeking habit which must not be encouraged. But this was so clearly not the case that Miss Throstle finally took matters into her own hands and insisted that Mrs. Bennett should send for Dr. Thomas at once. Well! That did it, apparently."

Charity scarcely heeded the details. Only one thing now concerned her. "What did the doctor say?"

"Well, as to that . . . now, you mustn't worry yourself, my dear . . ."

"Tell me, please!"

The quiet, raw agony of Charity's voice moved Mrs. Fitzallan deeply. "I gather he spoke of a severe congestion of the lungs. Oh, believe me, child, I have been through it all a great many times! Why, I cannot count the number of times I have thought mine at death's door and in a day or two, there they were running about again, as fit as fleas!"

But not at Emily's age, and not with her delicate constitution, Charity wanted to scream. She was angry—furious, in fact—when she thought of the patient hours she had spent building up the frail scrap of life that Emily had been in the weeks following her birth to a point where she at last began to thrive. And her anger was directed not so much against the nurse, who was merely stupid, but against the duke and his uncaring son, who had willfully set at nought all that had been achieved. Now it would all have to be done again, and not by the governess and Mrs. Bennett who, at best, could only share the nursing or hire someone to do it for them. And it was suddenly very clear who that someone must be.

"I shall go to her at once," she said with implacable resolution.

8

"Captain Fitzallan—it is Captain Fitzallan, is it not?"

The voice, smooth but with an undercurrent of cynicism, greeted Fitz as he left Gentleman Jackson's establishment, where, so he had been reliably informed by friends, Alistair was frequently to be found at this time of day. But not on this particular day.

The face of the languid, exceedingly elegant gentleman who had thus addressed him was vaguely familiar, but try as he might, Fitz could not call the name to mind.

"Darian," murmured the baronet with a graceful bow.

"Of course—Sir Rupert," Fitz stammered, embarrassed by his lapse of memory. "Do forgive me, my mind was elsewhere. We have met, I think—at Lady Sefton's?"

"Quite so. You were with a rather charming young lady, as I recall. A Miss Wynyate."

"Yes."

Sir Rupert smiled faintly, and made no attempt to pursue the subject. "You follow the Fancy, I see. Such energy! But then, I daresay your life will have accustomed you to physical exertion." He saw that Fitz was looking puzzled, and nodded in the direction of Jackson's rooms.

"Oh, I see. Well, yes, I do—but that isn't why . . . as a matter of fact, I was looking for Ashbourne. You haven't seen him, I suppose?"

"Regrettably, no. However, if our paths should cross, I will be happy to tell him you are looking for him. Can I give him a message, perhaps? No? Ah well, so be it."

He bowed again, and strolled on up Bond Street, leaving Fitz with a decidedly uncomfortable feeling, the kind of feeling he'd had one time in a bivouac on the plain beyond Salamanca when he'd opened his eyes to find a snake lying quite still not more than a few inches away from him, staring him in the face. He shuddered, remembering how he had stared back, transfixed, until it finally slithered away.

It was well into the evening when Fitz finally came upon Alistair and his friend, Mr. Trowbridge, in White's. They were just emerging from one of the gaming rooms, and from the good-natured observations of his friend, it would appear that his lordship had been on a winning streak.

"Come and sit down, Fitzallan, and take a drink with us," Mr. Trowbridge said with a droll smile. "I am sorely in need of one," he continued, disposing himself comfortably opposite Fitz. "I tell you something you might care to bear in mind—never throw against the bank when Stair is holding it."

"A simple run of luck, nothing more," drawled Lord Alistair, stretching out his long legs and crossed them at the ankles. "Do you gamble, Fitz?"

"No. Not one of my vices, I'm afraid."

"Don't apologize. It has ruined many a good man." He took a sip of port and lifted his quizzing glass to squint down at the gleaming toe of his shoe. "Ned came pretty close more than once, I think?"

"Once or twice," Fitz admitted, loath to criticize his dead friend. "But he seldom got in so deep that he couldn't come about, and never, or almost never, after he became a family man."

"H'm." His lordship's chin sank a little deeper into his cravat. "But I doubt there was much to leave them when he went?"

"I have no idea," Fitz said flatly.

Alistair's rather heavy eyelids lifted and the slate gray gaze fixed on him keenly. "No need to poker up, man. I'm not trying to make you say anything you've no wish to say." His expression was enigmatic. "You were ever a good friend to my brother. Would that we could all say as much."

"Oh, I don't know . . ." Fitz moved uncomfortably. "I

always thought you and he got on rather well. He spoke of you often.''

"Did he, indeed?''

Surprised by the unexpected note of bitterness, Fitz glanced across at Theo Trowbridge, who gave a puzzled shrug, and waited for Alistair to say more. But he made no attempt to fill the awkward gap in the conversation, and it was Theo who finally said, "Haven't seen you about recently, Fitz-allan. We rather thought you must have gone away.''

"Been visiting my parents,'' Fitz said, wondering if this was the opening he had been seeking. He decided to fortify himself with a further generous measure of port.

"Ah,'' Theo nodded sagely. "Did the same thing m'self a short while back. Not overfond of the country, mind, but one must make the effort occasionally.''

Alistair did not even appear to be listening as he lounged in brooding silence, swirling the wine around in his glass and contemplating its rich depths. So that it came as a surprise to both his companions when he said abruptly, "And Miss Wynyate?''

The unexpectedness of the question almost caught Fitz off guard, but he was resolved not to descend to untruths, and managed to reply with tolerable composure, "Ah, well, the fact is, I managed to persuade her to come with me to Guil-ford. She is staying with my parents until she can obtain a suitable position. Her circumstances, as you must be aware, are . . . difficult. However,'' he added, seeing the set of Alistair's mouth, "you need have no fear that she will try to communicate with the children. Even if she had not given her word, Charity is very conscious that it would merely serve to unsettle them to no purpose.'' It was unquestion-ably the opening he had been waiting for, and he felt the dry mouth and flutter of apprehension that had always attended those final moments immediately preceding a battle.

"However,'' he began, saw one frowning inquisitorial eye-brow lift, and hurried on, "it does bring me rather neatly to what I wish to say. You see, to be plain with you, Alistair, this is no chance meeting. I came to London with the particu-lar intention of seeking you out.''

"I confess, you surprise me," drawled his lordship, at his most ironical. "Should I be flattered?"

"Probably not. In fact, you may well wish me at Jericho, but I must risk that. The thing is, although Charity has not been in communication with anyone at Ashbourne Grange, I have. Ned and Arianne always made me free of their rooms in Brussels, and Harry and I always got on famously, so it seemed very natural in the circumstances that I should go to see him."

"Mighty civil of you. And?"

Again the irony was marked, and Fitz felt anger stirring in him. "*And*, Alistair, I shall not scruple to tell you that I was shocked at the change in the boy."

His lordship sat forward unhurriedly. "He is not unwell?"

"In the physical sense, no—a little pale, perhaps. But as for his spirit—lord, I never saw such a change in anyone! What Charity would do if she knew the half it, I shudder to think. Why, the lively, inquisitive child I knew has almost been crushed out of existence. That Friday-faced governess has him so that he's almost afraid to utter a sound for fear of incurring her wrath."

"Are you not perhaps being a trifle oversensitive, Fitzallan?" Theo put in soothingly, having glanced at Alistair's face. "Young children do need discipline."

"Discipline, yes. My two young rips of brothers are disciplined by their tutor, but it don't kill all the fun in 'em. I couldn't get two words out of him until we were well away from the house, and even then he was half-afraid to let go. I was so sorry for the lad, I went back the next day to give him a ride on Ben's pony, knowing how mad keen he always was on horses, and I tell you he was so grateful, it was pathetic!" Fitz looked Alistair straight in the eyes. "He seemed to have formed the impression that you were going to make some provision in that direction?"

Theo, waiting for his sometimes intemperate friend to answer, wondered if Fitzallan knew how dangerously he trod in attempting to take Alistair to task, an undertaking so delicate that even he approached it with caution.

"And I suppose you now expect me to be so moved by

your touching story that I shall drop all my engagements to ride *ventre-à terre* to Surrey?''

The withering sarcasm, however, far from unnerving Fitz, simply made him realize how futile it would be to make any further appeal to his good nature. The Alistair he had known of old clearly no longer existed. He stood up, every inch the young officer who had distinguished himself in battle and earned the respect of his peers as well as those who had served under him.

"I would not presume to tell you your business," he said quietly. "That must rest with your own conscience. I have said what I came to say, and now," he bowed stiffly, "if you will excuse me, I will take my leave."

"Must you?" Theo queried kindly. "I should be sorry to see you depart in such a fashion." He glanced reproachfully at Alistair, whose vivid face was set in harsh, discouraging lines. After a rather tense moment these dissolved into something nearer to impatience.

"Theo's right, man," he growled, and then, impatiently, "Oh, dammit, Fitz, don't be so stiff-rumped! Come down off your high ropes, and we'll broach another bottle."

Fitz shook his head. "Thank you, but I think not. The wine might choke me." He bowed. "Servant, Trowbridge. Alistair."

"Damn!" muttered his lordship, watching Fitz depart, straight-backed. "Impetuous young fool—and all for the love of a woman!"

"You think so?" mused Theo. "Well, perhaps. A masterly performance, nonetheless. And as for youth, Fitzallan is no younger than you or me, and has in his time, so I hear, acquitted himself nobly."

"Inferring that I have not?" growled his ungracious companion. His smoldering glance met Theo's, and he shrugged. "Well, you may have a point. The devil of it is, so has he. I also knew the lad was mad about horses—and, yes, I did give him to understand that I would do something about it. It simply slipped my mind."

"Ah!"

Alistair squinted at him suspiciously. "Do I deduce from

that highly eloquent monosyllable that you expect me to rectify the matter with all speed?''

"My dear fellow, as Fitzallan so succinctly put it, I would not presume to tell you your business."

"Careful, Theo. Even you can go too far." From the chuckle which greeted his remark, he deduced that the warning had fallen wide of the mark. He sighed. "I suppose I shall have to go down there and judge for myself what is going on, regardless of the fact that this whole rotten mess is none of my making. Would that my father could be brought to see sense."

"He might, given time."

Alistair tossed back the last of his wine and stood up. "He might—but I wouldn't hazard good money on't."

Melissa, as might have been expected, was less than pleased to learn that he was to leave town on the following day, and could give her no clear idea of how long he would be away. Also, it was most unfeeling in him to tell her just as they were going down the dance at Mrs. Templeton's ball, so that she was unable to quiz him about it there and then, and when she finally did so, he proved curiously evasive.

"Come," he murmured persuasively, "confess that you will scarcely miss me. Whenever I have called in Cavendish Square recently, you have been talking trousseaux with your mama and have hardly given me a second glance!"

Melissa bit her lip. "That is not true, and if it were," she lowered her eyes demurely, "you will surely want me to be as beautiful as possible for you?"

Minx, he thought, aware of an unexpected rasp of irritation at his betrothed's never-ending obsession with beauty. But he dutifully paid her the compliment she sought, and indeed it was no less than the truth, for in her peach-bloom silk gown she did look incredibly lovely.

Much mollified, she returned to her attempts at persuasion. "And what of Lady Jersey's drum? We are both promised to her for tomorrow evening . . ."

"I shall make her my apologies. And you will surely still attend with your mama."

"But it won't be the same if you are not there! And then there is Thursday—you surely cannot have forgotten that you have invited Mama and Aunt Agnes to the Opera?"

"So I did." If anything could be guaranteed to reconcile him to his forthcoming mission, it was the knowledge that he would be reprieved from entertaining Lady Vane and her top-lofty sister. "How very unfortunate," he murmured, "but I'm sure your mama will understand when I explain that I have some urgent business to transact for my father which cannot wait. And she and your aunt may still enjoy the comfort of my box—Theo Trowbridge shall stand as my proxy," he concluded, cheerfully consigning his friend to the role of sacrificial lamb.

But this did not sit at all well with Melissa. "Well, I think it a shabby way to treat Mama! What she will say, I dare not—"

"Dearest," he cut in, his ironical drawl cooling a trifle, "you are beginning to grow tiresome. We are not married yet, you know."

There was nothing in his voice to suggest he was being anything but teasing, yet Melissa felt a tiny frisson that warned her to tread carefully. During the months of their betrothal she had come to recognize beyond Alistair's impeccable front a contained ruthlessness which, if provoked, might explode into violence: it was, if she was honest, this thrill of the unknown that had fascinated her, lending a certain spice to their relationship as she took an argument to the very brink of danger. It fed a side of her otherwise conforming nature that lurked, unsuspected, beneath the beautiful facade. Only one person, apart from her brother, had ever witnessed the curious excitement aroused in her by the kind of physical excesses no lady should even admit to knowing about—and that person, she had sometimes suspected, was capable of anything.

It was bitterly cold when Lord Alistair set out for Ashbourne Grange the following morning in his curricle, minus John Gage, who had been dispatched to look over some possible mounts for Harry and would follow later. It there-

fore fell to his valet, Flagg, to ride in solitary state in the
light travelling coach, surrounded by his lordship's baggage,
a signal honor which he would as lief have relinquished.
When last seen, Flagg had been sitting apprehensively in one
corner of the coach, a thin finicky man, clutching upon his
knee a square wooden box containing all his precious lotions
and potions, and no doubt calling upon heaven to question
the sanity of his master in choosing to leave the comforts
of St. James's Square in a March squall for the dubious
amenities of a country house. Flagg had very little opinion
of the countryside, though he must perforce endure its short-
comings from time to time. It was a part of the price one
paid in order to have the dressing of a nonpareil such as his
lordship.

It was well into the afternoon and growing gloomy with
the onset of a fine rain when Lord Alistair reached his
destination, only to discover that, in the absence of his
groom, there was probably no one competent to stable the
horses. He cursed his lack of foresight, aware that John Gage
might well not arrive until the morrow.

He sprang down and led the team slowly forward. To his
surprise, the interior of the stable was immaculate, tackle
that hadn't seen use in years, polished and hanging neatly
in place.

"Hello?" he called, and almost at once a bent figure
shuffled out of the shadows and touched his forelock.

"M'lord."

"You are?" he barked.

"Adam, m'lord."

"Adam? Great heaven! So you are." He stared with a
sense of shock at the man who had shaped his own love of
horses as a boy. This shabby old man? He no longer looked
capable of unsaddling a horse, let alone cope with a team
and curricle.

"Is there no one else here?"

The old man ran a hand lovingly over the sweating flank
of the near-side leader. "No one but me, m'lord. E'nt been
no call for any stabling—not since your sainted mother passed
on, God rest her."

"Yet you keep everything in good order, I see."

"Aye, well, old habits die hard, sir, and anyways, it gives me something to do."

"I suppose it does. Well, Adam, you'll be pleased to know that there will be a limited amount of work for you from now on—just a couple of hacks, and a pony for Master Harry."

"Ah! Now, there's a chip off the old block, m'lord, if you don't mind me saying so. Quite took me back, seeing the lad. Several times I've caught him hanging around here when he can escape from that old—" He met Alistair's frowning glance, and thought better of what he was about to say. "Anyways, it'll be grand to have some life about the place again."

"Meanwhile, there is the immediate problem of dealing with these horses. My groom will be here some time tonight or tomorrow with the horses, but it is not likely he'll arrive before my traveling coach." There was a note of doubt in his lordship's voice. "Do you know of anyone who could give you a hand?"

"I can still cope an equipage like this 'un, m'lord, for all that some might think me good for nothing." And then, pride satisfied, he deigned to consider the possibilities. "But I daresay as I could get young Fred from the farm to help out for a day or two."

A short while later up at the house, Mrs. Bennett came hurrying into the hall, summoned by an incoherent maid-servant, to find his lordship had tossed his beaver hat and his gloves down on the table and was already beginning to divest himself of his greatcoat.

"Goodness me, my lord, I had not expected . . . Fancy you turning up like this, almost as if it was meant! And to think that I was on the point of writing to you. Mary, don't just stand there! Do you take his lordship's coat, and then go and tell Jacob to light fires immediately in the drawing room and the master bedchamber."

"Don't fuss, Mrs. Bennett. I shan't take any immediate harm for the want of a fire."

"That's as maybe, sir, but you must be halfway frozen,

and that bedchamber in particular will take a deal of airing. And as for what I'm to give your lordship for dinner . . . well, I'll have to see Cook. She's doing a nice piece of boiled mutton with caper sauce for us, but—"

Alistair stemmed his impatience. "That will do splendidly, ma'am."

Mrs. Bennett looked relieved. "If you're sure, sir. And I believe there might be a bottle or two in the cellar, left over from her ladyship's day."

"Yes, yes, I'll look presently."

"Well then, for now, perhaps you might care to step into my back parlor? It's not what your lordship's used to, of course, but there is a good fire in there . . . ." A sigh escaped her. "Only what with Nurse walking out like that, without so much as a thought for anyone else, and that poor child as near death's door as made no matter, with the doctor coming and going—"

"Mrs. Bennett!" He cut in on her so abruptly that she stopped in mid-sentence, while he shook off an unfamiliar feeling of alarm that swept through him at these somewhat garbled revelations. "What is all this talk of death and doctors? Be plain, if you please! You say Nurse Fenton has gone?"

She looked bewildered, almost apprehensive, in fact. "But I thought for sure you must know, my lord, and that was why you were here."

"No," he said. God, give me patience! he thought. "I came because—well, never mind why I came. Mrs. Bennett, do by all means let us repair to your parlor. Then you can tell me everything plainly from the beginning."

She led the way at his behest, and within a short time he was sitting beside a blazing log fire, fortified with a glass of her elderberry wine, while she sat uneasily facing him, recounting the gist of all that had happened. However, his relief that the patient was not Harry, was almost immediately superseded by quite another emotion as Mrs. Bennett concluded, ". . . we did all we could, of course, but goodness knows how we should have managed without Miss Wynyate—''

"*Who* did you say?"

"Miss Wynyate, m'lord. Such a pleasant, capable young lady. She is the children's aunt—''

"I know who Miss Wynyate is," he said grimly.

Mrs. Bennett was too engrossed in her narrative to heed his change of manner. "Well, I supposed you might, sir. It was ever so strange, though, when you think about it, that she should just happen to be staying not above two miles away with the Fitzallans . . . as if it were meant for her to be there on hand. Naturally she came, the moment she heard . . .''

"Oh, I'm sure she did!" he murmured, but the sarcasm was lost on Mrs. Bennett.

"And as well she did, my lord, for that little Emily was in a terrible way! She still isn't quite out of the woods, but considering that when Dr. Thomas first saw her, he as good as said she'd no chance at all, it's little short of a miracle— and the good doctor makes no bones about who should take the credit!''

Alistair stood up. "Thank you, Mrs. Bennett. Your account has been most—illuminating.'' He strode to the door and, pausing there, said, "I wonder, would you be so kind as to ask Miss Wynyate to spare me a few moments of her valuable time? I shall be in the drawing room.''

"Certainly, my lord. It's high time the poor young lady had a spell out of the sickroom.''

The drawing room was univintingly cold, though the curtains had been drawn and a passable fire now crackled in the huge grate. The twin chandeliers had not been lit, but a number of candelabra had been placed about the room, and their flickering tongues of light made soft welcoming pools among the shadows. For an instant his thoughts were distracted by memories—he could almost fancy that he heard his mama's enchanting laugh, caught a drift of her perfume lingering on the air, and he despised himself for indulging in mawkish sentiment.

The candle flames dipped and steadied as the door opened. He turned to see the figure of a woman etched in the opening, slim and still, as though reluctant to step inside. His voice traveled harshly across the space between them.

"So, Miss Wynyate, this is how you keep your word!"

9

Charity had had only a few minutes to prepare herself for an interview which she knew would be unpleasant, to say the least. Ellen, the housemaid, had slipped upstairs to tell her that his lordship had arrived, and she heard the news with sinking heart, knowing that it would only be a matter of time before she was sent for, and knowing herself at that moment to be ill-equipped for an argument.

Emily was fast asleep when Mrs. Bennett came with his lordship's summons. "He'll be wanting to thank you for all you've done, I daresay," she whispered, all unsuspecting. "You go along now. I'll stay here until you get back." She sank gratefully into a chair. "I'm not used to all this bustle, and what with arriving so late on and no warning . . . I'm sure I don't know how he'll take to the boiled mutton, but there it is. I've sent Jacob to the farm to see if they've a brace of chickens to spare for tomorrow, and by then Cook is confident of being able to contrive something passable, though his lordship hasn't said how long he intends to stay."

Charity made no comment, but went quickly to wash her face and hands. Her dress was crumpled, but a fresh one would do little to alleviate the tiredness that ran achingly through her body, and as for appearance—she did not much care whether or not Lord Alistair found the sight of her displeasing.

Nevertheless, it took a supreme effort of will to open the drawing room door. He was standing in the center of the room, and did not immediately seem aware of her presence. He was staring into space, and just for an instant she imagined there was a slight droop to the elegant figure, as though his thoughts brought him deep unhappiness. And then he turned, and even the poor light could not hide the sudden change in his expression.

His mood was confirmed by his greeting, which was very much as she had expected, yet the hurt it caused ran surprisingly deep, driving her onto the offensive. Her weariness banished, she lifted her head and gave him back look for look.

"You assured me that the children would be well cared for—is this how you keep *your* word, my lord?"

His eyes narrowed as he came closer. "So that is to be your argument. Well, it will not wear, madam. Shall I tell you why? Because you came down here with Fitzallan long before any word reached you of Emily's illness—expressly, as I venture to suggest, that you might inveigle your way in here at the first opportunity." He paused fractionally. "I see you make no attempt to deny it."

Charity realized that she still held the door open. Now she closed it, though she continued to lean against it for support. She wondered vaguely how he came to know so much about her movements, and then shrugged the thought away as of little account. He had moved very close, so that she was pressed back against the door, looking up at him.

"Why should I trouble to deny anything? Your opinion, preconceived and highly prejudiced, as I would expect, matters not one whit. My own conscience is clear, and that is all that need concern me. Can you say as much, my lord?"

Alistair, for all his anger, could not but admire her spirit, though it did not in any way affect his judgment, which was that she had knowingly and willfully set out to defy his father's edict, and similarly to ignore his own warnings. If anything, the very pallor of her face merely served to anger him the more.

"How dare you attempt to call up conscience as some kind of talisman when your very actions speak for themselves! You may think yourself lucky that I shall not in this instance inform my father of what has happened. Had circumstances been otherwise, I might well have been moved to do so. As things are, I suppose you had better remain, at least until another nurse can be found, after which—''

''No!''

''I beg your pardon?''

His face was very close, oppressively so, and, wrapped in shadow, it looked doubly awesome, but suddenly Charity didn't care.

''I said, no, my lord, I shall not leave—at least not without the children. I gave you fair warning. And this time you will not frighten me with threats of what your father might do, or how this travesty of a life is for their own good. I made the greatest mistake ever in going against my own instincts, and convincing myself that they would have a better start in life among their father's family. Oh, how wrong I was! From now on, they go where I go, and I shall take care that you don't find us. Times may prove hard, but at least we shall be together, and the children will be loved—something that all the money and all the privilege in the world can't buy!''

''Have a care, Miss Wynyate,'' he said softly. ''Until this moment, I have treated you more liberally than you deserve.''

But by now, she was in the grip of a powerful exhilarating force that refused to be quelled. ''My dear Lord Alistair, I don't give a fig for your liberality. My mind is made up. But I would like some answers.'' Charity's voice trembled in spite of all her efforts to steady it. ''I would like to know how you came to give your niece and mine—a babe not yet twelve months old—into the charge of a woman so blinkered that she discouraged all contact with her brother, and so incompetent that she allowed Emily to sink to the very brink of death without thinking it necessary to have recourse to a doctor, in spite of the constant exortations of Mrs. Bennett and Miss Throstle? Ah, I see that surprises you. Well, you may ask Mrs. Bennett if you doubt my word! Also, I would very much like to hear you ask, just once, how Emily does— or do you really care so little?'' Tears of sheer weakness and anger were by now streaming, uncontained, down her

face. "Last of all I w-would like to—no, I demand the right
to stay until . . ." All at once, Lord Alistair's face seemed
to be coming and going, and though she was begging him
to be still, no words would come. And then she felt herself
being lifted and was aware of the not unpleasant sensation
of floating . . .

"Miss Wynyate! Can you hear me?"

It was Lord Alistair's voice. He still sounded angry, but
in quite a different way.

"Of course I can hear you," she muttered complainingly,
"there is no need to shout."

He uttered a sound which might, had she not known it to
be impossible, have been a choked laugh. Then she heard
Mrs. Bennett's voice.

"Poor young lady. Worn out, that's what she is—and small
wonder, for she's had little sleep, day or night, though we've
done all we can to help. I never saw such devotion."

This was becoming embarrassing. Charity opened her eyes
to find them both staring down at her, Mrs. Bennett with
genuine concern, and his lordship—well, it was as hard as
ever to divine what he was thinking. She struggled to sit up.
The room swam and then steadied.

"Oh, do have a care, Miss Wynyate," begged the housekeeper. "I am sure you had much better lie still. Does your
lordship think that perhaps a little brandy might be in order?"

But before he could make answer, Charity had forestalled
him. "Thank you, ma'am, but there is no need for a fuss.
I am already feeling much more the thing."

"Well, you don't look it," said Lord Alistair abruptly.

"Thank you, my lord," she murmured faintly. "With such
encouragement I must be on my feet in no time!" She
attempted to suit the action to the word, and found it quite
beyond her. "Oh, this is really very silly. I never ail. In fact,
in general I am as strong as a . . ."

"Mule?" suggested his lordship, and saw her bite her lip.
"I fancy that in this instance, ma'am, you have driven
yourself too hard and for too long, and must now pay the
price." Fearful of being sent away, she began to protest,

but he had already turned to Mrs. Bennett. "See that Miss Wynyate's bed is made ready."

"Yes, of course, m'lord. A good night's sleep, that's what you need, Miss Wynyate—and I'll have Cook make you one of her very special possets. And you needn't worry about the little one—we shall manage somehow." She hurried away, deaf to all protests, leaving behind her a curious atmosphere of unreality.

Charity, very conscious of Lord Alistair's brooding gaze upon her, was unaware that he was reliving the shock of seeing her crumble at his feet—and wondering to what extent his own intolerance was responsible for shattering the thin shell of her composure. He was seldom given to indulging in self-recrimination; life, on the whole, had always gone on very much the way he ordained it. Even Melissa, though it went against the grain with her, seemed prepared to dance to his tune. So that he had never felt it necessary to put himself out for anyone, with the possible exception of his father—never, that is, until the advent of Miss Wynyate with Ned's children in train, Charity Wynyate, who refused to conform to any of the accepted conventions simply because they were there, who would fight like a tiger in defense of her rights, and seemed determined to turn his peaceful life upside down.

"This is all quite unnecessary, sir," she said, breaking the silence at last. "I really am feeling a great deal better already, and with your permission, I think I should be getting back to the nursery."

"You aren't going anywhere, except to your bed."

There was note of finality in his voice, but she chose to ignore it. "In other circumstances, that would be very pleasant, my lord. But for now, it is hardly practical. Your arrival has put a great deal of extra work on Mrs. Bennett and her very limited staff. It would not be fair to place upon them the added burden of caring for Emily."

"Dammit, woman! Will you, just for once, do as I say and stop worrying about those confounded children?"

She blinked at his sudden ferocity. "They are not confounded," she said weakly, trying to put from her mind the blissful thought of sleep. "They are very lost and alone, and someone must worry about them, you know." To her horror, tears were beginning to choke her, and there was nothing she could do to stop them. "Oh!" she cried, mortified beyond measure. "Now look what you've done!"

Had she attempted to use tears as a weapon, he would have had no compunction in giving her a setdown. But her obvious disgust of her own weakness, and the subsequent attempt to lay the blame for it at his door, gave her a quite unlooked-for vulnerability which in turn had the oddest effect upon him.

He said with surprising gentleness, "I'm sorry. I had not meant to make you cry."

"No, of course not." Charity took a handkerchief from her pocket and scrubbed at her eyes. "You are quite right—I *am* tired. Emily is no longer in any danger, and I shall be much more use to her after a good night's sleep." She blew her nose, put the handkerchief away, and stood up, holding on to the arm of the sofa to steady herself.

"Are you able to manage?" he asked.

She smiled wryly. "Thank you, yes."

He watched her walk very slowly toward the door, and after a moment moved to open it for her. "Nevertheless, I believe I will see you safely up the stair."

"Really, my lord, there is no need," she began, and then stopped, her breath catching on a half-sigh as she thought of that long climb. "Well, part of the way, perhaps. Pride is all very well, but I confess I should be grateful for the support of a strong arm."

But he insisted upon accompanying her right up to the nursery floor, appalled that she should be living in such cramped conditions when there were rooms a'plenty on the floor below.

"I have lived in worse," Charity said, her breath labored as she paused at the doorway of a dimly lighted room. "And here I am on the spot, you see. I will just look in on Emily before I retire."

"Miss Wynyate . . ." he began with a trace of exasperation.

"It's all right, my lord. I am not that much of a fool. And in any case, there is no reason to suppose that Emily will not sleep the best part of the night through now that the crisis is passed." She hesitated, then said awkwardly, "Thank you."

He bowed. His last glimpse of her as he turned away was of her slim, tired body bending solicitiously over the crib.

Flagg arrived in time to lay out his lordship's clothes for dinner. He had not enjoyed the journey, and although years of experience with Lord Alistair had brought discretion, his very silence conveyed his horror at the lack of the most basic creature comforts, thus confirming all his worst fears.

"Not quite to your liking, eh, Flagg?" Alistair murmured, as the valet prepared to shave him.

"It is not my place to comment, my lord," came the heroic reply, which was somewhat marred by a peevish addendum, "though I have never before been called upon to fetch my own hot water."

"My heart bleeds for you! If it is any consolation, I do not anticipate a long stay."

The dinner confirmed him in this resolve, though it was redeemed in some measure by the discovery in the cellar of a dozen bottles of a very respectable burgundy and an even more handsome pipe of port, so that by the time he repaired to the drawing room once more, taking the port with him, he was in a rather mellower frame of mind, having resigned himself to an evening of boredom.

He stretched out in front of the fire and presently fell to reviewing his life in general and wondering what the devil he was to do about Miss Charity Wynyate. If anyone had told him six months ago that he was about to become embroiled in this contentious family saga, he would have dismissed it as an impossibility.

A sizeable inheritance from a wealthy godfather had enabled him to set up his own establishment in St. James's Square while still in his early twenties. And for the ten years since then he had been content to pursue an agreeable and totally selfish existence, earning for himself a reputation as a noted Corinthian and leader of Fashion; a gentleman with many acquaintances, but few friends. He was also known for his ability to put people down with a glance, should they incur his displeasure, which did not prevent his being much sought after in first circles by mothers with daughters to bestow.

It was even hinted by those doomed to failure that Melissa Vane had succeeded where their own offspring had failed because Lady Vane's son, who lacked his sister's charms, had once been on the recieving end of one of Ashbourne's famous cuts, and her ladyship's subsequent statement that she would not favor a match between him and Melissa had been in the very spur needed to provoke Lord Alistair's interest—and that Melissa's own determination to have him had done the rest. Alistair was not unaware of the malicious rumors; there were even moments when he acknowledged to himself a certain element of truth in them, but what was done was done, and his upbringing had long since innured him to disappointment, likewise to the wounding power of words.

He visited his father regularly out of a sense of duty, but neither of them could pretend to the remotest degree of affection. It had been made cuttingly clear to him from a very early age that, as the youngest and sickliest of the three boys, and the one most dearly loved by his mother, he ranked a very poor third in the duke's estimation. The early death of his mother, and his subsequent harsh upbringing, left a mark upon him thereafter that was to shape his life. He worked quietly and unceasingly to become strong, both physically and mentally, and refused to give up until he excelled in every manly pursuit in order to win his father's approbation, only to find upon achieving his aim, that he no longer needed it. The bequest that came to him shortly after made his independence complete. His father's grudging acceptance of him no longer hurt, and so they had learned to tolerate one another.

A sound within the room disturbed Alistair's thoughts. He

listened and then decided it must have been a log settling in the fireplace. He refilled his glass and again pursued his train of thought.

It had never been his intention to involve himself in the affairs of Ned's family; sheer coincidence had led him to Ashbourne House on that first morning to inquire after his father's gout just as Miss Wynyate arrived with Harry. He had never had any dealings with children, who were to his way of thinking best kept within the confines of their nurseries and schoolrooms until they reached an age where they could hold their own in society without putting anyone to the blush. Even so, Harry's friendly open manner had had a curiously unsettling affect upon him, and it had taken a very real effort of will to dismiss the boy from his thoughts. But it seemed that Harry was not so easy to dismiss, and as for his aunt—

The sound came again, and this time he knew there was someone else in the room. He had no weapon, but was confident of being more than a match for any adversary.

He sat forward easily, so that he might be ready to spring if the necessary should arise. "Who is there?" he said, his eyes scanning the shadows for the least sign of movement. "Come along, for I know you *are* there, and if you do not show yourself immediately, I promise you will be very sorry."

10

For a moment or two nothing happened. And then, out from the shadows at the far end of the room came a small night-shirted figure.

Alistair could scarcely believe his eyes. "What in—Harry! What the devil are you doing here? Come here at once where I can see you."

Harry came very slowly into the light, blinking and some-how managing to look dejected and comical at one and the same time, so that in spite of himself Alistair was hard put to it not to smile.

He said brusquely, "Now then, what is the meaning of all this?" There was no immediate answer. "You had much better tell me, you know."

The small head drooped very slightly. "I wanted to see you," Harry muttered.

"Speak up, my lad."

Harry's head lifted so that their eyes met. "I wanted to see you," he repeated more firmly.

"And was the need so important that it could not wait until morning?"

"It . . . it might be," Harry said uncertainly. "You might be gone away again in the morning."

"I see," said his lordship, beginning to understand. "And? Come now, you are surely not afraid of me?"

"Not 'xactly, Uncle Alistair." But already the child's courage was beginning to evaporate. There was a discernible tremble in the small frame as he looked down at his clasped hands, twisting them nervously. "Only Miss Throstle said

I wasn't to bother you. She said small boys should be seen and not heard.''

Alistair could hear her saying it. ''But you came anyway.'' Clearly, what Harry wanted to say was important to him, and with growing perception, he thought he could make a fair guess as to the gist of it. Without knowing quite why he did so, he held out an encouraging hand, and after a moment Harry stretched out one of his own. ''Why, child, you are half-frozen!''

''I've b-been behind the curtain for a very long time.''

Alistair swore softly. He looked about him for something to wrap round the shivering boy and finding nothing, took him on his knee and rubbed hands and feet briskly. It must have been painful, but though Harry bit his lip hard, he made not a sound. This done, he pushed a footstool close to the fire and sat him down on it, before picking up the poker to stir new life into the logs.

''Don't move from there until you are warmed right through,'' he commanded roughly. ''It will be heaven help me with your aunt if you take a chill over this piece of work!'' It seemed that Harry grew suddenly still as he crouched over the fire. He said more gently, ''Is it about your aunt that you wished to talk to me?''

''Sort of,'' admitted the small voice. ''I w-wondered if we could p'raps keep Aunt Charity as our nurse? Nurse Fenton made Emily nearly die.'' When his uncle said nothing, he went on huskily, ''I'd do everything I was told and not cause trouble . . .''

''Have you been very unhappy here, Harry?''

''Not *so* much since Aunt Charity came,'' was the prompt reply.

Damnation! Alistair thought. ''If it were my decision, Harry, there would be no problem. But I'll see what can be done.''

Harry's shoulders straightened, and he swivelled around on the stool with a look of suppressed eagerness. ''I knew you would! An' if you told grandfather about Nurse Fenton, he'd see, wouldn't he, Uncle Alistair? He wouldn't want Emily to die!''

If only it were that simple. "No, he wouldn't want that," Alistair said slowly. "And if you don't want to incur Miss Throstle's wrath, you had better get back to bed. Are you quite warm now?"

"Um." Harry stood up, reluctant to leave, but allowing himself to be led to the door. Outside, Ellen was taken aback to see the door open and Lord Alistair's face peer almost furtively around it. Until that moment she had been in dread of him, but his eyes met hers with a hint of almost ludicrous dismay, and then he smiled, and she was instantly enslaved.

"Ellen, isn't it? Tell me, Ellen, do you happen to know whether Miss Throstle is still at supper?"

If the maidservant thought the question an odd one for a lordship to utter, she was much to overawed to show it. "She was a minute or so back, m'lord. I seen her with me own eyes."

"Good. Then, would you oblige me by bundling Master Harry back into his bed with all speed before he is—er, rumbled."

Ellen stared, and then as the little boy emerged, giggled, said, "Oh, my! what a to-do, to be sure!" and took his hand. Alistair watched them out of sight as they ran lightly up the stairs amid whispers and much stifled laughter, and then he walked thoughtfully back into the drawing room.

To his surprise, and even more to Flagg's, he slept the dreamless sleep of the just that night, and wakened early, surprising the valet almost out of his skin by appearing unusually alert for the hour.

"It's the country air," he explained, his usually languid manner overlaid with a good humor that Flagg found most unsettling. "I shall walk down to the stables before break-fast."

The rain of the previous evening had cleared off and the morning was fresh and sunny, with a brisk breeze moving the still bare branches of the trees. In the stable yard he found John Gage already about. With Adam, he was busy trying the paces of the stable's newest occupants, and reassessing their good points.

"Not bad, John," said his lordship, having given them

a cursory inspection. He returned to pat the flank of the stout little sorrel pony. "This should be just the thing."

"Aye, he's a bonny creature, is Gyp. Sound in wind and temperament, m'lord." Gage took an a side glance at his master. "I take it the young shaver don't know anything about it?"

"No. I mean to bring Harry down here myself later this morning."

There was a note of pleasurable anticipation in his lordship's voice that the groom hadn't heard there in many a long day. "Well, then, Adam and me'll have his coat shining like the sun for the occasion."

"Meanwhile, I have a fancy for a good gallop. Saddle the big fellow, if you will, and I'll try his paces."

The ride gave Alistair an appetite, and when it was satisfied, he sent for Miss Throstle. She stood before him, prim, hands folded before her as he lounged back in his chair, toying absently with a knife and eliciting a progress report as to how his nephew did.

"He is a bright child, well advanced for his age," she conceded. "Though we have had a few battles over routine and discipline. There is still a tendency toward ebullience which can occasionally disrupt our routine—particularly of late," her tone was ambiguous, "though that can hardly be accounted the child's fault."

"Quite so. I am aware of events. However, there are a few changes I wish to implement. Harry's routine—" he invested the word with a wealth of meaning, "will in future be rather less confining. For instance, I wish him to spend at least one hour a day in the open air—preferably riding, for which I have already made provision." As she gathered her breath to take issue, he added with a softness that masked a hint of steel, "Harry is still very young. I would not like to see all that . . . natural ebullience crushed. I am sure we understand one another."

She flushed a painful shade of red. He had been talking to that Captain Fitzallan, no doubt. "If your lordship is not satisfied . . ."

"I have not said that, Miss Throstle. I simply require you

to relax the reins a touch—give him room to run. Beginning this morning. You may bring him down to me in about an hour's time, but don't tell him why I wish to see him.''

She disliked the horseman's cant, but bowed to his authority, for she knew only too well how fortunate she was to have a place where there was no mistress to make life difficult, and interference in her work was minimal. From the sardonic look in his lordship's eyes, it seemed that he read her thoughts all too accurately.

Well satisfied, Alistair pulled the bell to order fresh coffee, there being no ale on the premises, and rocked indolently back in his chair as he turned his mind to the rather more taxing problem of how best to tackle his father. When the door opened again he did not look up, saying merely, "That was quick, Ellen. Set it down, if you will. I'll help myself."

"It isn't Ellen, my lord," Charity said quietly.

His chair came down with a thud as she walked forward and stretched across the table to set the silver jug on its stand. "The devil!" he exclaimed. "Don't tell me you have taken on the duties of maidservant in addition to your nursery skills? Small wonder you are worn to a thread."

She smiled—a little nervously, he thought. "No, sir. I met Ellen in the hall. She seemed rather flustered with so much to be done—and as I wished to see you, anyway . . ."

Alistair came belatedly to his feet. "Did you, indeed?" His eyes raked her face. "Well, you look better than you did last night, which isn't saying a great deal." He pulled out a chair. "Pray, sit down. You may as well take some coffee with me while you say whatever it is you came to say."

After a moment's hesitation, she complied, watching as he reached for an unused cup and poured the coffee before sitting down himself. How often in his life, she wondered, had he been obliged to perform such menial tasks for himself? Seldom, if ever, was the probable answer. He pushed the cup across to her and their eyes met.

"A novel experience, would you say?" he murmured, reading her thoughts with disturbing accuracy.

"I wouldn't presume to comment, my lord," she replied primly.

One eyebrow quivered. "*Really?* such meekness. Can this be the same young woman who ripped up at me to such devastating effect but a few hours since?"

Charity had the grace to blush, and took a sip of coffee to recruit her courage. "That, my lord, is why I have come. I feel I owe you an apology." Drat the man! She had known this would not be easy, but there was no need for him to *enjoy* her discomforture quite so openly. Her own manner altered accordingly. "Not that I mean to take back one word of what I said, but I am aware that the way in which I said it was—"

"Arbitrary? Brazen? Downright discourteous?" he suggested helpfully.

"Unfortunate," she insisted in a stifled voice, "for I am aware that it cannot have helped my cause, or indeed your opinion of me. which only matters," she added hastily, "insofar as it might well influence any decision you may take."

In the silence that followed, Charity was very much aware of the clock remorselessly ticking away the seconds—ticking away her future, her life. She stole a glance at him, and found him wrapped in thought, his chin sunk in the folds of his cravat. A shaft of sunlight brought a chestnut gleam to the swirl of dark hair and picked out the scar running down from his eye. For one crazy moment she felt an irresistible urge to touch it. Even as she banished it, he raised his head as though having taken some vital decision.

"Harry will be coming down shortly, Miss Wynyate. We are to take a walk together. If you can leave your charge for a while, perhaps you would care to join us?"

Later, as they traversed the ill-kept gardens, with Harry skipping happily between them, she wondered if she would ever understand Lord Alistair. At times his moods fluctuated like quicksilver, so that she was left with no clear idea of what he was thinking. Harry, it seemed, experienced no such difficulty. He was chattering away to his uncle like an excited sparrow—for a moment she experienced a twinge of jealousy, but it was swiftly banished. Any rapport established between them must surely be a hopeful sign.

Charity was unfamiliar with the layout of the grounds, so that it was Harry who first realized that they were approaching the stables.

"Did you come in your curricle, Uncle Alistair?" he asked eagerly. "Can we please go in and see your team?"

She was about to tell Harry not to pester his uncle, but he was already agreeing, taking the boy's hand as they went from stall to stall and explaining to him the good points of each of the horses, while she followed more slowly.

The pony had been put in a stall at the far end, so that it was not immediately visible. But Charity saw her young nephew suddenly stand still—it was almost as if, for that moment, he had stopped breathing. Then he looked uncertainly up at Lord Alistair, and she heard him ask in reverential tones, "Is he for me?"

Hurrying forward, she came level with his lordship in time to see Harry step forward and duck under the bar to join John Gage, who had the pony on a simple leather halter. The groom introduced them to one another, and watched with approval the child's natural affinity with the animal. "That's what I like to see, m'lord—instant trust on both sides."

"And he is truly mine?" Harry still couldn't quite believe it. "Not like the one Captain Fitzallan brought for me to ride?"

"He's all yours, Harry. Do you want to take him out?" Lord Alistair nodded to Adam, who was beaming from ear to ear. "Right. Saddle him up—and the big fellow I rode this morning." He turned to Charity. "Well, Miss Wynyate?"

She ignored the implicit irony to say impulsively, "Very well indeed, my lord. For once I have no criticism to offer."

He inclined his head. "I would imagine that you also ride? I thought as much. The third mount was chosen with you in mind."

Charity began to feel as though coals of fire were being heaped on her, but with the neat bay gelding showing her a limpid welcoming eye, she could only offer him her unqualified thanks. "My riding habit is still at the Fitzallans,' but I shall fetch it at the first opportunity."

It was only later that the full implications of his lordship's generosity came home to her. Her threat of the previous evening to remove the children from Ashbourne Grange must inevitably have been fraught with difficulties, but now, Harry would be loath to leave his new companion. Was it pure coincidence, or part of a strategic battle for Harry's allegiance? Not for the first time a feeling of impotence washed over her—was she destined to fight the Ashbournes forever?

Charity had fully expected Lord Alistair to state terms and depart as swiftly as he had come, but as day followed day, he seemed more than content to remain where he was.

"I really don't know what to think," she told Mrs. Fitzallan on a brief visit to collect her riding habit and a few other items of clothing. "Not a word has he said concerning my ultimatum with regard to the children, but nor has he made any attempt to refute it by giving me the order to quit."

Mrs. Fitzallan protested that he would surely not think of doing any such thing. "It would be quite iniquitous in view of all you have done, as he must surely see."

"Ah, but it is the duke who calls the tune. Lord Alistair is merely the instrument of his malice."

"Oh, I doubt that very much," said Mrs. Fitzallan. "I have not met him for some years, of course, but people do not in general change and even as a boy he was very much inclined to go his own way, the more so after his mother's death—he was devoted to her, you know."

Charity didn't know. This insight into Lord Alistair's past was fascinating and she longed to ask more, but did not wish to appear inquisitive. "Well, I must wait and see, I suppose. And if it does come to a fight, I am resolved to stand firm."

But Lord Alistair showed no evidence of wishing to come to cuffs, except in that rather capricious verbal fashion she was coming to know so well, and once she had learned to recognize it, she was more than able to hold her own. True, he had, in his high-handed way, issued several edicts to which she had offered a token resistance—the first being that with Emily recovering steadily, Mrs. Bennett should make inquiries in the village with the object of engaging a nursery maid, so that Charity was no longer so tied to caring for her niece. To this, Charity willingly agreed, and a very pleasant girl, Alice by name, was taken on.

"So she has your approval, Miss Wynyate," said his lordship. "I am delighted to hear it. You will now have a great deal more time at your disposal, and should be able to resume a more normal existence."

Charity smiled wryly. "I'm not sure that I know what constitutes normal, my lord. My life has been for too long subject to change."

It was this attitude that so intrigued Alistair. There was a curious mixture of strength and serenity about her that constantly confounded him, so that he found himself wanting to know more about her. He had seldom met anyone so unimpressed by the trappings of wealth and power—at times she seemed almost to hold them in contempt.

He said dryly, "Well, for a start, it means that you should no longer have any excuse for declining to bear me company occasionally. I shall therefore be happy to see you at dinner this evening, and each evening for the remainder of my stay."

"I am obliged to you, sir," she said demurely. "You have such a gracious way of extending an invitation. But I fear you do me too much honor."

To her surprise, he laughed aloud. "Touché!" He came close and took her hand, smiling quizzically down at her. "Miss Wynyate, will you do me the honor of dining with me this evening?"

His sudden change of manner was almost her undoing. "Thank you, my lord," she replied a trifle breathlessly, "I shall be happy to do so."

Lady Jersey's drum had been tedious in the extreme without Alistair, and the opera seemed like to prove every bit as dull, with only Theo Trowbridge as escort. Nevertheless, Melissa had persuaded her mama to let her wear a new gown

for the occasion. It had been especially fashioned to captivate
Alistair, but there might be others in the auditorium who
would appreciate its finer points. It was fashioned of ivory
silk, cut daringly low, although to placate Lady Vane, the
neckline had been discreetly draped with a fichu of creamy
lace. Her hair had been dressed with a pretty ornament of
gold and pearls, and she knew that she outshone everyone
else.

Sir Rupert Darian, having espied her early on in the pro-
ceedings, had not been blind to the hint of discontent in the
lovely face, and made it his business to visit the opera box,
though not before the second interval, by which time, he
guessed, her boredom would be close to screaming point.
Lady Vane was deep in conversation with friends and Trowbridge was doing the polite with the aunt, and finding it heavy
going by his earnest expression.

Melissa was for the moment alone, her restless gaze
sweeping the theater in the hope of finding someone worthy
of her interest. In desperation, she awaited the moment when
no one was looking and slipped out into the corridor, where
almost at once she encountered Sir Rupert. Her heart
fluttered. Sir Rupert was not the kind of diversion she had
in mind, but, except for the two of them, the corridor was
temporarily deserted, so there was little she could do to avoid
him. It seemed to her that he had more than ever the look
of a satyr as he levelled his glass at her, the ruffles of his
shirt cuff falling away from a slim white hand.

"Ashbourne really should not leave you unprotected, my
dear," he observed, mockery as ever present in the smooth
voice. "If you were mine, I would guard you more closely."

"Well, I am not yours," she avowed with a touch of
hauteur, even as her pulses quickened. "Nor should I ever
wish to be so."

"No? And yet I have a feeling that we might deal rather
well together. We do, after all, share a number of interests,
do we not?"

She glared down her well-bred nose at him, though by now
her heart was pounding. "I'm sure I don't know what you
mean."

Sir Rupert laughed softly. "As you will, Melissa. But some day it might be . . . entertaining to persuade you to change your mind." He watched her heightened color with interest. And then, changing the subject yet again, asked casually, "Does Ashbourne stay long in the country, do you know?"

She was obliged to confess that she did not, though not by as so much as a blink did she reveal that Alistair's whereabouts were unknown to her—not, that is, until Sir Rupert went on to wonder what could have taken his lordship down to Surrey so precipitately. "Mayhap he has had a change of heart where his young relations are concerned. That would not please you, I think. But such a coincidence, don't you think, that Miss Wynyate should be staying close by with the Fitzallans?"

Melissa hardly knew what she answered; a variety of emotions swirled around in her head. She could not drag her gaze away from his, and it took every ounce of her self-control to remain coherent.

"And such a pity if your ambitions were to suffer in consequence." As if divining her thoughts, he lowered his voice. "Should that come to pass, I might be persuaded to exercise my considerable talent on your behalf by ridding you of your little problem. I'm sure we could come to some agreement as to what you might be prepared to offer in return."

Melissa felt that she could hardly breathe. Her heart was by now beating right up in her throat. What he was suggesting—what she assumed he was suggesting—was monstrous, impossible! And yet, Alistair could not—must not stoop to befriend those children! It was unthinkable when the boy was set to deprive him of what was rightfully his! And as for *that woman*—the scheming creature, when the duke had forbidden her to have any dealings with them.

"You talk in riddles, sir." She forced the words out.

"Do I? But then, riddles are meant to be solved."

He saw Trowbridge, his face tiresomely stern, coming to spoil sport, and sighed. "Your servant, ma'am." He made Melissa a sweeping bow and, having greeted Theo with the utmost politeness, sauntered away.

"It was not altogether wise, m'dear, to come out here alone. You should have told me if you wanted a little exercise."

Theo's gently chiding voice did nothing whatever to soothe Melissa's exacerbated feelings. She turned her back on him with an angry flounce and began to retrace her steps toward the box.

"I did not want exercise—I was bored," she snapped. And then, stopping to fix him with her jewel-sharp sapphire gaze, "Theo, what exactly is Alistair doing down in Surrey?"

11

It had been the Duke of Orme's custom, since the onset of his gout, to take a late breakfast and thereafter to repair to the library to read his newspaper and attend to the post, which his secretary, Mr. Fisk, had previously opened and laid ready for him on the desk.

There was seldom much of interest. People in general only wrote to him when they wanted something. This morning was no exception, and he speedily disposed of the correspondence until almost at the last he recognized the familiar hand of his sister. Euphemia was five years his senior and always addressed herself to him as though he were not yet out of short coats. She lived in the wilds of Warwickshire, too far away, thank God, for anything but written communications. In this instance she had dismissed her steward, and wished him to apply his mind to the vexing question of engaging a new one, but as she invariably dismissed the fellow at least once every year, and as speedily reinstated him, he grunted and consigned the letter to the pile to be answered by Fisk with his usual tact. He reached for the last one with a sense of relief.

His angry bellow was heard by his secretary some way down the hall. Mr. Fisk had been waiting in nervous anticipation, and now, as he hurried to obey the summons, the palms of his hands were perspiring freely.

"Where did this—this piece of anonymous filth come from?" inquired his grace in tones so silky soft that, in spite of all his years in the duke's service, Mr. Fisk quailed.

"Its source, I fear, remains something of a mystery, your grace. The porter informs me that it was handed in by a maidservant at the same time as the post was being delivered.''

"Maidservant! Bah!'' The look he bent upon his secretary was awesome. "There is not a word of truth in it, you understand? Not one word.''

"Quite so, your grace. If your grace will pardon the liberty—there are always people out to make mischief . . .''

"Mischief! I'll give 'em mischief when I run them to earth! Tell Hamlyn I want the traveling coach made ready in an hour's time.''

Mr. Fisk was torn—the duke's gout was a little on the better side, but he was in no fit case to be traveling to Surrey, for there was no doubt in the secretary's mind but that that was where he was bound. He ought to have followed his first instincts and torn the letter into little pieces. But his grace had a devilish queer way of learning things, things you'd swear he couldn't possibly have known about in any ordinary way. It must be a family trait, for Lord Alistair had something of the same omniscience about him. So Fisk bowed to the inevitable, and consoled himself with the thought that whatever ructions there might be at Ashbourne Grange, he at least would be well out of reach of his grace's wrath.

"Aunt Charity?'' Harry asked, as they walked to the stables for their morning ride. "Is Uncle Alistair going to stay here for ever and ever?''

She had begun to wonder something of the sort herself, though in less dramatic terms.

"I wouldn't at all mind if he did, would you?'' Harry persisted.

Charity hardly knew what to answer. So short a while ago the answer would have been "God forfend!'' Yet so many of her previously held opinions of him had undergone a change. Not that *he* had changed in any particular, but perhaps she had come to understand him rather better.

It was now several days since his lordship had arrived and turned everything upside-down, and contrary to all her expectations, he had as yet shown no sign of boredom. When he was not out riding, either in their company or on his own, he occupied his time in taking stock of the house and instituting the refurbishment of some of the more shabby rooms, enlisting her aid in the choice of designs.

"I was under the impression that this was your father's property," she had remarked over dinner one evening when he demanded her opinion of some particular improvement in the brusque way she was coming to know so well. "Will he not mind that you are making all those changes?"

"I very much doubt, my dear Miss Wynyate, whether he will ever know a thing about it."

Much emboldened, she continued, "Mrs. Fitzallan told me once that your mama spent much of her time at Ashbourne Grange."

"True." He frowned and subjected her to a chilling glance. "The country air suited her better. She was ever delicate, and when her health broke down, she moved to the Grange permanently—spent the last six years of her life here, in fact," he concluded in a tone that warned her not to proceed.

Charity would have liked to know more, but felt it would be a pity to spoil the atmosphere of harmony that was beginning to grow up between them, so after a moment of silence she went on to talk of other things.

Alistair lounged back in his chair, toying with his glass and watching her through slightly narrowed eyes. He had never known anyone quite like her—able to combine restfulness and tact with an ability to look you straight in the eye and stand up for what she believed in without equivocation. His mother had the former in abundance, but she had been too gentle in spirit to withstand the excesses of the duke's overbearing personality.

"Does nothing daunt you?" he asked suddenly.

The question took Charity by surprise. "Many things, my lord."

"Name one," he demanded.

"People who ask me questions like that without warning," she replied, quick as a flash.

He laughed aloud—and with a spontaneity that had an immediate softening effect. "You know, increasingly I find myself wondering why you have never married.''

The observation surprised her, but she answered without hesitation, "Quite simply, my lord, I was never asked.''

"Never?''

She smiled, not unflattered by this expression of outright disbelief. "You see, my sister and I were almost invariably together, and the gentlemen saw only Arianne.''

"More fools, they!''

"Ah, but if you had ever seen my sister, you would understand.''

"I did, once,'' he said carelessly. "Ned introduced us. She was certainly beautiful, if a trifle pea-brained. As I remember, Ned hoped at the time to enlist my support against father in his obsessive opposition to their marriage.''

"Which you declined to give,'' Charity exclaimed, remembering.

Alistair shrugged. "There seemed little point. I was never, as you may have gathered, a favorite with my father. Any interference on my part would merely have inflamed an already impossible situation. In any case, his grace would never change his mind, and I could see that Ned was totally besotted with your sister and would marry her with or without parental consent, so in that sense, the die was already cast.'' He saw the indignation in her eyes. "It would seem I have incurred your disapproval.''

"It's a bit late for that,'' she said reprovingly. "But I'm bound to say I find your attitude a bit poor-spirited.''

She expected him to take offense, but to her surprise he chuckled. "Well, no one can accuse you of that particular failing, ma'am. Are you quite sure there was not one single gentleman with wit enough or discernment enough to prize a lively mind above mere beauty?''

"One or two, perhaps—though for the most part they were already married.'' Charity could not remember when she had last enjoyed such a stimulating conversation. She selected a sweetmeat and bit into it with relish. "But I would not have you suppose that frustration has made me old cattish—the children have given me much joy. And I feel bound to tell you that years of observation have led me to the conclusion that, in general, gentlemen do not favor any great degree of intellect in a wife, fearing perhaps that it might pose a threat to their own superiority."

Alistair quirked an eyebrow. "You are hard on us, ma'am," he drawled.

"Perhaps, my lord. I have no doubt there are exceptions as there are with most generalizations, but I would be willing to wager that given the choice between brains and beauty, most gentlemen would choose beauty every time." With great daring she added, "You, after all, are to marry an exceedingly beautiful woman—but then, Miss Vane is undoubtedly as clever as she is beautiful."

For a moment Charity thought she had gone too far. He made no answer and seemed to be frowning quite awesomely. But after a moment he said, "Quite so," poured more wine, and they passed on to less contentious issues.

Lying awake that night, Charity found her thoughts returning to him with disturbing frequency. He was not the easiest of men. From the little she had gleaned from Mrs. Fitzallan and Mrs. Bennett without actually prying, it would seem that his lordship had known little in the way of real happiness—and with the duke for a father, who could wonder at it. She had seen for herself how things stood between them, and had he not made reference to it this very evening. Perhaps that was the root cause of his regarding the world at large with a somewhat jaundiced eye, for wealth alone was insufficient compensation for a want of love and companionship. She had been much interested to learn that Lord Alistair had adored his mother. There was a picture of her hanging in the small music room, portraying a delicate looking lady, not beautiful in the conventional sense but with a serene, gentle smile. According to Mrs. Fitzallan, she had died pitifully young and it would not be altogether fanciful to suppose that this early loss of her grace's softening influence might have had a profound effect upon the formation of Lord Alistair's character.

Charity could not help thinking it a pity that he was to marry Melissa Vane, who, she suspected, would bring out the very worst in him, when what he he really needed was someone to tease him out of his autocratic humors—perhaps even make him laugh at himself, as she had done that very evening.

In fact, the more she saw him, the more she became convinced that there was a different Lord Alistair beneath the face he showed to the world—she had seen fleeting evidence of it in these last few days as, while outwardly dismissing it as something of a bore, he permitted Harry to take up more and more of his time. At first it was just riding, but gradually and in the face of Miss Throstle's obvious disapproval, other pursuits had crept in, and he had not seemed in the least bored as he patiently explained the intricacies of casting a line and how to aim a cricket ball. Was he perhaps, belatedly, recognizing a parallel between his own early life and that of his nephew?

As she drifted into sleep, Charity's subconscious tantalized her with thoughts of how dangerously easy it would be to fall in love. "I could manage him so easily," was her last coherent thought. But common sense returned with the dawn, and with it came an acknowledgment of the futility of harboring impossible dreams.

Breakfast on the following morning was a quiet meal, more so than usual, and Charity was on the point of excusing herself when Ellen came to announce shyly that Captain Fitzallan had called and was asking for Miss Wynyate.

Charity's face lit up. "Ah, so he is back. Do pray ask him to come in—" She stopped suddenly, and looked across at Lord Alistair. "That is, if you have no objection, sir?"

He lounged back in his chair, his manner deeply sardonic. "Pray, feel free to give what orders you please, ma'am."

She ruefully bit her lip, but after a moment decided to take him at his word and nodded to Ellen.

A moment later Fitz was in the room, full of life, and Charity rose to welcome him, hands outstretched. He grasped them eagerly and bent to kiss her cheek. "Mama told me you were here . . ." At this point he suddenly became aware of his lordship's baleful eye on him, and was immediately embarrassed. "Ah, Stair! I am not intruding upon your breakfast, I hope?"

"Think nothing of it, my dear Fitz. Have you eaten? Pray do not hesitate to say if you haven't. I am sure Miss Wynyate will be delighted to order you anything of your choice!"

"No, really . . ." Fitz stammered, very conscious of the sarcasm beneath the words, and not wishing to make things difficult for Charity. But she seemed surprisingly undismayed.

"Pay no heed to his lordship, Fitz," she said, greatly daring. "He is seldom at his most agreeable at this hour of the morning. It usually falls to Harry to coax him into better humor."

"Is that a fact?" He looked at Alistair, who met his glance with a kind of sardonic challenge. After a moment he said quietly, "I am glad. Harry has sore need of a man to look up to."

"And you'd cast me in that role, would you? My good Fitz, you must have windmills in your head!" Alistair came suddenly to his feet. "I suppose you have ridden over? Well, you are come in excellent time to accompany Harry and Miss Wynyate on their morning ride. No doubt you will have much to discuss, and I may use my time more profitably." He nodded curtly to them both and strode out.

As the door closed upon him, Fitz turned to Charity in dismay. "Oh, lord—have I upset him? I really did mean well, m'dear."

"Yes, of course you did. And it is nothing that you have done so pray don't let it worry you. I suspect his lordship is finding it difficult to reconcile his developing attitude toward Harry with the image he has for so long striven to cultivate."

Fitz glanced at her in surprise. "You've changed your mind mighty suddenly! Not so long ago, you hadn't a good word to say for Alistair."

Charity shrugged and turned away to hide the warmth creeping into her cheeks. "Yes, well I may yet be proved to have misjudged his lordship. He has certainly made an

effort where Harry is concerned, and it has made a world
of difference to Harry, as you will see for yourself
presently.''

A short time later Lord Alistair was crossing the hall on
his way to the gun room when he heard Harry's childish
treble lifted in eager greeting—''Captain Fitz, Captain Fitz,
you're back! Oh, famous!''—and for the second time that
morning he felt a stab of something which he did not
immediately recognize as jealousy. It put him in an ill humor,
which he vented upon the large and fast-increasing rabbit
population on the neglected estate. The success of his efforts
delighted Cook, but did little to improve his lordship's
temper.

Charity saw nothing of him until dinner. This was not
unusual, for she still spent some considerable time with
Emily. The doctor expressed himself delighted with her
progress, and she was certainly growing stronger every day,
but although Alice had proved to be an excellent nursery
maid, Charity would not be wholly easy in her mind until
the child was completely well.

For all that she had made light of it to Fitz, Lord Alistair's
behavior had both disconcerted and disappointed her. It
seemed so much at odds with his much more relaxed attitude
of late, and although Fitz had dismissed it as being typical
of his odd quirks, she had the feeling that there was something more to it. In consequence, she approached dinner that
evening with some apprehension, dressing with particular
care and abandoning the gray crape which had served her
well for the past few evenings in favor of a cinnamon-colored
gown of twilled silk trimmed with cream lace—yet another
of Arianne's dresses which she had nimbly adapted. The
color was particularly becoming, and picked up warm lights
in her hair, which for that evening she had coaxed into a
soft fall of curls.

Lord Alistair was in the drawing room before her. As she
entered, he looked—and then looked again, lifting his
quizzing glass in that disconcerting way he had in order to
make a more comprehensive study of her appearance.

"Charming," he said at last. "Are we expecting
company?"

Charity colored, and was thrown on the defensive. "No,
my lord. I merely felt the need of a change."

"I see. Perhaps we should invite Fitzallan to dine. What
do you say to that?"

She hardly knew what to say, mistrusting as she did his
deceptively polite tone. In the end, she answered with equal
politeness that it was for him to decide.

"Did you enjoy your ride with Fitz this morning?"

"Very much." And lest he should try to make more of
her reply than was meant, she added, "So did Harry. They
always did get on well."

"And why shouldn't they? Fitz is a good man."

Charity had the feeling that there was more to the conversation than was actually being said, but for the life of her
she could not fathom it.

The odd atmosphere continued throughout dinner, with his
lordship becoming less and less communicative as the meal
progressed. Also he appeared to be drinking rather more than
usual, but since she had no doubt of his ability to carry his
wine, that was not in itself worrying. She endeavored to
evade trouble by matching her mood to his, returning answer
quietly and pleasantly when he did condescend to address
her. Otherwise she remained silent, and as soon as she could
do so without giving offense, begged to be excused.

"Already?" He glowered across at her. "You've had
mighty little to say for yourself this evening."

"I'm sorry, my lord. I was taking my tone from you."

"Were you, indeed?" he drawled. "Vastly civil of you,
I'm sure. And why, pray, do you think it necessary to humor
me?"

Charity knew that common sense dictated an answer that
could not be construed as contentious, yet she found herself
saying calmly, "Because I've no wish to have my head bitten
off at your slightest whim, sir."

It was a long time before he answered, time enough, certainly, for her to regret her tongue's errant ways. In the

silence, the spit of the logs freshly thrown on the fire and the ticking of the clock sounded inordinately loud. When at last she could bring herself to look him in the face, she was not encouraged to hope. But in the end, all he said was, "Go then, if you must."

Charity had always thought the drawing room a charming room, but now it seemed large and unwelcoming. After glancing through several magazines, she picked up one of the smaller branch candlesticks and went through into the small music room which led off the drawing room and was known more familiarly to the older servants as "the duchess's room." There was no fire here, but the sun had been on the windows for a fair part of the day and the room had retained sufficient warmth to be comfortable.

The pianoforte stood near a window which in daylight looked out onto the herb garden, and it seemed as though the scent of thyme and rosemary and sweet lovage and numerous other herbs lingered permanently on the air. The curtains were not drawn and Charity's reflection looked back at her as she set the candle down on a shelf close by the instrument.

She made no claim to be a musician, but the notes of a Bach prelude came easily to fingers trained in childhood, the calmly reptitive rhythm soothing away all the small irritations of the day.

She did not hear Lord Alistair come in, so she had no way of knowing how long he had been there when, as the last note died away, he said from somewhere just within the door, "And who the devil gave you leave to play my mother's piano?"

She started up guiltily. "I'm sorry, my lord. The room is never locked—I had no idea I was intruding."

He came nearer and in the light of the candles his eyes seemed to glitter strangely. From the rich aroma of port wreathing the air between them, Charity suspected that he was something less than sober, although he gave no other evidence of it. Almost before she knew what he was about, he had pulled her close. "My dear innocent girl, you have been intruding quite damnably since the first day we met."

His arms bound her to him, his face so close that she could see the scar standing out lividly. Surely he must feel the painful thudding of her heart, the unsteadiness of which betrayed itself in her voice as she strove to calmness. "Please, my lord, let me go. You are not . . . not yourself."

He laughed softly. "Why such sham delicacy all of a sudden? It don't sit at all well on you. I can see from your lovely troubled eyes that you think I am badly foxed—drunk as a wheelbarrow, in fact. Not true, of course, I'm not even half cut."

"I would not presume to judge, sir, though I think perhaps you should sit down . . ."

"Only if you will sit down with me, sweet Charity . . ." He savored the name, crushing her ever closer to him. "Charity means love, does it not? And I have a feeling you would love very sweetly." For an instant his face swam before her and then his mouth came down on hers, searching, insistent in its gentle probing—and she, who had long since abandoned all hope that anyone would find her desirable, felt an exultant tremor run through her body. So this is how it feels, she thought as everything in her responded; I shall remember it always, the magic and the shining! Time lost all meaning, but at last he lifted his head, leaving her mouth bruised and tingling from the fire of his touch, and longing for more. She heard him say softly, "Ah, yes—sweet Charity, indeed. I have been wanting to do that for some considerable time."

Still seduced by the languorous sensation which his very nearness had induced in her, the words brought but the faintest pinprick of unease. "And no doubt you are accustomed to getting what you want, my lord?"

He laughed softly, for he too had felt that betraying tremor, the eager response. It told him more about her than she could possibly imagine, her very innocence and inexperience evoking in him a feeling of protective tenderness such as he had not felt for any woman other than his mother until now.

"What if I am?" he quizzed her softly. "You were not wholly indifferent, I think. Come now, confess it!"

Had she really been such easy game? A sudden disgust

of her own behavior, of the ease with which she had
succumbed to—nay, enjoyed his embraces, made her draw
back. "If that is the impression I gave, then I am sorry."

"Why be sorry about something so pleasurable?" He
attempted to pull her close again, but she resisted. "Come,
I never thought you, of all people, would turn missish."

Tears of misery and disappointment were thickening in her
throat, making speech difficult. "If it is missish to be unable
to treat the matter as lightly as you, then I must plead guilty,
sir. No doubt to you this is a delightful game that you have
played a hundred times or more, but I am not accustomed
to bestowing my favors upon all and sundry, and I certainly
have no wish to become one of your bits of muslin!"

"Enough!" Alistair was angry out of all proportion to the
nature of her accusation, perhaps because it had too much
truth in it for comfort. "Unless I am much mistaken, Charity
Wynyate, you have not until now bestowed your favors, as
you are pleased to call them, on anyone—not even Fitzallan.
All your affections have been concentrated upon your sister
and those wretched children!" His lip curled. "I, on the other
hand, as you so rightly say, am well practiced in the art,"
his tone was ruthlessly cutting, "though I have never been
known to take anything that was not freely given."

"Oh!" Indignation almost robbed Charity of coherent
thought, but in her desire to hurt, she stammered, "Insult
me if you will, my lord, but there is no need to defame my
family! In my weakness, I at least have not shamed anyone
but myself! But as for you . . . I should think you would
do well to look to your conscience, betrothed as you are and
shortly to be married, yet boasting to me of your conquests!
And in this, your mother's room!"

For a moment she thought he would strike her. The
glittering anger in his narrowed eyes truly alarmed her, and
she was aware of his hands convulsively clenching and unclenching. "How dare you presume to bring my mother's
name into this! She means nothing to you!" His voice grated.
"As for Miss Vane—you are not the keeper of my morals,
and I will thank you to remember it!"

"Gladly, sir!"

They were so engrossed in acrimony that only gradually did they become aware of an even greater commotion out in the hall. Only as the drawing room door opened to admit the distraught Mrs. Bennett did Alistair recognize the all-too familiar voice upraised in furious condemnation of all within its hearing.

"Curse the lot of you! Y're as clumsy a set of ham-fisted idiots as it has ever been my misfortune to employ. Now, find me my stick and get out of my sight!"

"Good God! I don't believe it!" Their own quarrel forgotten, Alistair strode into the drawing room, followed more slowly by Charity. Shocked into instant sobriety, he was coolly assembling his thoughts even as he moved. "Stay there," he commanded, unceremoniously pushing Charity back into the music room and shutting the door.

Mrs. Bennett hurried toward him, breathless, her face creased with worry. "Oh, my lord, what am I to do? Why, I've never seen his grace above half a dozen times in all the years I've been here, and how I'm to cater for his needs at such short notice, I don't know, since, saving your lordship's presence, and for all that he's your father, I remember only too well how impossible he was to please then."

He cut her short. "For a start, you would do well to have a bedchamber prepared with all speed. Or, better still, he can have mine and you can find somewhere else for me. Inform Flagg that he is to render all possible assistance to Parsons, his grace's valet. As for his grace's needs, you may leave me to deal with them. Now, I can hear him coming, so I'll just move this wing chair closer to the fire—and perhaps you would bring that footstool over before you go."

Even as they completed the preparations, the door was flung open and the Duke of Orme entered, a daunting figure swathed in a black cloak and leaning heavily upon his stick, his free hand grasping the shoulder of a small stout person of sober mien, also impeccably clad in black from top to toe. The inimitable Parsons had been with his grace all his working life, enduring the worst of his humors with a stoicism which often, as now, assumed heroic proportions. The duke looked up, saw his son, and scowled.

"Hah, Alistair! So you *are* here—that much at least is true."

Alistair, though mystified, greeted him calmly and with a speaking glance at Parsons which brought a nod of understanding, begged his father to make himself comfortable before they talked.

"Comfortable—bah! Don't talk like a dolt. When, pray, was I last comfortable. Don't fuss, woman," he snapped, as Mrs. Bennett endeavored to move the footstool closer. "Dammit, leave it to those who know what they are about!"

She uttered an incoherent sound and, receiving a sympathetic nod from Lord Alistair, hastily curtsied and fled the room.

Parsons, fully aware of the pain his grace was suffering, was impervious to insult and invective as he went quietly about the unenviable task of settling his master and making his bandaged leg as easy as possible. Then, having done all he could, he begged to be excused so that he might supervise his grace's sleeping arrangements.

"Yes, yes, leave us, man. I want to talk to my son, and what I have to say don't warrant an audience."

Alistair had a few words with Parsons before he left the room, and then walked slowly back to the fire where he stood with every appearance of ease, leaning a shoulder against the mantelshelf, one foot resting on the fender as he stared down into the flames and wondered what the devil had prompted his father to make a journey which must have entailed considerable pain and inconvenience—and how he would take the situation into which he was come.

"Well, Alistair?" The duke eyed his elegant son dourly, taking in the diamond as big as a fingernail adorning his fancy cravat, the new-fangled black trousers which, he had been informed by Parsons, were fast replacing the knee breeches which had been *de rigeur* for evenings for as long as he could remember.

"I might ask the same of you, sir. It would be idle to pretend I am not surprised to see your grace," Alistair said, stalling for time.

"Aye, and what is more, I'll wager you're less than

pleased! Thought y'rself safe enough from prying eyes here, I daresay.''

The suspicion was growing that somehow, and he knew not how, his father had got wind of Miss Wynyate's presence, but still Alistair feigned innocence. ''If you mean to talk in riddles, sir, we shall get nowhere. I came down to see how my young nephew did, since you made it very clear at the outset that you had no wish to visit this house or its occupants.''

The duke seized on his words. ''Its occupants. Yes, well, there you have it in a nutshell, sirrah. Perhaps you would care to tell me who precisely are its present occupants?''

Apart from a slight narrowing of the eyes, his son gave no hint of his thoughts. But it was enough for the duke. ''Or shall I hazard a guess? Where is she—that cheating jade?''

''She is here, your grace,'' said a clear strong voice from the other end of the room.

12

The drawing room was very quiet after all the histrionics of a few hours earlier. Too restless to sleep, and finding her room too cramped to contain her, Charity had finally in desperation crept downstairs hoping to find the place deserted, and so it was. The candles still burned and although the fire was little more than a dying glow, it retained some warmth. Her one fear—that Lord Alistair might still be around— proved unfounded, and for that much she was glad. Yet another scene on top of all the rest would be one too many.

He had, as she had anticipated, been furious with her for revealing her presence to the duke, whereas she could see no point in deferring such a revelation when his grace had but to ask one of the servants in order to learn the truth. However, she had no wish to get anyone else—even Lord Alistair, for all the bitterness of their recent encounter— into trouble. In the event, her hope had been a vain one.

But now, thank heaven, all was peaceful once more and, as earlier, she made for the music room, where she curled up in a chair turned away from the door with her dressing gown tucked around her. With luck, anyone coming to snuff out the drawing room candles would not venture this far, and would not see her if they did. Moonlight bathed the room in silver light and gradually the tension in her head and shoulders eased and she was able to review the evening's events more calmly. It had been a long, exhausting evening, and tomorrow, no doubt, the arguments would all begin again—if the duke had not made himself ill with the force of his anger.

He had taken up very much where he left off at their last

encounter, ignoring the attempted intervention of his son and reviling her and threatening her with everything he could conjure up from his fertile imagination. But this time she was better prepared, and was determined to stand firm.

"Oh, for pity's sake, can we not leave all this for the morning?" Lord Alistair had said wearily, seizing upon a moment of silence during which his father was working himself up to a fresh outburst. "I've no doubt your leg is plaguing you like the very devil after the journey. Surely you would be much better advised to go to your bed, sir, and let Parsons make you one of his possets."

"Don't be impertinent, sirrah," roared his incensed parent. "You won't fob me off with any shim-sham prating about my health. I wouldn't be here now if y'd done what I told you to do in the first place instead of conniving with this creature who don't even have looks to commend her—"

"Enough, Father." Lord Alistair's voice was silky smooth, its tone causing even the duke to pause. "The lady's name is Miss Wynyate, and I must ask you to accord her the courtesy of using it in her presence and mine."

"Thank you, my lord," Charity said. "I appreciate your concern, though I hope I may be able to fend for myself."

"Quite a pair, aren't you?" sneered his grace. "Lord, I took this for a scurrilous lie when I received it—" he thrust the letter at his son, "but it seems I grow naive in my dotage."

Lord Alistair scanned the brief note with distaste, then crushed it into a tight ball. "No signature! If you give credence to this rubbish, sir, you are indeed less acute than I took you for."

"Ah, but am I?" Fierce eyes looked from one to the other. "As well I did give it a second thought. Betrayed by my own son, egad! Don't trouble to deny it. My orders were quite specific—"

"If your grace would allow me to explain . . ." Charity began.

"I don't want y'r explanation, madam. I want you out of this house, bag and baggage, first thing in the morning."

"I'm sorry, but that will be quite impossible. As I told

his lordship when he presented me with a similar ultimatum some days ago, if I go, the children go with me.'' She saw him glance sharply at Lord Alistair. ''I have quite made up my mind, sir. And since Emily has been extremely ill, entirely due, I may say, to the incompetence of the nurse in whose charge she was placed, I could not contemplate moving her until the doctor says I may safely do so.''

Alistair sighed and bent upon her a look of acute exasperation, which she met with defiant but unruffled calm. ''What Miss Wynyate says is quite true, sir. The child almost died.''

His confirmation, far from mollifying the duke, only succeeded in making him more choleric. And his spleen was vented upon the young woman who stood so quietly immoveable, facing him without a trace of fear.

''I'll have you thrown out!''

''Then I'll come back,'' Charity replied equably. ''And I'll keep on coming back however many times you try. And we shall see who tires first.''

''Infamous! I'll set the law on you!''

''Oh, I have no doubt you will. Your mere name can command most things, I daresay.'' There was contempt in her voice. ''Tell me, my lord duke, how does it feel to have so much power? Does it give you immense satisfaction to know that a word from you can cause untold misery to two small children?'' Contempt gave way suddenly to passion. ''If so, I feel sorry for you, because with such meanness of spirit there is one thing you will never know—not with all your wealth and all your power. You will never know how it feels to love and be loved!''

''Enough! Both of you,'' Alistair said, his voice taut. And as the duke opened his mouth to rebuke him, ''Yes, Father, I am well aware of how much I dare. I am also aware that this is your house and, in theory, you are at liberty to throw me out too—consign me to the devil. But for now, I am stronger than you. For now, I hold all the cards, and you must relinquish your hand.'' He stood over his father, and for a long moment their eyes locked in silent combat. Then Alistair's softened slightly. ''Sir, you will do great harm to your health if you continue with this nonsense in your present state, and strange as it may seem, it would not please me to have your death on my conscience!''

The duke, for perhaps the first time in his life, was deprived of speech, and Alistair, taking a grim satisfaction from this unexpected phenomenon, made use of the brief respite by swiftly turning his attention to Charity. "As for you, Miss Wynyate, you will oblige me by quitting the room before any further damage is done.''

At first she had tried to outstare him, then realized the futility of carrying on. "Very well, my lord. As it happens, I have said all I really wanted to say to his grace.'' She dipped a formal curtsy and turned away.

He had not seen her to the door, or wished her good night, but then she had not expected any such courtesy. All in all, it had been an evening best forgotten. Except that she could not forget. She rearranged the cushions and tried to compose her thoughts, at which point she heard faint sounds in the room beyond—one of the servants coming at last to put out the candles. Charity made no attempt to reveal her presence when the door was pushed ajar, wanting only to be left in peace.

But the figure outlined in the doorway was no servant. Lord Alistair stood motionless for what seemed an endless moment in time, and then stepped inside and moved slowly to stand in front of the portrait of his mother, his arms folded on the mantelshelf. The moonlight showed clearly the anguished profile and the dejected droop of his shoulders, so out of character with the image he presented to the world. Slowly his head came to rest on clasped hands.

Charity froze into immobility, unable to comprehend why he should be so unhappy. Anger, exasperation, these she could understand in the light of the evenings events, but this? She was shaken to the core by the effect his mere nearness had upon her. Everything in her longed to comfort him. And yet she knew how intensely he would hate to be discovered in such a vulnerable state—and by her, of all people.

How long they both remained thus she had no way of knowing; time was of little interest to her. But finally he raised his head, and with a last glance at the portrait he turned to leave.

Halfway across the room he paused. ''Is there someone here?''

Charity held her breath. She could have sworn she hadn't made a sound. Perhaps he would put it down to the usual creaks and groans of a sleeping house. It seemed she was right, for after a moment he moved quite suddenly, striding into the drawing room. But she had scarcely time to do more than draw breath again when he was back, holding aloft a branch of candles.

No chance now of escaping notice; she had but seconds to think, to act, if he was not to know that she had intruded upon a very private moment. He stood over her, and she blinked into the light.

''My lord—is that you?'' She moved stiffly. ''Heavens, I must have fallen asleep!''

''But not in your bed where you rightly belong.''

''I couldn't settle.''

He set down the candles on the pianoforte and came back to stare down into eyes that were dark fathomless pools. ''I can't think why I should be surprised,'' he continued, ignoring her explanation. ''You seem determined never to take the easy way.''

There was a deep irony in the observation. Charity made an undignified attempt to struggle to her feet, which was hampered by having remained for too long in a cramped position. As she winced, his lordship's hands came at once to steady her, and having done so, seemed loath to release her.

''Have you and your father . . . have you settled my fate between you?'' she ventured at last.

''No.''

So he did not mean to make it easy for her. ''My lord, about your father . . . I fear my tongue may have rather run away with me.''

''You could say that,'' he agreed, his mouth twitching. ''It seems to have a habit of so doing whenever your strongest passions are aroused.''

"Yes. But is he all right? He did become excessively over-wrought, and for all that I dislike him intensely, I would not deliberately wish him ill."

"Would you not?" Lord Alistair regarded her with renewed curiosity. "It seems your parents named you most aptly, Charity Wynyate. Speaking for myself, I would not blame you if you wished him very ill indeed."

"Well, I don't. Furthermore, on reflection—and for all that I meant what I said, every word—I now see that it was foolish and self-indulgent to risk alienating him all over again."

"I agree."

Charity thought that he was contradicting himself and told him so—a judgment he accepted with equanimity and a faint lift of the eyebrow. "You will allow that I was provoked?" she persisted.

"Oh, undoubtedly. Beyond all bearing."

"Well then," she rushed on, "how did he seem to you . . . after I had left?"

"Stunned is, I believe, the most apt description. I make you my compliments. Between us we achieved the impossible—it is the first time I have ever seen his grace deprived of speech."

Charity came very close to stamping her foot. "Please do not play games with me, my lord! You know very well what I am asking. Will he attempt to get back at me through the children? Even you must now realize what it would do to Harry!"

"I might have known." His fingers tightened momentarily on her arms, his mouth twisting wryly. "What a tenacious creature you are in defense of your young!" In her night-clothes and with her hair loose about her face, she looked little more than a slip of a girl herself, and the sight of her, her very nearness, had the oddest effect upon him. Quite suddenly he released her. "Go to bed, Miss Wynyate," he said quietly. "I won't let my father's bitterness hurt the children a second time."

For a moment her eyes raked his face. Reassured by what she saw there, she said simply, "Thank you, my lord," and stepped away. She had almost reached the door when he spoke her name again. She turned, but he was not looking in her direction. His gaze seemed to be fixed on his mother's portrait.

"One other thing—earlier this evening I believe I used you ill. Pray accept my apologies."

The memory brought a sudden constriction to Charity's throat. "Thank you, but I beg you will not regard it. I had already forgotten. Good night, my lord."

"Good night, Miss Wynyate."

Lord Alistair was not in the breakfast room when Charity came down the following morning. He had already eaten, Ellen said.

"Such a carry on there's been, miss," she confided, round-eyed. "What with his grace's arriving in such a state last evening, and then him being took bad in the night—"

"Oh no! Is it his leg?"

"Well, I'm not really sure, miss, except that doctor was sent for, and the valet of his grace's, Parsons, is going around with a face on him that'd turn milk! He was well named, that one."

Charity hurried through a sketchy breakfast with little appetite, and went in search of Mrs. Bennett. The house-keeper, however, could tell her little more than Ellen, except that there was some fear that his grace might have suffered a slight seizure. "But Dr. Thomas should be here again any-time, and we'll maybe have a better idea. Lord Alistair's been with his father most of the night, off and on, and he's there yet."

In spite of her efforts to keep busy, guilt was uppermost in Charity's thoughts, and it seemed an age before she heard the doctor's steady tread on the stair. She had already asked Mrs. Bennett to be sure to get him to look in on Emily before he left, though the child had little further need of his ministrations.

"Well now, what's this?" Dr. Thomas said gruffly when he came at last, filling the nursery with his bulky, reassuring presence. "Not jealous of our grandfather, I trust, eh?" He picked Emily up and she chortled with delight. "Not much wrong with this young lady that I can see, ma'am. Excellent recovery."

"Yes, indeed. I cannot thank you enough, Dr. Thomas," Charity said as he lay Emily back on her cushions. She smiled apologetically. "Do, pray, sit down for a moment. You see, I'm afraid I got you up here under false pretences. I wanted to ask you about the duke. Is he very ill?"

Dr. Thomas lowered his bulk into a chair fashioned for someone half his size. "It rather depends what you mean by very ill, ma'am. His grace is not by any stretch of the imagination a young man, and I gather from his man that he has been in great pain with his gout for some considerable time. Added to that—" the doctor quirked a rueful eyebrow, "he is occasionally a gentleman of somewhat immoderate temper . . ."

"Yes, I know. Last night . . ."

He nodded. "Last night I gather he gave full vent to it."

"Yes, but I fear I was largely to blame for his outburst," Charity admitted wretchedly. "And if as a result his grace should have taken some kind of fit . . ."

"My dear young lady, you must not distress yourself. I will admit that when I was sent for in the early hours of this morning, the duke exhibited all the symptoms of someone who had suffered a minor brain seizure. However," Dr. Thomas said reassuringly, "now that I have seen him again, I am by no means convinced that this is the case." He saw the beginnings of relief flicker in her eyes and his own eyes twinkled. "For a start, he was able to curse me up hill and down dale with a fluency quite beyond someone whose brain had been affected. Also, I now learn from Lord Alistair that upon retiring last evening, his grace had demanded a bottle of port, and, in the words of his valet, a splendidly competent fellow, his grace had sat up in bed and downed the lot."

"Good gracious!"

"An excellent vintage, mind—Lord Alistair was kind enough to present me with a bottle only last week." The doctor's eyes misted over with the memory of it was with obvious reluctance that he brought his mind back to the present. "However, in the circumstances—and bearing in mind an already high degree of excitability with the added complication of his grace's gout—it was quite the worst thing he could have done. I have therefore cupped him, and have every hope that this will be beneficial in subduing the evil humors. Naturally, this has left his grace feeling a trifle weak, which is only to be expected, but with complete rest and quiet for the next few days, he should soon be feeling considerably better. I'll call in again tomorrow."

Charity's relief left her feeling restless and in need of some form of activity. There was still no sign of Lord Alistair, and she had already decided to defer Harry's ride until later in the day, concluding that his natural exuberance would be better confined to the schoolroom until the state of his grace's health was resolved. In any case, the weather was decidedly chilly with a most unspringlike hint of snow in the air.

Even so, she felt the immediate need of fresh air and decided to brave the inclement weather. It took but a moment to change into her riding habit, and having worked off some of her fidgets by taking her horse for a gallop across the fields, she decided to call in on the Fitzallans. Mary and Eliza saw her from the window and came running down to meet her.

"Mama, here is Charity!" The girls led her, each hanging on to an arm and both chattering at once, into the drawing room where their mother was busy compiling lists.

Mrs. Fitzallan immediately laid aside her papers. "So much to be done before we leave for London," she said. "I confess I shall glad of an excuse to think of something else for a change. Do come and sit down, my dear, and tell us how you all go on up at the Grange. We have heard nothing from you for days. How is the little one?"

"Very much better, ma'am. Almost completely well, in fact."

"And the wicked Lord Alistair?" Eliza giggled, only to be instantly reproved by her mother.

Charity answered all their questions readily enough and was regaled by both girls with descriptions of their latest dresses and pleas for her to come and see them, which she promised to do before she left. But Mrs. Fitzallan was not slow to sense that there was much Charity was not saying. She promptly dispatched her daughters, under protest, to ask Cook to make them all some chocolate. "And some of her best shortbread biscuits."

When they had gone, she said quietly, "Something is troubling you, I think. You do not have to confide in me, if you would rather not, but I hope you know that I am always very ready to listen."

The mere pleasure of being able to confide in another woman brought the words flooding out. "And you may conceive how I feel," she concluded, "for I am still completely in the dark as to what the duke will decide, if and when he is finally fit to decide anything."

"My poor child! As if you had not endured enough. However, if as you say Lord Alistair has promised you his support, I am sure he will not go back on his word."

"No." Charity sighed.

"And you must put out of your mind completely this stupid guilt about having contributed to his grace's collapse. A man who cannot keep his temper within bounds must take the consequences. I am only sorry that we are so soon to leave for London." She heard the girls returning and said quickly, "But I will give you our direction. You may write to me anytime, and if, for whatever reason, you should find yourself in town, I hope you will not hesitate to seek us out."

The remainder of Charity's visit passed in a much lighter vein, and she left promising to bring Harry to tea within the next day or two. "He will be delighted," she said. "He has been longing to meet the twins since I first told him about them."

Fitz came in shortly before she left and immediately suggested that he should ride back to Ashbourne Grange with her. "You look a trifle pale," he said when they were on their way. "Nothing wrong, is there?"

Charity hesitated, then told him about the duke, but without going into detail. "Do you mind if we don't talk about it, Fitz?"

He shot her a quick look. "Whatever you say, m'dear,"

he said easily. "Did I tell you about my erstwhile commanding officer? I met him recently when I was in London . . ." And he went on to regale her with an anecdote so unlikely that they were both laughing uncontrollably by the time they reached the stables.

Alistair heard the laughter as he was on the point of riding out. At first he could not believe that Charity, who only a few hours previously had been in such low spirits, was now so obviously enjoying herself. But then she came into view—cheeks glowing and eyes still brimming over with mirth as if she hadn't a care in the world.

13

Harry had been awaiting his opportunity for a long time.

He had heard Alice and Ellen talking about his grandfather who had arrived some time during the night and had been "struck down." He wasn't sure what that meant, but his curiosity was well and truly aroused.

He had asked Alice what the words meant, but she had told him that it was wicked to listen to other people's private conversations, and if he wasn't careful, he'd be struck down himself. This puzzled him even more. Had his grandfather been listening to Alice and Ellen talking? He decided that the best thing to do would be to find out which room the duke was in, and try to see for himself.

Only it wasn't easy. His grandfather's coming seemed to have upset everyone, including Aunt Charity—and had deprived him of his morning ride with Gyp, so that he was obliged to have an extra reading lesson with Miss Throstle instead.

But now Miss Throstle had one of her bad headaches and had gone to lie down for an hour, leaving him a set piece of work to copy in his best hand, and with instructions to Alice to look in on him now and then. He now knew his grandfather was in Uncle Alistair's room. Aunt Charity was out, and if he was very quick, he might be able to creep downstairs and back without being discovered.

When he reached his uncle's room everywhere was very quiet. He stood uncertainly, his courage almost failing him; then he reached out and turned the door knob very carefully. It was very quiet inside the room, dark and a little frightening with the heavy curtains partly drawn and great shadowy shapes of furniture. Harry swallowed nervously, his whole attention fixed on the huge canopied bed which dominated the room. It seemed very high—perhaps he wouldn't be able to see over the top.

But as he crept nearer he saw a great many pillows supporting an awesome head with flowing blackish, silverish hair spreading out around a long sharp face that looked a bit like a falcon he had once seen in a book, except that his grandfather's skin was kind of waxy-looking, like candle grease. And there was a great hump further down the bed which intrigued him. Was that what being "struck down" did to people?

Harry's disappointment could hardly be contained; he had so wanted his grandfather to look like Papa. He looked again at the two small pictures of his Mama and Papa joined together in a simple silver frame, which he had brought from beside his bed, seeking vainly for some hint of resemblance, but there was none. He sighed and turned to move away, and as he did so, the heavy eyelids lifted.

"Who is there? Parsons, is that you?"

Harry froze, watching the head turn fretfully and holding his breath until he was afraid he would burst.

"I know someone is there. You had better show yourself, or by God, you will be sorry!"

The voice was surprisingly strong, and after a moment Harry drew near, half terrified, half intrigued, and saw fierce dark eyes glaring at him.

"The devil!"

The duke seemed to hiss the word, and he shrank a little.

"N-no, sir," he stammered. "I am Harry . . . your grandson, Harry."

"Are you indeed?" growled his grace. "And who gave you leave to come in here?"

"No one, sir. I just sort of came by myself . . . t-to see you." Harry thought it better not to mention the bit about being "struck down." "I wanted to see if you looked like Papa," he added wistfully, glancing once more at the miniatures.

"Well, I don't," came the curt reply. "What is that you are holding?"

Harry, with slightly more confidence, held the miniatures out to him. He heard his grandfather draw in a sharp breath, and then there was a long silence. Then a shaky finger pointed. "Who is this?"

Harry stood on tiptoe. "It is Mama. Isn't she pretty?"

There was no reply. Harry saw that the duke's face had acquired two red patches, and that he looked sort of funny, as though he was in pain.

"Get out," he muttered. "And send your aunt to me this instant."

The child was bemused. "But, my pictures, grandfather?"

"Do as you are told, boy!"

Harry turned and ran, the tears streaming down his face. Out on the landing, he saw Aunt Charity in her riding dress, on her way to her room. He sobbed out a garbled story, the gist of which she understood well enough to make her heart sink. Poor Harry. She took him back to the schoolroom, reassured him that nothing dreadful would happen, to her or to anyone else, and settled him down to his work before hurrying back to face the duke.

"Come in, come in," he called testily in answer to her knock. "Parsons is resting. Been up all night fussing over me—wouldn't be told!"

Charity's first thought was that he was an ungrateful curmudgeonly man who didn't deserve a servant as devoted as Parsons, but a closer look obliged her to revise her opinion. His grace might bluster, but in spite of some kind of cage beneath the bedclothes to protect his leg, he did look quite ill and was, she suspected, a little less sure of himself than usual.

"Well, don't stand over there. I don't propose to shout what I have to say!"

She moved to the side of the bed. "My lord duke, I am sorry if Harry's visit distressed you. He is a very outgoing little boy, but I had no idea he would attempt anything so foolhardy."

The duke grunted. "Like his father, more's the pity."

"I am persuaded your grace doesn't really mean that."

"Have done. I didn't send for you to read me a lecture, or to discuss the child—" He saw the indignation in her eyes. "And there's no call to get on y'r high ropes, either. The doctor says I must have peace and quiet."

The piercing eyes barely concealed his triumph as he produced this trump card, and there was something so like Harry in his conviction that in other circumstances Charity would have laughed.

"I sent for you because of this." The duke leaned forward, ignoring her protests, and thrust the framed miniatures under her nose.

"Why, this is Harry's most treasured possession," she exclaimed, taking it from him.

"But the woman?"

"My sister, Arianne—Ned's wife."

"Yes, yes, I know that. I'm not a fool, for all that you might think it." There was an urgency about him suddenly. "Would I be right, Miss Wynyate, in thinking that your sister greatly resembled your mother?"

The question came a total surprise, making her slow to answer. "My father was used to say that she was the very image of her as a girl."

"And her name—before her marriage?" He seemed to force the words out.

Charity was by now completely mystified, but answered readily enough. "She was Emily Pargeter, the only daughter of the late Sir Humphrey Pargeter of Sittincombe."

The duke made no answer, but fell back against his pillows with a deep groan, his eyes tightly closed. Alarmed, Charity bent over him. "Sir, are you ill?"

"Get out!"

"But, your grace . . . I cannot leave you like this . . ."

"Get out, I say!"

There was so much anguish in his voice that she deemed it safer to comply with his command, and went at once in search of Parsons.

*   *   *

It was some time later that Lord Alistair came in search of Charity. She was sitting in the drawing room with a gown she was smocking for Emily lying idle in her lap. She looked up as he came in and saw that he was tight-lipped with anger.

"The duke . . ." she began, alarmed. "Is he all right?"

"No thanks to you, ma'am," he said. "Could you not have ceased your passion for feuding, at least until my father is better able to hold his own?"

The injustice of the accusation inflamed Charity. "My lord, I have done nothing to deserve your censure, whatever you may have been told. You must think me quite unfeeling to suggest otherwise!"

He frowned. "But you did go to him?"

"Only because he sent for me. Even you will allow that he would have been infinitely more upset if I had refused. Besides, I knew why he wanted to see me, or thought I did . . ." She saw that she would have to explain the whole thing from the beginning. Having done so, she insisted, "You must not blame Harry, either. It is perfectly natural that he should be curious about his grandfather."

"That is exactly what I would expect you to say," Alistair argued, though with less heat. "Personally, I think a cuff around the ear wouldn't go amiss."

"Oh, no. Besides, the more I think about it, the more convinced I become that it wasn't Harry's intrusion that upset your father so much as that miniature of Arianne, and its likeness to our mother." Charity shook her head, puzzled. "Almost as though he had once known her. Does that sound ridiculously fanciful?"

"No more so than all the rest," he said shortly. "My life was pleasant and uncomplicated before you came along, but you seem to have done nothing but put my family all on end from the moment you set foot among us."

"Oh, how unjust!" she protested. "But I shall not stoop to argue."

For a moment her indignation brought a half-smile to his eyes. Then he shrugged and turned away.

It was late in the afternoon when the duke again sent for Charity. Lord Alistair was not around to be consulted or offer

her support, so for the second time in a day she found herself
in the presence of his strange and complex parent. This time,
Parsons was there to usher her in and put a chair where his
grace could see her without undue strain. He was in fact
looking much better, sitting up against the pillows, wearing
a magnificent wine-colored dressing gown and with his hair
tied back in a queue. He dismissed Parsons and sat fixing
her with that intense, hard stare.

"Well, Miss Wynyate, I daresay you think y'r entitled to
an explanation?"

Charity inclined her head. "I will own that I am curious,
but it is for your grace to decide."

He uttered a grunt. "Mighty polite all of a sudden. Been
told to treat me with care, have you? Well, you needn't
trouble yourself—I'm not about to turn up my toes for a good
while yet."

"I am delighted to hear you say so, my lord duke, though
your health must inevitably be a matter for concern. However, in this instance I was simply stating the obvious—you
are not obliged to explain anything to me—" her mouth
curved irrepressibly, "but I very much hope you will do so."

Charity saw his fingers curl suddenly around the miniatures
which still lay on the quilt beside him.

"You may not have her looks," he said gruffly, "but the
smile is unmistakable."

She said nothing, fearing to interrupt his train of thought.

"When I first saw Emily Pargeter," he went on, "she was
barely eighteen and the loveliest creature ever fashioned by
an indulgent God. I worshipped her from that first moment,
and knew no rest until I could find someone to introduce us.
When they did, I discovered that she had a strength of spirit
to match mine and yet remained as good and unspoiled as
she was beautiful."

Charity felt that she could see him as he must have been
then—proud, strong-willed, and handsome as a young hawk,
very much accustomed to having his own way in all things.
And she could see her mother, too, as a young girl, full of
life and gaiety.

"I could at that time have married any one of a dozen

beautiful, eligible women, but from that moment on I courted Emily with a single-mindedness that knew no bounds—never doubting that she would be mine. Sir Humphrey looked kindly upon my suit, but when his beloved daughter proved difficult to convince, he refused to coerce her. For Emily''—the duke's voice grew bitter—"Emily, it seemed, was in love with a nobody, a schoolmaster, if you please, and would have no other.''

"My father," Charity whispered the words, scarcely able to believe what he was telling her.

"So it would now seem." He ground the words out. "I never knew his name, though I cursed him to hell for many a long day. I suppose you can have no idea what it is like to be subjected to the ignominy of rejection in the full glare of publicity, and in the knowledge that people were laughing behind their sleeves to see me given my congé!'' She could see his fist clenching and unclenching. "Well, it was the end of loving for me. I vowed that no one would *ever* cause me to suffer like that again. And to prove to the world that I was heartwhole, I married a well-born mouse of a young woman whose father, unlike Sir Humphrey, put the prestige of a dukedom before any mimminy-pimminy whims of his daughter.''

He glared freely at Charity as if daring her to condemn him. "I did not love Phoebe. I did not even consider whether or not she was happy so long as she gave me heirs. And she did—three, in fact—at great cost to her health. She was a gentle soul and did not deserve my indifference. But if there is a God, he has exacted a terrible retribution, for one by one he has quite ruthlessly taken away that which he gave me. Only one son remains, and he gives me his duty but not his love. You will say I am well served, and no doubt rightly so."

Quite suddenly the surge of energy that had carried him through this extraordinary baring of his soul seemed to leave him, and he closed his eyes and sank weakly back onto his pillows. Charity, alarmed by his pallor, wondered if she should ring for Parsons. She half-rose from her chair.

"Don't go," he said urgently, though without moving.

She sank back, trying to analyze her emotions, which were nothing like as cut and dried as either of them might have supposed. She ought to feel disgust—if ever there was a case of vindictiveness breeding vindictiveness, it was evident in this spectacle of a man spurned and lashing out at all around him in an attempt to assuage his own hurt. And yet, to her surprise, the emotion uppermost in her breast was pity; for all that he would deny it most vigorously, the duke was the loneliest man she had ever known. And quite suddenly she saw a glimpse of hope for him.

"It is never too late," she ventured quietly. "Perhaps you have already been shown the way to make amends if you would but take it, for you were wrong to say that only Lord Alistair remains. You have been given two grandchildren— Ned's children. And what is more, Harry and Emily are more than just your grandchildren—they are in fact the fruit of a union between your son and Emily's daughter. Is it fanciful of me to suppose that this is more than mere coincidence?"

At first she thought her words had fallen on deaf ears. His face had grown taut, reminding her irresistibly of Lord Alistair at his most unapproachable, and her heart sank. Then she saw that two tears had squeezed from beneath those heavy closed lids to course down his ashen cheeks. She sat on in silence, feeling her own throat constrict.

And so it was that Alistair found them. He saw his father's distress, and misinterpreting its cause, angrily rounded on Charity and was about to order her from the room when the duke intervened.

"Let her be," he said, his voice surprisingly strong. "We have been getting to know one another."

Alistair's frowning look encompassed them both. "If you say so, sir."

"I do," came the pugnacious retort. "We have been discovering that we have more in common than we could ever have known."

Charity smiled and stood up. "Nevertheless, I fear you have overtired yourself, so I will go, an' it please your grace." She hesitated. "I wonder? Do you think I might give Harry back his picture? It means a great deal to him."

He was holding on to it so tightly that for a moment she thought he would refuse. Then he pushed it across the bed. "Take it. The past is the past."

That day marked the beginning of a whole new era, especially for Harry. From the trauma of that first meeting with his grandfather, he quickly progressed to the point where he was spending much of his free time in the duke's company.

"I have never seen such a change in anyone as in his grace," Charity told Mrs. Fitzallan when, as promised, she took Harry to tea. "Not that his basic nature has altered—I don't suppose it ever will. But I think he is secretly delighted that Harry shows no fear of him, even when he is at his most ill-humored."

"Children are the oddest creatures," Mrs. Fitzallan agreed, watching Harry and the twins racing across the lawn beyond the window. "Mr. Fitzallan decided that the boys should go away to school this coming autumn, and I had worried myself into a state at the thought of how they would hate to leave the pleasant freedoms of the countryside and dear old Mr. Frank, who has tutored them for so long, only to discover that they considered it the greatest adventure ever!"

She had earlier been intrigued by the circumstances that had brought about such a change in the duke. "Only fancy Emily Pargeter's being your mama. I wish I had known earlier. We came out in the same year, you know, and I well remember how Emily bewitched his grace, and how ardently he pursued her—it was one of the Season's most enlivening *on-dits*. We were all quite wild with envy, of course, for he was a considerable prize. I suppose it was not kind in us to derive entertainment from the rakish duke's discomforture when your mama declined to entertain his suit and chose instead a complete stranger—a very studious young man, but at the time no one could have guessed how deeply it went with him, or that it would sour the rest of his life," Mrs. Fitzallan sighed.

"What I cannot understand is why Papa never told us— not even when Ned asked him for Arianne's hand in marriage."

"Mayhap he did not know," the older woman suggested. "I rather had the impression all those years ago that your father was not a very worldly, man, something of a dreamer, in fact."

"He still is," Charity admitted ruefully. "We always understood that he met Mama when he was teaching at a school close to the Pargeters' country home. It was some years before they came to London—after Sir Humphrey's death, in fact, when Papa took a post in a small seminary in town."

"Well, there you are, then." Mrs. Fitzallan nodded with the satisfaction of one who has solved a tiresome puzzle. "And how has Lord Alistair taken this latest turn of events?"

Charity made some noncommittal answer. In fact, she had been dismayed to find that, far from being pleased by the news, his lordship had been at first incredulous and later, more disquietingly, had grown almost taciturn. But then if, as she supposed, the duke had been as frank with his son as he had with her, Lord Alistair must have been made more than ever aware of the callous indifference with which his grace had selected his duchess, as well as his later treatment of her. She remembered that moment in the music room which had revealed so much of his lordship's feeling for his mother, and feared that such painful revelations could only serve to widen the rift between them.

Whatever the cause, the pleasant mood of camaraderie that had grown up between herself and Lord Alistair seemed to vanish almost overnight. Their pleasant dinner conversation became stilted and awkward, and as the duke claimed more and more of Harry's attention, so his lordship showed less and less inclination to continue their outdoor pursuits, despite Harry's pleas.

Even so, it came as a shock to Charity when over dinner one evening he announced his intention of returning to London the following day. "I have already stayed much longer than I ever meant to do."

"But you can't!" And, as she saw his brows draw together, "I'm sorry, my lord, but there is your father to be thought of—you cannot mean to go and leave me to . . . to deal with him?"

His mouth curled. "Oh, I'd say you are dealing together more than adequately already. After all, you have so much in common. So fortuitous that you should discover yourself to be the daughter of the woman my father *loved* . . ." He almost spat the word out. "In fact, Miss Wynyate, matters have turned out rather well for you, wouldn't you say?"

It was as though he had struck her. Charity felt the blood draining from her face. "You speak as though I am somehow to blame! My lord, I had no idea . . ."

"Even so, it does change the whole situation. You have no further need of me, and, circumstances being what they are, I have no wish to remain here one moment longer than I have to."

He was indeed hurt, deeply hurt, and she could not find the words to comfort him. In the end, she said simply, "You must do as you see fit, my lord. But we shall be sorry to see you go . . ." She faltered, then as a last appeal, "Harry will miss you greatly."

His mouth twisted in a way that it had almost ceased to do of late. "Oh, I think not, Miss Wynyate. He is much occupied with his newly discovered grandparent, who, having done a complete *volte-face*, is now the hero of the hour! As for Harry's more energetic pursuits, Fitzallan can no doubt fulfill them to everyone's satisfaction. He already seems to spend most of his days here."

There was so much bitterness, perhaps even a hint of jealousy, in the words that Charity longed to comfort him. "Nevertheless, he would still rather have you," she said impulsively.

And oh, so would I, she realized with blinding perception. But she could not say the words.

14

Mr. Trowbridge was walking through St. James's Square on his way to White's when he saw Alistair's curricle being led away to the stables by John Gage, and, curious to know what had kept his friend away so long, he immediately crossed the square and mounted the steps.

Alistair was about to mount the stair as the butler admitted him, and he turned and put up his glass to eye the young exquisite with unhurried thoroughness. "Theo. I had naturally expected that I would be missed, but this is devotion above and beyond the call of friendship! I do hope you have not been camping out, metaphorically speaking, on my doorstep in expectation of my return—and in that coat, too. An' I am not mistaken it is new, is it not? Rather handsome buttons. Weston, of course."

"Never let anyone else have the dressing of me, as you well know." Mr. Trowbridge grinned sheepishly. "It's good to have you back, Stair—I've missed you. How are you?"

His lordship's expression gave nothing away. "Fatigued, my dear. All that country air, you know. Well, now that you are here, you may as well come up and regale me with all the latest scandal broths."

Mr. Trowbridge, following him up to the drawing room, was not deceived. Something had shaken Alistair badly. He knew the signs—the bland pose, the profession of boredom—and as he accepted a glass of Madeira and settled into a comfortable chair, he was consumed with curiosity. It was no secret that the Duke of Orme had left town, and in a mighty hurry at that, but although rumor was rife, most of it instigated by Sir Rupert Darian, no one could say with

absolute certainty that his grace was headed for Ashbourne
Grange.

Mr. Trowbridge would have dearly loved to know the
answer, but was only too aware that Alistair would not lightly
tolerate any unwarranted prying into his private affairs, even
by friends who meant no harm. So he sipped his wine and
said casually, "Everything goes on very much as usual here.
Town already grows much busier and is beginning to acquire
the air of bustle which inevitably precedes the onset of
another Season."

"I suppose so," Alistair replied vaguely, as though his
mind was preoccupied with more important things. "D'you
know, Theo, I must be getting old—there was a time when
I actually enjoyed the prospect. Now, it simply fills me with
ennui."

His friend grinned again. "Maybe that's because your days
of freedom are at an end, so to speak. Less than two months
to go now. Said it yourself more than once, Stair—a man
who's as good as leg-shackled can't expect to experience the
scent of the chase in his nostrils quite as he used to!"

For a moment he thought Alistair was about to administer
one of his blistering setdowns, but the expression in his
friend's eyes was so fleeting that he had no time to define
whether it was pain or rage; or even whether he had imagined
the whole incident. And while he was still pondering the
question, Alistair remarked with no more than a hint of
cynicism that he was doubtless being proved right.

"And how is my betrothed, Theo? Not pining away, I
trust?"

Mr. Trowbridge shot him a quick look. He didn't precisely
sound like a man in the throes of passion, but then one never
knew with Alistair—not one to wear his heart on his cuff.
Still, wiser perhaps not to mention the curious attitude of
Sir Rupert toward his bride-to-be ever since that rather
tedious night at the opera, or that Melissa, already vexed
by Alistair's absence, had become further incensed by his
failure to communicate with her, and had quite deliberately
and in defiance of Lady Vane's strictures, set about

encouraging the attentions of a young French nobleman but recently come to town.

"There can be no doubt that Melissa has missed you," he said, adhering scrupulously to the truth. "I daresay that you will be wishing to set her mind at rest as soon as possible, so I won't detain you."

Without waiting for answer, he set down his glass and rose to leave. Alistair made no effort to detain him, and again Mr. Trowbridge had the distinct feeling that his thoughts were elsewhere.

The news of Lord Alistair's return traveled swiftly. It reached Melissa during the course of a select little soirée given by one of her friends. As she had already admitted that she had no idea when Alistair might return, it took every ounce of her not inconsiderable capabilities as an actress to explain away this latest evidence of her fiancé's quixotic ways.

"Wicked man! I vow, he is always looking to confound me!" she exclaimed, uttering a trill of delighted laughter. "But, be sure I shall make him pay dearly this time—and our wedding only weeks away!"

The coterie of young ladies around her dutifully joined in her laughter, some with carefully concealed malice, for Miss Vane was not universally liked among her contemporaries. But there were others, very young and newly come to London, who were more than a trifle in awe of her beauty, to say nothing of her *savoir faire*.

However, the handsome young Marquis de St. Jules, who hovered on the fringe of the group, affected to be outraged. "Me—I consider this fiancé to be not at all worthy of you," he declared gallantly. "Say only that you wish it, and I will become your champion and challenge this unfeeling cur to a duel!"

Melissa felt a thrill of excitement run through her. She glanced at him through veiled lashes. "Would you really?" she murmured.

Hand on heart, he reiterated his declaration.

The pink tip of her tongue flicked provocatively over the full sensual curve of her lower lip. "Sword or pistols?" she persisted.

"That will be for his lordship to decide," said the marquis. "It matters nothing to me. I am confident of dispatching him with either."

"I wouldn't advise you to try, monsieur le marquis," drawled the finicky voice that Melissa had come to know only too well. "Lord Alistair is considered to be more than a match for anyone, regardless of the weapon."

The marquis turned to look at Sir Rupert.

"You know this from your own experience, perhaps?"

Sir Rupert looked him up and down, smiling thinly. "It is not always necessary to pit one's own strength against that of another in order to assess his merit," he said, skillfully evading a direct answer. "You do not have to take my word—ask Jackson, or anyone who has seen Lord Alistair in action at the Fives Court."

"So? More and more you make me wish to meet this gentleman."

But Melissa had grown weary of the discussion, as always happened the moment she ceased to be the center of attention. "We are growing much too serious," she declared with a charming little moue. "A fine thing it would be if my bridegroom were to be injured so close to our wedding day."

She arrived home with her mama to find that Lord Alistair had called, and finding her from home had scrawled a brief unloverlike note informing her that he would call again at eleven o'clock on the following morning.

"How tiresome of him!" she exclaimed. "Not a word have I had from him, and now—to arrive so casually when I have been looking for him these days past, and making excuses for his absence." She flounced away to stare out of the window. "I have a mind to be out when he comes."

But this was going too far for her mama, in whom the nightmare of every bride's mother—that until her daughter was safely shackled she might yet be left standing at the altar, with all the attendant shame and scandal—suddenly loomed large. Lord Alistair could be mighty high in the instep at times, and it would never do to alienate him at this late stage. Lady Vane might not be totally enamored of her son-to-be, but even with the dukedom now in question, there was still a certain cachet to be derived from the family name—and a house in St. James's Square and an income, so his lordship had informed her husband, of some thirty thousand pounds a year was not to be so lightly put in jeopardy.

"You will not be out, my girl," she told Melissa. "Nor will you treat his lordship to any of your megrims. He is not the man to stand any such nonsense, as I have no doubt you have already discovered for yourself. But he is *your* choice—a luxury not afforded to most girls in your position as you well know—and we have been put to considerable trouble and expense to send you off in style, so be warned. When you are married, you may behave as you please, but if you do anything stupid now, your father will wash his hands of you." Lady Vane pressed home the point. "And don't think you would find it an easy matter to attract another husband—you may flirt all you choose, but when it comes to matrimony, gentlemen are inclined to eschew cast-off wares."

Melissa bridled, but was obliged to acknowledge that there was an uncomfortable degree of truth in her mama's argument.

So it was that when Lord Alistair called on the following morning, he found a compliant fiancée most becomingly attired in a chintz morning gown, who ran forward with hands outstretched and professed herself overjoyed to have him back once more.

"For I declare I have been quite wretched without you," Melissa exclaimed, lifting her beautiful face for his kiss. "Do come and sit beside me on the sofa, and then I shall know that you are really home." She lowered her eyes demurely. "Mama has very kindly allowed us to be alone together for a short while, as it is now so short a time to our wedding day."

Alistair looked into her lovely sapphire eyes and said all

the right things, but found his thoughts constantly straying to expressive gray eyes that mirrored a character of infinite complexity.

His preoccupation was not lost on Melissa, and for the first time she felt a twinge of unease; until recently she had never doubted her power over him, even though they had come close to a confrontation on more than one occasion. But now Alistair's lack of ardor amounted almost to coolness; for one dreadful moment she was terrified that he might have discovered who had informed the duke about what was going on at Ashbourne Grange. But that could not be—she had taken the greatest care, and in any case he would have confronted her with it at once.

Nevertheless, her mother's words, coming back to her, seemed to have a hollow prophetic ring, and Melissa resolved there and then that nothing must be allowed to mar the weeks leading up to their nuptials. She would devote herself to wooing him afresh.

But it would seem strange if she made no reference at all to his absence, so she asked innocently, "I hope the business you were conducting for his grace went well? I could not help but worry when someone told me they had seen your papa's carriage leaving town, for fear that something had gone amiss, as I am only too aware that his grace's health does not permit him to travel any distance."

It seemed a long time before he spoke, and he looked so forbidding that her unease returned. But at last he said in a colorless voice. "You need have no fear for my father's health. He possesses an inherent instinct for survival," an answer which, if not satisfying, at least served to calm her fears.

In the days that followed, fashionable London began to stir itself to face another Season. One by one, houses that had been closed and shuttered through the long winter were invaded by armies of servants who swept and dusted and polished in anticipation of their imminent occupation.

In the parks, the trees defied chill winds by producing buds which grew fatter day by day, with here and there a faint burgeoning of new green. Now and again London's residents were to be seen taking the air, but before long the sound of carriage wheels would announce the arrival of the first intrepid visitors, and in no time the leafy branches above would be echoing with the laughter and conversation of the fashionable with here and there the occasional whispered confidence.

The Fitzallans were among the early arrivals. They took possession of the house in Mount Street that Mr. Fitzallan had rented for the Season amid a great deal of excitement and confusion, so that Mrs. Fitzallan needed little persuading to send the twins off to Hyde Park almost immediately in the care of one of the grooms, with strict orders to behave.

"I hope you realize that they won't heed your words for one moment, Mama," Fitz said, and saw her eyes twinkle.

"I know, dear, but if they had remained in the house one moment longer, they would have driven your father to despair! And I doubt they will come to any great harm— George is very good with them."

"Well, if you don't need me for anything, I believe I shall take a walk to Bond Street—see if there's anyone I know in Jackson's."

She wrinkled her nose at him. "Horrid fisticuffs!"

Almost the first person Fitz saw when he arrived was Theo Trowbridge. "I wouldn't have taken you for a follower of the noble art," he said, eyeing the young exquisite's pale yellow pantaloons, the unwrinkled perfection of his blue superfine coat, and his cravat which fell in complex folds.

Mr. Trowbridge shuddered faintly. "I am merely a spectator, dear fellow. As a matter of fact, I came looking for Alistair. You haven't seen him, I suppose?"

Fitz shook his head. "Can't oblige, I'm afraid. Only just arrived in London."

"Thought for sure I'd find him here. Comes most days to spar with the great man—Jackson thinks very highly of him. But seemingly he's been coming at some unconscionably early hour for the last few days. Odd, that, wouldn't you say? Not like him at all. Almost as though he were avoiding his friends since he returned from Surrey." He cocked a eye at Fitz. "You wouldn't happen to know why, I suppose?"

"We-ll . . ." Fitz hesitated, but only for a moment. After all, Trowbridge wasn't just anybody. He gave him a brief account of recent events insofar as they were known to him.

"I see." Mr. Trowbridge recalled Alistair's odd manner on that first day back in London, and going further back still, the curious atmosphere between his friend and Miss Wynyate on the only occasion he had seen them together. "Yes—well, it might explain a few things," he said thoughtfully. "My thanks, Fitzallan. Do you stay here, or will you walk with me to White's?"

Fitz gladly accepted the offer of company, and the two young men went on their way together.

Alistair pushed aside his half-eaten breakfast and stood up. He had been back in London for more than a week, though it seemed much longer, and it was a source of acute annoyance to him that he should be feeling so at odds with everything and everyone, as though a small worm of discontent were eating away at his insides.

He most heartily wished that he had never allowed his conscience to be swayed in the first place by the inference that the children were somehow his responsibility. It wasn't as if he cared much for country life, let alone for children, which made it even more difficult to understand how he had come to stay so long, involving himself in the simple pursuits of a small boy. As for Charity Wynyate's part in it all, he hadn't yet decided whether she was incredibly naive or exceedingly clever—either way, she had managed to turn everyone's life on end and in the process, had somehow achieved the impossible with regard to his father, though she might yet regret that particular victory. If so, she would have to live with her mistake.

As for himself—*this* was his world, a world in which he was the noted Nonpareil, an acknowledged leader, and the sooner he threw himself back into the hub of things, the better. He was well aware that he had been less than loverlike toward Melissa since his return, and now was as good a time as any to make amends. Suiting the action to the word, he gave the order for his curricle to be brought around in half an hour and told Flagg to put out his new coat.

"And the buff pantaloons, my lord?" murmured Flagg, happy to be back in the bosom of civilization once more, and hopeful that this sudden bustle on his lordship's part signaled the end of what had been a most trying time.

John Gage was also relieved to see the spring back in his lordship's step, though he was less certain that the mood would last. Howsoever, there was certainly a new air of purpose about Lord Alistair as they set off at a spanking pace through quiet streets, the object of the journey becoming clear as they drew to a halt outside the premises of Messrs. Rundle and Bridge, jewelers. A new trinket for Miss Vane, no doubt.

Lord Alistair handed the reins to his groom and stepped down. "Walk them if they get restless, John, though my business shouldn't take long."

Later in the day he called on Melissa. He was admitted to the hall just as she was descending the stairs, looking at her most becoming in a pelisse and bonnet of deep blue velvet. He stepped forward and took her hands.

"You are going out?"

"Yes. Oh, how vexing! And you may not even come with us," she exclaimed archly, "for I am to be fitted for my wedding gown." And then, seeing the faint hint of a frown, "But Mama is not down yet, so we have a few moments to spare."

Melissa drew him swiftly into the nearby saloon and shut the door, then turned and lifted her face for his kiss.

He brushed her mouth lightly with his before stepping back and taking the small parcel from his pocket. "A trifling gift," he said, "in atonement for my recent ill-humor."

She tore away the elegant wrapping with impatient fingers and sprang the clasp of the tiny velvet box. "Oh! It is beautiful!" A sapphire and diamond pendant winked up at her . . . if this was his idea of an apology before they were married, what might he not give her later with a little encouragement!

Alistair thought she looked like a child with a new toy. "Would that its color might more truly rival your eyes," he said.

The door opened to admit Lady Vane.

"See, Mama—is this not beautiful? I may keep it, may I not?"

Lady Vane's gaze lifted from contemplation of the pendant to meet Lord Alistair's. She inclined her head graciously. "Your lordship is very generous. In the circumstances, I see no objection."

Why, Alistair wondered, as he drove home by way of Grosvenor Street, did Melissa's obvious delight in his gift not give him more pleasure? He was still debating the answer when he became aware of a considerable degree of activity in the vicinity of Ashbourne House.

Several carriages were pulled up outside with a small army of servants swarming around them like bees. So, his father was home. Filial courtesy dictated that he should stop and inquire after his grace's health, although bearing in mind the rigors of the journey, and the fact that he had but that moment arrived, now might not be the ideal moment.

Even as he was debating the matter, a small figure, having evaded the watchful eyes of his elders, dashed from the house to watch the unloading of the carriages. What in the name of heaven was Harry doing in London? He pulled back on the reins and in the same instant Harry saw them.

"Uncle Alistair! Uncle Alistair! And John Gage—oh, famous!"

"Hello, young 'un," called the groom. Then they were at a standstill, the reins were thrust into the groom's hands, and his lordship was springing down, his face like thunder.

15

Harry's joyous cry reached the hall where Charity had just surrendered Emily into the arms of Alice. Oh, no—not Lord Alistair so soon after the rigors of the journey! She stifled the sudden feeling of panic, and, seeing that Miss Throstle was already on her way to collect her errant charge, moved reluctantly in her wake.

". . . and it took three whole carriages, one for Grandfather and one for us and one for all the baggage! And Grandfather said I could have Gyp with me, too—one of the grooms is bringing him!"

His lordship, clearly unimpressed by Harry's account of the complexities of the removal, waited in grim silence until his nephew had been carried off, protesting, before stepping into the hall where Charity waited somewhat nervously among the servants who were coming and going with portmanteaux and bandboxes under the eagle eye of Hamlyn.

The butler came hurrying forward upon seeing Lord Alistair, and begged pardon for the hubbub, which he assured him would be over in a matter of minutes. "Perhaps, my lord, if you were to step into the Blue Saloon for a few moments."

"Where is my father?"

"Gone to his room, my lord. His grace was much fatigued by the journey."

Alistair nodded abruptly. Then his fingers closed vicelike around Charity's arm and he propelled her, unresisting, to the door which William already held open. He bowed, murmured a polite "M'lord," and bestowed a beaming grin of welcome on Charity.

"Now," Alistair said as the footman closed the door behind them, "perhaps you will oblige me by telling me what all this means."

Charity had guessed he wouldn't like it. She had done her very best to persuade the duke that it would not be a good idea. Now, nervousness made her flippant.

"It is surely obvious, my lord. Your father wished to return to London, and not wishing to be separated from Harry, he decided that we should all come."

"I see. And naturally, you agreed."

A rueful smile momentarily lit Charity's eyes as she recalled her vain attempt to disagree. "Knowing how vehemently his grace reacts to being crossed, I thought it wiser not to persist when my objections were strongly resisted."

"Quite the surrogate daughter already, I see," he said with cutting sarcasm.

Charity caught her breath. "I have not the least idea what you mean."

"Oh, I think you have. You might so easily have been my father's daughter, might you not?—had circumstances been otherwise. Or perhaps now you hope to aspire to even dizzier heights."

"If I understand you aright, that is a terrible thing to say!" Two spots of color burned in her cheeks. She was so angry, she could scarcely think coherently, let alone defend herself with conviction.

"Is it? I think not. I confess I am disappointed, Miss Wynyate. It was clear from the first that there was precious little you wouldn't do for those children, but I had not thought you so lacking in integrity that you would deliberately seek to ingratiate yourself with my father!" He heard her gasp, saw a kind of angry shock in the widening eyes, a glint of tears, but was driven on by force he couldn't control. "Well, you may think to have him eating out of your hand, but do not imagine for one moment that I shall allow you to bamboozle him—"

"Stop—oh, stop! I'll not listen to any more . . ." She ran to the door, dragging it open and slamming it behind her.

Charity scarcely knew how she got through the rest of that day. It was as though she were two different people—the one saying and doing all the right things, calming the overexcited children, supervising the unpacking of their belongings in the rooms alloted to them, smiling and being generally pleasant, while the other raged inwardly, going over and over in minute detail every word that had passed between herself and Lord Alistair. It was perhaps fortunate that the duke required nothing of her, for she would have found it almost impossible to face him with any degree of equanimity.

It was not simply the nature of his lordship's accusation, deeply wounding though that was, but rather it was the disappointment of knowing beyond all doubt that the rapport which had sprung up between them during those days in the country had been no more than a device on his part to help while away his boredom. And his kiss—even now, knowing the falseness of its tender insistence and the betraying way she had responded, the memory of it brought an aching response that sent the blood racing through her veins.

Charity deliberately used the pain of recollection to stiffen her anger, firmly castigating herself. She had been a fool! So inexperienced that for a short while she had been in danger of deluding herself—of reading more into his lordship's interest than it merited, and in consequence her pride had suffered a severe blow. But pride could be mended, and lessons learned. She would waste no more time in useless repining, but look positively toward the future.

She had, after all, finally achieved what she had set out to do, which was to unite Ned's children with their grandfather. And although she entertained no hope of being able to bring about any miraculous change in his grace's overbearing nature, she was reasonably confident that, in spite of Lord Alistair's veiled hints of intervention, he would not disown them now. He had already grown too fond of Harry, and while the child's engaging ways might not perform miracles, they did seem to have had a great effect.

The duke's growing interest in her did, however, afford her some small concern; it was not, she assured herself, anything like as marked as Lord Alistair had inferred, but there was no denying that his manner toward her had undergone a change; in fact, had she been the kind of woman his lordship believed her to be, she might have had almost anything she wished. But his motives for wishing to indulge her, she was convinced, were rooted in the past rather than in any regard for her personally—as though her mother's shadow somehow hung over them both, prompting him to salve his conscience.

Charity therefore felt that it was up to her to ensure that his misplaced benevolence did not go beyond reasonable bounds, which took a considerable amount of tact, a determination not to allow herself to be coerced, and the judgment to know when to give in gracefully. His grace's gout was much improved, largely due to the ministrations of Dr. Thomas, but his temper remained volatile, and she had no wish to provoke another collapse.

Her skill was tested to the full after dinner one evening as she sat with him in the handsome cream and gold drawing room, plying her needle in a way that he found curiously restful, even though it irked him that she should find it necessary.

"Humgudgeon!" he declared when she professed herself adequately provided with dresses. "D'ye think I'm past noticing what a young woman wears? You've three passable gowns at most, even if you do keep refurbishing them with frippery bits like that thing you're sewing now. Small use they'll be to you when the Season gets underway. I shall send you out shopping tomorrow—never knew a woman yet who didn't like pretty things—buy whatever takes your fancy and charge it to me."

Charity looked up with a smile, allowing the lace collar she had been finishing off to rest in her lap. "Your grace is more than generous, but I cannot possibly agree to any such thing. It would be most improper. And a needless extravagance, for other than a few evenings with the Fitzallans, I doubt the Season will much concern me. It might, perhaps, if I were eighteen and in the market for a husband. As it is, I am more than content."

"Then you're a fool, my girl," he grunted. "Turning your

back on life's pleasures as though you were an antidote! How old are you, anyway? Not much above twenty, I'll warrant.''

"Almost four and twenty," Charity confessed equably.

He uttered a short bark of laughter. "Honest to a fault, even when it hurts, eh? Well, you don't look y'r age, so there's no call for you to be living like a nun! As for my so-called generosity—there is nothing improper about it. You are Harry's aunt, and therefore one of the family." He frowned fiercely at her. "I never thought to admit it, but I am daily made more aware that that boy's openness of character owes everything to your care of him. If my grand-daughter turns out half as well, she'll be fortunate indeed. For this you must allow me to show my gratitude in the only way open to me.''

"Sir, I cannot . . .''

"In the only way open to me," he repeated inexorably. "I may no longer go into company, but I am not, I believe, without influence, and you will oblige me by allowing me to use that influence." His eyes narrowed, reminding her irresistibly of his son. "You ain't preceisely a beauty in the way y'r mother was, but you have certain less obvious qualities, I think, and with a touch of town bronze you should acquit yourself well enough.''

It was the longest speech Charity had ever heard him make, and its unexpected magnanimity almost took her breath away. "Your grace, I scarcely know what to say.''

"Good. That's settled then.''

"No . . . at least, I really cannot permit . . .''

At once the brows came together. "Not permit?" he growled.

She had by now spent enough time with him to sense when a strategic compromise was necessary. What Lord Alistair would make of it, she dared not think. But his opinions were no longer of interest to her—and it would be so pleasant, just for once, to indulge herself, to buy whatever took her eye without a thought of the cost.

"Well," she conceded, "perhaps just a few purchases.''

"Good girl. I'll instruct Hamlyn to have the carriage put at your disposal tomorrow morning—" his mouth quirked into a half humorous smile, "before you change your mind."

The town coach bearing the Duke of Orme's crest, its four fine horses distainfully tossing their manes, outside one of London's most exclusive modistes in Conduit Street was a sight so rare as to cause more than one eyebrow to be raised.

Charity had not at first known where to take her custom, and reflected wryly that it was at such a time that the disadvantage of having no woman friend to consult became apparent. It was true that the Fitzallans must by now have arrived in town, but poor Mrs. Fitzallan would have quite enough to do with Mary and Eliza, and would hardly thank her for landing upon her doorstep with a cry for help.

However, she was young enough to savor the prospect of indulging in undreamed-of extravagance, and spent some time wandering happily among the shops in Bond Street and Piccadilly with the little maid called Annie who had been assigned to accompany her. And then she remembered how Arianne was used to long for Ned to be sufficiently in funds to enable her to visit a Madame Fanchon. The coachman, when consulted, knew the direction instantly, and so her problem was solved.

The discreetly luxurious interior of the establishment did give her a twinge of unease, as did Madame's rather haughty manner upon first seeing her. Had Charity but known it, Madame felt equally uneasy, and was on the point of suggesting that this most unpromising would-be client might be happier elsewhere when she happened to glance beyond the door to where the duke's coach waited. At once the modiste became graciousness itself. The Duke of Orme was known to her only as the father of Lord Alistair Ashbourne, but if the father were one half as indulgent as the son . . .

Charity spent the next hour in a state of delicious confusion so foreign to her that after attempting for a while to discover what this gown and that pelisse would cost, she totally lost her head, and surrendered completely to the sybaritic delights of being flattered by Madame, as together they explored the rival merits of silks and muslins, spangles and beads, velvet and finest broadcloth. Miss Wynyate was indeed fortunate, observed the unctuous modiste, in that she was possessed of the kind of tall slim figure which would show off the current styles to advantage. And Charity, by now quite carried away, accepted the compliment graciously.

Not until she was well on her way home did she come down to earth and realize with dismay what she had done—but by then she lacked the courage to turn back and cancel the order. If she had done so, she would undoubtedly have encountered Miss Vane, who was on the point of entering Madame Fanchon's, having watched in furious disbelief the sight of the duke's coach driving away.

On an impulse Charity directed the coachman to Mount Street, though whether out of a desire to confess her terrible extravagance to someone, or merely to put off the moment when she must explain it to his grace, she knew not.

Mrs. Fitzallan was at home and greeted her warmly, giving her news of the family who had not five minutes since gone walking in the Park, before succumbing to her curiosity to know how her young friend came to be in town. Her eyes grew rounder by the minute as Charity explained, and when she arrived at the halting explanation of the morning's events, they began to twinkle.

"Oh, you may laugh, ma'am, but I am quite mortified. Such appalling extravagance! I don't know what came over me. I am sure that I have ordered a great many more clothes than I can possibly need—and haven't the first idea how I am to tell his grace!"

"My dear Charity, this is not like you . . ."

"I know. That seems to make matters worse."

Mrs. Fitzallan chuckled. "Nothing of the kind. I am sure that you are worrying yourself into a state unnecessarily. You have spent so long having to count every penny that I daresay your notion of extravagance will differ considerably from the duke's."

"I do hope you may be right," Charity said, though it seemed highly unlikely. Either way, she could not be happy until she had made a clean breast of the whole to his grace.

"It was an unforgivable abuse of your generosity," she concluded haltingly, and waited for his wrath to erupt.

The duke looked at her in silence for a long moment, wondering if she realized just what a change the morning's work had wrought—how, in spite of her very real anxiety, her eyes already sparkled with new life. When he spoke, his voice was gruff.

"The cost is of no interest to me. The only thing I should find unforgivable is if what you've chosen wants for style, and I think that unlikely. So you will oblige me by ridding yourself of y'r sackcloth and ashes—they don't become you. And in any case, I wish to speak to you of more important matters."

Relief, followed by a sudden desire to laugh, temporarily robed Charity of speech, but he seemed to notice nothing amiss.

"I have been writing to a friend of long acquaintance— Lady Tufnell, an amiable creature—"

"Yes, indeed!" Charity exclaimed, and saw his brows come together.

"You know her?"

"Not exactly, but Fitz—Captain Fitzallan, that is—took me to one of her parties when I first arrived in London and she was very gracious to me. I also accompanied him to Lady Sefton's," she added, half-apologetically, "but that was a much grander affair, and I doubt her ladyship would remember me."

"Hmp!" He regarded her with a jaundiced eye. "And who else might you just happen to have met, miss—eh?"

"No one that I can recall, sir. Fitz only asked me out of kindness at a time when I was very unhappy . . ." She felt she was on dangerous ground and hastily concluded, "The fact is, I was very much out of my depth, I fear."

"I see," he said dryly. "Well, this time you will acquit yourself with more confidence, I trust. I have asked Matilda to take you up, give you the benefit of her vast experience. I'll prime Lady Sefton as well, since you are more than likely to meet up with her again. And don't, pray, tell me again how kind I am, for I never do anything without good reason."

Charity would have liked to ask what reason he particularly

had in mind, but felt that it might be wiser to hold her tongue.

On the following day, Fitz called to see her.

"Mama said you were here—I could scare believe it!" He looked down at her quizzically. "It seems you have charmed your erstwhile enemy into submission?"

"Hush, Fitz!" Charity besought him. "Oh, so much has happened, I still find it all very hard to believe."

"And Alistair?" he asked. "How has he taken the change of heart?"

Her face closed up at once. "His lordship is impossible—I have seldom known anyone to be so unreasonable," she declared with a ferocity that made him blink.

"Hardly surprising when you think about it, I suppose. However," Fitz continued, wisely turning the subject, "to return to you—I wondered if you would care to come riding tomorrow afternoon in the Park? I have a friend with a nicely mannered hack that he will willingly loan you."

Charity accepted with pleasure. And when, on the following morning, Madame Fanchon delivered all but a few of her new gowns, her joy was unconfined. As she and Annie unwrapped them, she knew at once that, mad as her behavior may have seemed at the time, her instincts had been sound. The duke must surely approve her choices.

That afternoon, in her eagerness to show off to him, she donned the riding habit of bronze green with black frogging, her fingers shaking slightly as she fastened the little jacket which was cut on military lines and tilted the black shako with its tuft of green feathers pertly over her eyes.

His grace was sitting beside the fire in the library, with Harry chattering away at his side. They both looked up as Charity came in, and after a moment of stunned silence, Harry ran to her.

"Aunt Charity! You look as fine as fivepence!" He swung around. "Doesn't she look fine, Grandfather?"

The duke's expression was so severe that for a moment Charity's heart almost misgave her. Could she be wrong? And then he cleared his throat. "That one of La Fanchon's creations, is it?"

She nodded, holding her breath.

"Well, if the rest are anything approaching it for style, you have done very well."

As she presently rode into Hyde Park with Fitz at her side, Charity was still glowing with the recollection of his words. Fitz, too, had been highly complimentary. He was still teasing her about her looks as they turned in at the Stanhope Gate, when she looked up and saw the now familiar curricle with its famous black horses.

In the same moment Lord Alistair looked up and saw them. He was not alone. Miss Vane, her face stiff with annoyance, leaned toward him to say something.

"Oh, lor!" murmured Fitz. "We must stop, I suppose."

But before they could do so, Lord Alistair touched his hat briefly and the curricle swept past them.

16

"You see?" cried Melissa. "You would not believe me when I told you I had seen your father's coach outside Madame Fanchon's. But I was right. That riding habit is one of Fanchon's—I would swear to it!"

Alistair made no answer. He was almost too angry to speak and almost all of his anger was directed against Charity for killing once and for all any lingering hope that he might have misjudged her. The road was quiet and he gave the horses their heads, as if by so doing he might somehow erase the image of her, clothed in her new elegance, so vividly imprinted on his mind, which all but blotted out the unspoiled young woman who had for a while captured his imagination. The wheels rattled over the road, and above the noise, Melissa's voice rose ever more petulantly.

". . . it is insupportable! I refuse to have that woman parading herself in public as your father's . . ."

"Have a care what you say, my dear." He did not raise his voice, yet it cracked like a whip. "His grace is indeed my father, and as such I will not hear him abused by anyone—even you."

"But . . . but surely you will do something?"

He hauled back on the reins as a dog ran out a few yards ahead—it skittered away in the nick of time, and he said with quiet savagery, "What do you suggest? That I read him a lecture on morals?" An abrupt laugh escaped him. "Egad! I'd not care to try it."

"Even so . . ."

"Enough!" he snapped. "For the last time, Melissa, I am not my father's keeper. If he chooses to make himself a laughingstock, he may do so—and welcome. It is of no real interest to me.''

Charity was very quiet for some time after the curricle had disappeared from sight, and Fitz, seeing more than she herself realized, had the sense to hold his tongue. At last she turned to him with a rather strained smile.

''A salutary experience, but no more than I expected after our last encounter.''

''Do you mind very much?'' Fitz asked quietly.

''Good heavens, why should I mind?'' She caught his eye and colored slightly. ''Well, it is never very pleasant to be on the receiving end of a cut, especially when it is so unjustly delivered. But I am sorry that you should have been involved.''

''Oh, my dear girl, think nothing of it. It don't trouble me, I assure you.'' Except, thought Fitz, that it grieves me to see you hurt. He did not say so, however, for he had long since recognized the nature of her feelings for Alistair. He cherished the hope that one day, when Ashbourne was safely married, Charity might look with kindness upon his suit. But for now he turned the conversation to lighter matters, and was pleased to see her gradually showing something of her former good spirits.

When Charity returned to Grosvenor Street, she found Lady Tufnell with his grace, accompanied as always by the effusive Miss Berridge. Her ladyship was kind enough to say that she remembered Charity, and professed herself delighted to be renewing the acquaintance.

''Yes, indeed,'' murmured her irrepressible companion, who then looked nervously in the duke's direction.

''His grace has been explaining your situation to me,'' Lady Tufnell continued amiably, ''and it will give me great pleasure to lend you my support. I enjoy the company of young people. Ain't that so, Celia?''

''Oh, absolutely! You always say that they help to keep you young!''

The duke shot Miss Berridge an impatient look, and Charity strove to keep a straight face.

"Well, that's settled, then." His grace's tone conveyed that his toleration threshold was fast approaching.

Thankfully, at the same moment Lady Tufnell chose to depart. She gathered herself together, folded a heavy silk shawl edged with ermine across her immense bosom, and stood up to take her leave. Miss Berridge was up on the instant, fussing around her with gloves and reticule until even Charity's patience was tested, yet her ladyship seemed to find nothing amiss.

"I am holding a ball this coming Friday, Miss Wynyate—tradition, y'know—helps to get the Season off to a good rousing start," she said, pulling on her gloves. Her eyes twinkled. "I daresay young Fitzallan would be happy enough to bring you along, and we shall see what transpires. As for you, Henry, I am happy to meet you again after all this time. See that you take good care of that leg, now. Remember the compress I told you about—night and morning without fail. My George used to swear by it."

"God give me strength!" the duke exploded testily the moment the door closed behind his visitors. He laid his head back on the cushion, eyes closed, and Charity noticed with some disquiet how tiredness had sharpened his features. "I hope you appreciate the extent to which I sacrifice my finer feelings on your behalf, Charity Wynyate—it would not please me to know that I had endured all that for nothing! Half an hour of Tilly is five and twenty minutes too long, but how *does* she put up with that twittering imbecile all day and every day?"

Charity smiled sympathetically. "They are used to one another, I think—and Miss Berridge is very well-meaning."

"Ha! A damning phrase, if I ever heard one." His eyes snapped open. "Did you enjoy your ride?"

She thought of Lord Alistair's snub. "Very much, sir, thank you."

"I should do something about a mount for you, I suppose."

"Oh, no. Fitz's friend is more than happy to loan me his horse."

"Even so. I must see Alistair about it—when he next condescends to visit me." Preoccupied with his own thoughts, he did not notice Charity's look of distress. His eyes gew suddenly keen. "Like young Fitzallan, do you?"

She pulled herself together, choosing her words with care. "He is a good friend. I knew him first in Brussels."

There was a silence. Then: "He and Ned grew up together, y'know."

"Yes, so I have heard." Something in the way he said it brought a tightness to her throat. She waited for more, but it didn't come—and when she looked, his eyes had closed again.

On the Friday evening, it seemed to Charity that almost the whole of London must be attending Lady Tufnell's ball. The crush of carriages outside was as nothing to the mass of people thronging the staircase within.

"Is it always like this?" she whispered to Fitz as they advanced one step at a time.

"Believe so. No experience, myself," he confessed. "Went straight from Oxford into the Grays, but Mama says Lady T's ball is always a sad crush."

"I believe I saw your parents a little way ahead of us."

"More than likely." He grinned. "The girls aren't with them. Mary didn't in the least mind waiting for her official come-out, though Eliza couldn't understand why she wasn't fizzing at the thought of missing all the excitement."

Charity felt very strange. It was all so different from the few functions she had attended earlier, making even Lady Sefton's reception seem modest by comparison. But however apprehensive she might feel inside, her outward appearance must give every cause for satisfaction. The duke had made sure of that.

"Let me look at you," he had commanded when she had come down to await Fitz's arrival. And she stood very still while he put up his glass very much as his son might have done.

The dress she had chosen for this, her debut, was a slim sheath of palest peach *mousseline de soie* over cream satin falling from a high waist, its scalloped neckline cut with a brevity which exposed more of her bosom than she was wont to show. But she need not have worried; the warmth of color flattered her complexion, giving it a creamy pallor which emphasized her clear eyes, now bright with excitement and not a little apprehension. Her light brown hair, under the magical fingers of a hairdresser commissioned by his grace, shone with red highlights and tumbled in a complex cluster of curls threaded with tiny seed pearls.

"Hmp. I commend y'r taste," was all the duke had said, but she took it as the highest compliment. He turned away for a moment to pick up a velvet box from the table close to his chair. "Mayhap these will add a finishing touch."

The pearls glowed in their bed of silk. Charity had stared at them, motionless, deprived of speech.

"Well," he barked at last, "are you going to take them, or aren't you?"

"I am persuaded I should not," she said huskily, "but they are very beautiful." She lifted the pearls from their case almost with reverence, and fumbled with the clasp.

"Here, give them to me." The duke had rested his stick against the table and taken the pearls from her hands. His fingers trembled slightly against the cool skin of her neck. "There," he said, his voice curiously ebullient in spite of its gruffness. "It's many a long year since I fastened a string of pearls around a pretty woman's neck."

Charity turned swiftly and kissed his cheek. "Bless you, dear sir."

He had reached for his stick. "Now, now, don't turn mawkish on me, for pity's sake," he growled, but she thought he was not displeased.

Lady Tufnell was a sight to behold in folds of purple silk, her matching turban nodding with black osprey plumes as she greeted Charity and approved her appearance.

"Charming," she exclaimed, her plump beringed hands lifting Charity up from her curtsy. "Quite delightful!" Beaming, she turned to Fitz. "Lucky young dog. Y'r mother's here somewhere, have you seen her yet?"

Fitz grinned and said that he had not. "But that is hardly surprising, ma'am, among all these people."

"I suppose not," she said, glancing around complacently. "Now then, I'm sure I can leave Miss Wynyate in your safe-keeping while I greet my remaining guests." She lowered her voice, "A little later, my dear, I mean to introduce you to lots of interesting and influential people."

"Oh, dear," Charity sighed, as they wandered through the anterooms in search of Mrs. Fitzallan, "I do wish his grace had not conceived this notion of wishing to launch me into society, but it is quite impossible to shift him once his mind is made up."

Fitz gave her a quizzical look. "What an odd girl you are, to be sure. If Eliza is to be believed, it is the sole dream of every right-thinking young woman!"

"I suppose so." She wrinkled her nose, half laughing at herself. "And of course it *is* very exciting, but I cannot rid myself of the feeling that it will all end in tears."

Had she but known it, Lord Alistair was thinking along similar lines as he stood in the doorway of the brilliantly lit ballroom. He had meant to seek out Melissa, but instead found himself watching the dowager's dais where Lady Tufnell was busy making Charity known to all the most influential ladies of the day, among them some of the most formidable doyens of Almack's. He had no idea what game his father was playing, but enlisting the aid of Lady Tufnell was a stroke of genius, and judging by the ease with which Charity was adapting to her new role, she had every intention of making the most of it. But she might yet regret being thrust to the fore—Society was a fickle jade. The musicians were tuning up and he saw Fitz come from the colorful crowd to lead her into the dance.

"Looks well, don't she?" observed Mr. Trowbridge, following the direction of his gaze. "No wish to appear patronizing, of course, but you'd scarcely know her for the same young lady."

"I couldn't agree more," came the curt reply.

Charity would have been less than human had she failed to enjoy herself, although always at the back of her mind was the fear that she might encounter Lord Alistair. She had caught a brief distant glimpse of him when he arrived, rather later than most of the guests, but he had made no attempt to seek her out—viewed realistically, there was no reason why he should do so, and she certainly had no intention of letting his unreasonable behavior spoil her evening. So many people had been gracious to her, the ballroom was a magical setting, and the music made her want to dance on and on.

It was indeed an unforgettable experience, as she later told Mrs. Fitzallan. "But my mind is in such a whirl! Lady Tufnell is the most generous hostess imaginable, ma'am, but she has introduced me to so many people that I scarce remember who is who, and live in dread of making a faux pas!"

"I shouldn't trouble your head about that, my dear," said Fitz's mother with unusual dryness. "They will know who *you* are, which is all that really matters. Unless I am much mistaken, you will be showered with invitations. I do hope, so popular as you are like to become, you will not forget Mary's come-out a week from now."

Charity's response was so enthusiastic that Mrs. Fitzallan immediately rebuked herself for even thinking that her young friend might be carried away by the attentions of so many new acquaintances. She seemed quite genuinely not to realize just how great an accolade was being bestowed upon her. It was to be hoped she would not get hurt, for already her good fortune was the focus of much speculation among a small but influential group of the *haut ton*, and some of their conclusions were less than kind.

But no hint of gossip reached Charity's ears. She did not want for partners, and it was some considerable time before she found time to draw breath, making her excuses to Lady Tufnell and going in search of the ladies retiring room. Miss Berridge was less easy to shake off, however. She insisted upon showing Charity the way, and it was only with the greatest difficulty that the birdlike little woman was persuaded that her charge could find her own way back to the ballroom. In the event, this proved more difficult than Charity had anticipated. She followed the distant sounds of revelry, to little avail, as having taken one wrong turn too many, she at last found herself in the conservatory.

With no clear idea where this stood in relation to the ballroom, and with not a soul in sight to enlighten her, she ventured inside. It was like another world, a humid haven of tranquility, with moonlight filtering through the Gothic windows. Charity sank gratefully onto a small bench among the fronds of greenery. The sound of distant music merged with the faint trickle of water, and a pungent earthy smell assailed her nostrils. She sighed, leaned back, and closed her eyes.

Time lost all meaning, but suddenly a curious prickling sensation warned her that she was no longer alone. She opened her eyes to find Lord Alistair looming over her in the half light. She sat up, blinking.

"So this is where you are hiding," he said. "Surely your triumphant debut has not begun to pall already?"

"Not in the least," she replied with a touch of defiance, stung by the sarcasm in his voice. "I was merely catching my breath."

"Well, if you have now done so, I am here to escort you back to the ballroom."

"You?" She stared up at him in the dimness, striving to read his expression.

He placed firm hands beneath her arms and lifted her, resisting, to her feet. "The next dance is a waltz, and you are going to take the floor with me."

"But I can't possibly dance with you!"

His humorless smile appeared vaguely menacing in the half-light. "I am sorry to seem disobliging, but I must insist. The whole assembled male company is clamoring for the privilege. Why should I be the exception?"

"Because you"—she caught her breath—"you have made it abundantly clear that you no longer wish to know me."

"Ah, but wishing doesn't come into it, ma'am. If it did, I would be anywhere but here, I assure you."

The formal *ma'am* stung, as did his cutting tone. "Then why?"

"Oh, come! You cannot be so naive as to suppose that my father's efforts on your behalf have escaped notice?" His glance rested momentarily on the pearl necklace and instinctively Charity put up a hand to cover it—a gesture that did not go unmarked. "Or have you been so carried away by the manner in which you have been received tonight that you have not heard the whispers?"

"Whispers?"

He still held her fast, so that she was obliged to lean back in order to look up at him; in her uplifted face Alistair could see that her mouth was trembling and felt an overpowering longing to crush it beneath his own. The treachery of his own body whipped his anger up afresh. "That my father is an old fool who has become enamored of an unscrupulous woman young enough to be his granddaughter—and that he is allowing her to lead him by the nose."

"Oh, no!" Charity began to feel that she was living through some kind of nightmare. "But it isn't true. You must know that. You, above all people, know how impossible it is to gainsay his grace once he has made up his mind. Besides, Lady Tufnell would never have agreed to . . . to sponsor me if she thought . . ."

"Lady Tufnell sees only the best in people, but there are others less kind."

"If you are right, then there is only one thing for it—I shall ask Fitz to take me home at once!" She tried to pull away, but his fingers tightened cruelly.

"And give the gabble-grinders further cause for destructive gossip? Oh, no, my girl. For my father's sake, if not for your own, you will waltz with me and show the world a happy face. That way, at least, it will appear that I find nothing untoward in the relationship."

"Well, of course there isn't!" she exclaimed hotly. "You know there isn't!"

"Do I? But then, it isn't me you have to convince. Come now, or we shall be too late."

They reached the ballroom just as the couples were taking the floor and he swept her into their midst with a flourish. The music was liltingly lovely and his lordship a most accomplished dancer, but what should have been a wonderful experience was rather a kind of refined torture; through the fine silk of her dress, the pressure of his hand burned with an intimacy that mocked her, and as he whirled her around, the taut line of his thigh pressed against hers quite deliberately, sending the most exquisite sensations coursing through her.

It was as if he was cruelly and quite deliberately punishing her for having succeeded with his father where he had failed—and for appearing to flaunt her success before his friends. And all the while he exuded charm, maintaining a flow of small talk while his eyes glinted down at her in a way that all but she must take for an excess of amiability, for only she was fully aware of the nature of that look, and the way his scar stood out lividly.

"Smile, my dear," he murmured, his head bent intimately toward her, and smile she did, thinking of the duke and wondering if the music would ever end. But when it did, the agony did not end, for he continued to hold her firmly as they quit the floor, still engaging her in conversation.

Miss Vane was decidedly not amused. It was mortifying enough to watch Alistair flirting with Charity Wynyate, but even worse, she herself was already promised to him for this waltz. She had been approached by several gentlemen— excellent dancers, all—and had been obliged to refuse them. Now she was left without a partner, a thing unheard of for her, and so must sit among a scattering of empty chairs, occupied only here and there by dowagers and unclaimed ingenues, fluttering her fan to feign tiredness, and filled with murderous rage.

"Careful, Melissa." Sir Rupert Darian had approached with his usual catlike stealth, elegant as ever with that misleading air of ennui. "Your expression betrays you."

Her pose forgotten momentarily, she put up her chin, glaring at him. "I have no idea what you mean."

"No?" Sir Rupert's smile was tinged with malice. "Ah, well—may I?" He indicated the little gilt chair beside her. Lady Vane, ever vigilant, turned from an engrossing conversation with a friend several places away, nodded abruptly to him, and resumed her narrative. Darian took this gesture for acquiescence, and settled himself with some care.

"They make a remarkably fine couple," he observed, putting up his glass. And, hearing the muffled squeak of rage beside him, turned, all innocence. "Forgive me, Melissa. That was a tactless remark to make when your nuptials are almost upon you—except that his lordship does seem very engrossed, not in the least like a man on the brink of marriage."

Melissa's glance was drawn irresistibly back to the dipping, swaying couple just as Alistair bent to his partner in a particularly intimate way. She longed to get up and rush away—away from Sir Rupert's insidious speculation. She gritted her teeth and tried not to listen.

"Odd, wouldn't you say, when it is rumored that they are scarce on speaking terms. But then, I keep forgetting that Miss Wynyate is almost family—and all families have their squabbles, the Ashbournes more than most, except that *they* are not noted for making up."

"Sir Rupert!" Melissa hissed from behind her fan. "If you are hoping that I shall be so indiscreet as to . . ."

"Nothing of the kind, my dear," he murmured, his voice as soft as silk. "You are, as I well know, the very soul of discretion. No breath of scandal has ever attached to you—and, I trust, never will."

Beneath his smoothness, the hint of menace was unmistakeable, and Melissa's stomach muscles contracted with that familiar thrill of fear. How he delighted in letting her know that he could, if he so wished, destroy her with a word. She felt the color run up under her skin, hidden from view by the spread of her fan which she fluttered to conceal a betraying shake.

"One cannot say as much for Miss Wynyate," the smooth voice continued. "She is as full of surprises as Pandora's box, and is like to cause as much trouble. Of course, one should never underestimate an unworldly woman—their apparent simplicity can of itself serve as a weapon. Miss Wynyate has already achieved much—doting aunt to the duke's heir, inseparable companion to the duke himself, who is already lavishing gifts upon her. Who knows where it may not end?" Sir Rupert's heavy-lidded eyes were speculative

as they held hers. "If what one hears is true, she may yet
precede you to the altar. Will you enjoy having her for a
mother-in-law, do you think?"

It couldn't have gone that far? The very thought was
anathema to her. It must not be. "You must be mistaken,"
she said in a stifled voice, her fan pressed against her mouth,
her wild glance meeting his cool one over its rim. "His grace
would not . . . Oh, this is insupportable! You are making
it up to tease me!"

But although the words throbbed with the force of her
emotions, her accusation lacked conviction. And he knew
it. The music was coming to an end—time to play his trump
card.

"Can you afford to take the chance, my dear Melissa? Or
would you rather put your trust in me?" His eyes fixed her
as a snake fixes its prey. "For certain guaranteed favors,
I might be persuaded to rid you of both impediments to your
future happiness—the lady and her inconvenient nephew."
The final chords faded away, and amid the general swell of
conversation, he concluded softly, "Well, Melissa, what do
you say?"

17

Charity was unusually subdued during the days following Lady Tufnell's ball. The duke could not understand it, and was in consequence irritable. Her debut had gone exceedingly well—her ladyship had confirmed as much to him, and even if she had not, the number of invitations arriving daily was proof enough. People had even taken to calling, which pleased him less. Mostly, he kept out of the way, but he had been foiled by that accomplished tattler, Sally Jersey, who had come ostensibly to tell him that Lady Tufnell would be receiving vouchers for Almack's on Miss Wynyate's behalf, but he wasn't fooled. She hoped for some sniff of scandal to carry back to her cronies.

"Oh, I really don't . . ." Charity scarcely managed to hide her dismay when he had later congratulated her on storming that particular sacred bastion of society so soon. "That is, I would as lief not go, sir."

"Not go?" he barked. "My dear girl, you don't refuse vouchers for Almack's. Those women would crucify you, all seven of 'em! Well, not quite all, perhaps. Lady Sefton and Emily Cowper are too amiable to cut you completely, but they wouldn't love you for it, and you would certainly not be offered a second chance."

Charity found it impossible to tell him that she didn't want a second chance, any more than she could tell him what was being said about the nature of their relationship. She felt a sudden overwhelming longing for obscurity.

"I suppose that son of mine was there with his mock-virtuous, self-complacent bride to be?"

The duke's voice dragged her back. It was painful to speak

of Lord Alistair, let alone of Miss Vane, whose measure the duke had so accurately assessed. She said briefly that they were and attempted to turn the subject. But the duke was not so easily deceived. "You and Alistair quarreled, have you? Is that why I've seen neither hide nor hair of him since I came back to London?"

"Quarreled is too strong a word," she said stiffly. "It is true that his lordship chooses to hold certain opinions about me—which is his privilege. I, however, do not feel obliged to listen to them, any more than I will stoop to disprove them. If he is staying away on that account, I am sorry, but short of leaving, I don't really see what I can do about it."

"All right, young lady, no need to get on y'r high ropes with me," said the duke with astonishing mildness. "So, you've quarreled. Pity. I had hoped he'd see sense before it was too late. Trouble is, he can be as stiff-rumped and stubborn as I am m'self. In fact, of the three boys, I suppose he has inherited the worst traits of my character," He observed the effect of his words, and, apparently satisfied, added gruffly, "If it's any consolation, he also inherited some rather more commendable ones from his mother, which is probably why I have always tended to be hard on him."

This was an extraordinary admission for him to make; in fact, if she had understood him aright, his whole attitude was so extraordinary that Charity wondered if he were feeling quite himself. But he appeared very much as he always did, so she replied firmly and with only the slightest flush denoting her still ruffled feelings, "I am sure I have no interest in Lord Alistair, or what motivates him to behave as he does."

"Quite so," he readily agreed, adding with a sigh, "But you know, I never thought to miss his visits as much as I do, brief though they were."

Harry also missed his uncle, and wanted to know when he would come. "I'd like him to take me riding. It's fun going with you and Captain Fitz, of course," he added ingenuously, "but it *was* Uncle Alistair who gave Gyp to me."

"I daresay, but he leads a very busy life, which leaves him little time for small boys." For a moment he looked hurt and Charity regretted her unnecessary curtness. But Harry was never down for long.

Next to riding with his uncle, his latest joy was driving out in an open landau with his grandfather, something which had only happened twice so far, when the weather turned unexpectedly warm. But although the duke deliberately avoided the fashionable hour, the second of these outings, on which Charity had reluctantly agreed to accompany them, coincided with the visit to the Park of a small riding party comprising Lord Alistair, Melissa and a small group of friends. It was the thing Charity least wanted to have happen.

Harry was quick to recognize his uncle. He called out excitedly, and although he immediately subsided upon being reproved by the duke, the damage was done. The meeting could not be avoided. Charity's heart sank and she wished herself anywhere but where she was. Even the fact that she was looking her best in a new redingote of soft blue-gray, closed high at the neck and edged with swansdown, did nothing to raise her spirits, for it merely shouted aloud her new-found extravagance. And as Lord Alistair rode across to the waiting carriage with Miss Vane trailing reluctantly behind him, she was convinced that the sight of them, looking very much a family in the duke's landau, must surely lend credence to the worst kind of rumor.

The next few moments were the longest Charity could remember, and contained all the elements of a tragicomedy, with the duke high-nosed and unapproachable, Melissa scarcely able to be civil, and she herself striving for invisibility. Lord Alistair, as starkly formal and tight-lipped as his parent, touched his hat briefly to her and to his father, before giving his whole attention to Harry. It was Harry who saved the situation from total farce; quite oblivious of the undercurrents surrounding him, he chattered away happily to his uncle and managed to wring from him before he left a promise to take him riding very soon.

But it was the end of their drive. The duke ordered the coachman to take them home, and the moment they arrived he retired to his room and was not seen again that day.

* * *

In the Park, the atmosphere was equally charged with tension as Alistair and Melissa rode slowly, side by side, not attempting to catch up with their party, each preoccupied with private thoughts.

Alistair was seeing Charity's face, lifted briefly to him, enchantingly framed by the soft blue silk of her bonnet brim, her eyes wide and clear as a child's meeting his with fleeting apprehension. And as he cursed her for having the power to move him, even now. But the more he sought to banish the memory, the more it plagued him.

Melissa's thoughts were darker. She had watched Alistair with Harry. It was the first time she had seen the boy, and she knew now what she was up against. There was genuine affection between uncle and nephew; it was obvious in spite of the strained circumstances. Equally obvious was the bond between the three people in the carriage, giving some credence to Sir Rupert's hints concerning the duke's change of heart. But what had frightened her more than all the rest was that one fleeting glance between Alistair and Charity Wynyate, which had revealed more than either of them could know they were betraying.

In that instant she saw where the real danger lay—saw too that she must do something before they ruined everything by recognizing their love for each other. And in the same moment she saw how, with boldness and a certain degree of luck, she might yet gain everything at a stroke.

But speed was of the essence. Ideally, the deed would be better left until she was married and far away, but now she dare not wait so long. It was less than a month to the wedding, but time enough for Alistair to succumb to temptation, to risk all—the censure of his peers, not to mention the total destruction of her future happiness—by running off with Charity Wynyate. If that were to happen, she would die of shame!

So, it was up to her to prevent it happening—and soon. It would take careful planning, for something must be contrived to make it seem at first that Miss Wynyate had merely run off with the child. That way, the duke would merely be very angry, and probably institute a search. Only later, when her marriage to Alistair had been celebrated with all the attendant pomp and ceremony, would the tragic news of the violent deaths of his grandchild and Miss Wynyate be revealed to the duke; and, knowing how he doted upon them, she felt certain that the shock would kill him, and she would become the Duchess of Orme. *That* was to be the *pièce de résistance* in her beautifully contrived drama.

Melissa had no idea how to achieve all of this on her own, but Sir Rupert's devious mind would doubtless devise ways and means. He had made no attempt to see her alone since the night of Lady Tufnell's ball, but she had no doubt that he had meant every word of his thinly veiled suggestion that he should rid her of the boy and his aunt. Outrageous as it seemed at the time, the idea had nevertheless lain at the back of her mind, tempting her with its very audacity. Now, somehow, she must contrive a meeting.

Even Sir Rupert's hint about the price he meant to exact, and Melissa had few illusions as to what it would be, held a spice of danger that both thrilled and repelled her. But it did not deter her. She was confident of finding some way to thwart him when the time came.

Her equanimity restored, Melissa determined that Alistair should have no cause to question her devotion during the next few weeks. She rode a little closer to him and said with a smile, "I am so glad that I have met your nephew at last, dearest. I confess I was quite taken with him."

And Alistair, belatedly realizing that he had been less than gracious, made an effort to meet her conciliatory overture with equal warmth. "Harry is a scamp," he said with the ghost of a smile.

"Yes, but such a bright little boy. I hope we may see a lot more of him when we are married—and his sister," Melissa added, mentally crossing her fingers.

He stretched out a hand to cover hers where it rested on the pommel. "That is generous of you, my dear. I am aware that the last few weeks have not been easy for you."

"Mama says it is often so just before one's wedding," she confessed with a demure fluttering of eyelashes.

"Yes, I daresay." Alistair was silent for a moment before

asking abruptly, "How did you think my father seemed?"

"Oh, what a question! I confess I would not find it easy to judge. I scarcely know his grace . . . and he is such a terrifying old gentleman that it is all I can do not to quake visibly in his presence." But this question of failing health might work in her favor. She let a small silence elapse before saying with a pretty display of concern, "Are you worried about your father's health?"

"Not really. I have not seen him for some days. Perhaps it was the sunlight which emphasized the sharpness of his features and made him seem less robust. He is obviously in less pain from his gout, but I did wonder whether his recent illness had taken rather more of a toll than we thought at the time."

Melissa was well aware who the *we* included. "Well, your father is no longer a young man," she said innocently. "And the presence of small children about the place, however well-controlled, can be tiring. It must be a source of comfort to you to see Miss Wynyate so at ease with his grace. I do so admire her courage in coping with his ill humors."

"H'm. She certainly seems to have found the way through his armor. But then, she never did want for tenacity."

She was not displeased to see him frown, and made no further reference to Miss Wynyate. By this time they had almost come up with the rest of their party, and Melissa watched the young French marquis wheel his horse and lift a hand in welcome.

"Mademoiselle," he called out. "We were desolate lest you might have left us forever!"

His woebegone face made everyone laugh—with the exception of Alistair, who merely curled an ironic lip.

It was a pity about Henri St. Jules, Melissa thought. She had enjoyed their brief flirtation. But there would be time enough later—married ladies enjoyed greater freedom in which to pursue these little diversions.

Charity tried her best in the days that followed to hide her initial misgivings. And Lady Tufnell seemed so pleased by the favorable comments of her friends in respect to her protégé that if there were any adverse gossip, she clearly took no heed of it.

Fitz was surprised that Charity should be taking the matter so seriously. "Lord, someone is forever tattling. Mama says it's the breath of life to them, but it don't mean a thing to most people."

Charity had already begun to realize this for herself, just as she had realized how impossible it was to turn back the clock. She had visited her father two or three times, and had felt just as much out of place in Wimpole Street, fending off Maria's attempts to secure an invitation to Ashbourne House. But one thing she was now sure of—her father knew nothing of any connection between the duke and her mother. And so she slowly came to terms with her sense of guilt at taking so much from the duke, and decided that people would have to like her for what she was, or not at all. By the evening of Mary's come-out she was feeling much more cheerful. Even the presence of Lord Alistair and Miss Vane could not diminish her pleasure.

It had been decided quite early on that the house in Mount Street would not accommodate the number of people to be invited, but Mrs. Fitzallan's dear friend, Lady Sefton, had a niece making her debut at the same time, and she had most generously offered to host a joint celebration for the two girls.

"Mary, you look lovely this evening," Charity said warmly as she greeted her young friend standing nervously beside her parents to receive their guests. The obligatory white could so often look insipid, but Mary's simple muslin gown was exactly right for her, setting off her chestnut hair which had been burnished until it shone. Eliza, who had been permitted to attend on this special occasion, though not to dance, might look a little more ethereal with her golden curls, but her ebullient nature only served to emphasize Mary's gentleness of character.

"She does look well, does she not?" said her mama with a very proper degree of partiality, complacent in the knowledge that Julia, Lady Sefton's niece, though a charming girl, had just the suspicion of a squint.

"I only hope I shall not be sick," Mary whispered, biting

her lip to the disgust of her more gregarious sister and the apprehension of her mama.

"I'm sure you won't," Charity said encouragingly. "Try a few deep breaths. I find it usually does the trick when I am nervous."

"That was kind of you," said Mr. Trowbridge, coming to stand beside her a little later.

She smiled. "Well, Mary is very shy, and it must be quite an ordeal for her—something I was spared, thank God."

There were still people arriving, and one gentleman in particular took her attention. He was striking in a rather foppish way, and she recalled having seen him at every function she had attended.

"Do tell me, who is that gentleman?" she asked Mr. Trowbridge. "He must have a great deal of address, for I seem to see him everywhere I go."

Theo glanced across the room. "Sir Rupert Darian," he said, and something in his voice made her turn to look at him.

"You don't like him much, I think?"

"Not a particularly likeable fellow. Got a vicious way with him when he chooses. Stair knows him better than I do, and he can't stand him." Theo turned with a droll smile. "How is that for cutting up a character?"

"Oh, well, I did ask you. And what you've told me does explain my own feeling about him. We have never met, but I have quite often found him staring at me in a way that makes me feel decidedly uncomfortable."

Theo's smile faded. "Devil take the man! Tell you what, I'll drop a word in his ear, if you like."

"Oh, no. You are very kind, but it really isn't important."

They were still standing within view when Lord Alistair presently arrived with Miss Vane and her mama. His lordship was looking quite disturbingly handsome in his severe black and white. Charity watched as Lady Vane and her daughter went through the formalities with a studied politeness and the merest inclination of the head, but Lord Alistair earned her reluctant admiration by making a point of stopping a moment with each of the young girls and leaving them starry-eyed.

The whole evening seemed destined to go off without a hitch. The band of the Scots Greys had been engaged to play, and there was little doubt that by the end the two young girls would be able to claim that they had never wanted for a partner. Charity was almost equally in demand. Fitz claimed one of the country dances and a waltz, while Mr. Trowbridge led her into the cotillion and entertained her with his rather droll wit. Lord Alistair made no attempt to speak to her, let alone ask her to dance, and she told herself she was glad.

Miss Vane, on the other hand, was surprisingly gracious when she encountered Charity between dances, and even went so far as to admire her gown—a slim half dress of ivory crepe, ruched at the hem. "But then, Madame Fanchon is so superior to any other modiste, don't you think?"

Charity confessed without embarrassment that she had very little experience in such matters. Miss Vane smiled, happy in the knowledge that not only was her own peach bloom gown every bit as stylish as her companion's, but her looks were so far superior that anyone seeing the two of them together would not give Miss Wynyate a second glance.

In this she was deluding herself. Several people, seeing them in conversation, found Miss Wynyate's air of quiet elegance more than a match for the other's beauty. Lord Alistair found the comparison even more dramatic. Ever since that day in the Park he too had been deluding himself; now, seeing the two young women together, it was suddenly blindingly clear where his heart lay. Melissa's beauty was revealed as a shallow thing when compared with Charity's wonderful poise and quiet charm; and it was Charity who filled his heart to overflowing, who was everything that he wanted, everything that was good and true and honest. The mere thought of seeing her and not being able to touch her, let alone possess her, was a physical pain. He now realized how little he even *liked* Melissa, let alone loved her! And he felt trapped, for there was no honorable way of extricating himself from a marriage that was becoming more abhorrent to him with every moment that passed.

He turned away, his mind in turmoil—and failed to see Sir Rupert Darian, who had followed him from the card room. Sir Rupert found the little scene he had just witnessed most illuminating. Had it been anyone but Ashbourne he might have found it in his heart to pity him just a little. But there had been bad blood between them for too long now for him to feel anything other than an exhilarating foretaste of revenge.

18

Several days later, as Charity was considering taking Emily for an early afternoon outing to the Park, Hamlyn announced Miss Vane. She had scarcely time to assemble her features into a smile of welcome before the fashionable vision swept past Hamlyn, her gloved hand outstretched.

"I do hope you will not mind my dropping in on you in this way," Melissa said, smiling graciously as she accepted an invitation to be seated and looked about her at the small saloon which Charity used when she was alone. "What a charming room."

She stripped off her gloves and brought her attention back to the young woman who sat quietly opposite, looking very much at home in her present surroundings. "The fact is, I was all set to accompany Mama to a tedious musical afternoon at Lady Arbuthnot's—you know the kind of thing? And then, as we were driving down Grosvenor Street, I suddenly seized my chance and persuaded Mama to set me down at your door."

Charity looked into the guileless sapphire eyes and waited, silent and composed, for her to continue. Melissa, shrewdly assessing her, knew that it would not do to underestimate Miss Wynyate.

"I have felt for some time that we should become better acquainted—we are all soon to be family, after all. Why, you will scarce believe it, but I have not exchanged more than a dozen words with the duke since Alistair and I were betrothed."

Suspicious of this apparent change of heart, Charity said, "Well, if you wish to see his grace, I'm afraid you have chosen a bad time. It is his invariable habit to rest in the afternoon and he seldom makes an appearance before four o'clock.''

Melissa seemed preoccupied with her discarded gloves, smoothing them with careful fingers. She looked up at last with an apologetic smile. ''I know—Alistair told me. To be honest with you, Miss Wynyate, it is really you I have come to see—to enlist your help. You see, Alistair is so fond of his young nephew that I feel I would like to get to know Harry too. Would you . . . that is, it is such a lovely day, do you think we might take him to the Park?''

''Now?'' There was surprise in Charity's voice. ''As a matter of fact, I *was* thinking of taking Emily . . .''

Melissa looked disconcerted. ''Cannot your nursemaid do that? I am not awfully good with babies, I'm afraid. And there will be time enough for me to get to know the little girl when she is older.''

''Well . . .'' There was reluctance in the hesitation. ''Miss Throstle does not take kindly to having Harry's lessons interrupted.''

''But surely,'' Melissa pressed her gently, ''you do not allow a mere governess to dictate to you?''

Charity flushed at this implied criticism of her authority. ''Of course not.'' She stood up. ''Very well. I will ask Hamlyn to have the carriage brought around. It will take me but a few minutes to get Harry ready.''

''There is no hurry, Miss Wynyate. Take all the time you need.'' While Charity was away, Melissa walked about the room. All was going splendidly. Alistair had gone with Theo Trowbridge to watch a prize fight, and would not be back until late. Too late, she thought exultantly. She picked up a china figurine, and put it down again. Old-fashioned. When she was mistress here, there would have to be changes. In fact, she would much prefer it if Alistair were to close this house up altogether—the one in St. James's Square was much finer.

Charity returned in a remarkably short space of time with Harry. He had been told to be on his best behavior, but

Charity still held her breath as he solemnly shook hands with Miss Vane, and looked at her curiously.

"You are going to marry Uncle Alistair, aren't you?"

"Harry!"

Melissa's laugh trilled out. "The dear boy! I don't mind his questions in the least!"

But Charity, knowing this to be tantamount to an open invitation, gave Harry one of her most repressive looks.

They were on the point of leaving when Melissa withdrew a letter from her reticule. "I wonder if this might be given to the duke? It is but a brief note assuring him of my warmest regards, and the joy with which I look forward to our closer union."

Charity, taking it from her, felt that she could make a pretty fair guess as to what his grace would make of it. As they crossed the hall, she handed the letter to Hamlyn. "Would you be so kind as to see that this is delivered to the duke after he has had his rest?"

"I shall deliver it to his grace myself, madam," said Hamlyn with a bow.

Harry chattered away happily as they drove to the Park. He didn't like Miss Vane anything like so well as Aunt Charity, but his odd upbringing had made him philosophical. Charity let him talk as it relieved her of the need to make conversation Miss Vane. Once inside the Park they left the carriage and walked away across the grass in the spring sunshine with Harry hopping between them, clearly wishing to take to his heels. There were not too many people around and at last Charity took pity on his fidgets and said he could play, but he must stay in sight.

Harry needed no second bidding, and spurred on by the distant yelps of a dog, he set off at a trot toward the distant shrubbery. Charity stifled a sigh, and wondered how short a stay would be considered adequate before she would be able to suggest politely that they return to the carriage. The dog's yelping was growing more frantic, and she saw that Harry was now in hot pursuit of the sound. She called to him, but he was too eager to take heed.

"Oh, no!" Charity gathered up her skirts and turned apologetically to Miss Vane. "Forgive me, I shall have to rescue him before he gets his clothes torn to shreds."

"Yes, do go by all means. I will wait here." Melissa waited until Charity had gone some distance, and then followed more slowly. As she approached the shrubbery, which concealed a small gate for the use of pedestrians, the yelping ceased and she heard a muffled shriek, followed by a thud, and was in time to see two men, one carrying a wriggling sack and the other supporting the limp figure of Charity Wynyate toward a nearby carriage. It was done.

She turned at once and hurried back over the grass, calling out to the coachman as she approached, "Quickly. You must take me home at once."

The coachman was clearly at a loss. "But—but what about Miss Wynyate, ma'am, and Master Harry?"

"Do as you are told, impertinent man," she snapped. "Miss Wynyate will not be coming. She has just driven off with the boy in a strange carriage, without a word of explanation. I have never been treated in such a fashion!"

Charity could not at first recall exactly what had happened. Her head ached abominably, and it was obvious that she was in a carriage traveling at a suicidal speed, bucking and bouncing over cobbles. When she opened her eyes, however, and saw the sack on the floor at her feet, memory came flooding back—the memory of seeing it being forced down over Harry and the dog, and of a hand wielding some kind of cudgel coming down to land with a sickening thud on the wriggling sack before being used upon her.

"Harry?" she whispered, and then screamed wildly, "Harry!" She slithered to the floor, her fingers frantic to untie the sack. At once a large rough hand shot out and, twisting cruel fingers in her hair, hauled her back onto the rocking seat, eyes smarting with the pain.

"Stow it, you!" he growled.

"Take your hand off me! Can't you understand? He will choke to death in that filthy sack!"

"Aye, and you'll join him, quicker'n wink, if yer don't stow yer mag!"

Terrified as she was that Harry might already be dead, Charity saw that no good would be served by making the man angrier than he was. "Please," she said quietly, "I just want to loosen the neck of the sack so that he can breathe more easily—and so that I can see he's all right."

This appeared to amuse him, but after a moment he bent down himself, swaying with the rocking motion, untied the rope, and pulled back the sacking. "Right," he muttered. "That's what yer wanted. Now let be."

Harry's face was sickly white except for a long trickle of blood. But she thought—she prayed—that he still breathed. The poor little dog, however, had stood no chance. She longed to ask him to move it in case Harry woke up, but was afraid that the man might take his anger out on the boy; for the same reason she bit back all the other questions that cried out for answers. In silence she prayed as she had never prayed before.

Had she but known it, Charity's prayers were even then being answered, for Alistair's curricle had been passing the Park gate, traveling in the opposite direction, at the precise moment she and Harry were being abducted. He was driving fast, looking neither to right nor left, and, sensing his mood, Theo Trowbridge made little attempt to converse with him. Pity. He had been looking forward to the mill, but he'd hazard a monkey that it wasn't the cancellation that had made his friend so out-of-reason cross. Alistair had been blue-deviled for days now, and although one might guess at the cause, it would take a braver man than himself to voice sympathy, let alone offer advice.

Theo's attention wandered to the scene around him, and suddenly his senses were alert. His exclamation made Alistair job clumsily at the horses's mouths and he swore softly and fluently.

"Sorry, but stop, man—for God's sake stop!" Theo, his gentle urbanity forgotten, was craning his neck around, and actually shouting. "I am certain I have just seen Miss Wynyate being hustled into a carriage against her will!"

Alistair hauled back on the reins and turned a livid face to him. "If this is some kind of jest—"

"Man, do I look as though I'm joking? See—that's the one, just moving off. Turn now, and you've a good chance of catching it. If I'm wrong, you may do what you will with me. But if I'm right, you'll need to be sharp not to lose sight of it!"

Making up his mind, Alistair called to John at the rear to hold the traffic as amid disgruntled shouts he wheeled the horses, a task requiring all of his consummate skill. A long way ahead he could see a closed carriage churning up the dust. What if Theo should be right? The mere thought was enough. He sent his whip singing out and the horses, though they were far from fresh, responded like the prime cattle they were.

Theo, no mean whip himself, had always marveled at his friend's ability to drive to an inch, but now urgency seemed to give him an extra edge. It was an experience never to be forgotten. The traffic thinned to a mere trickle and soon the two vehicles were alone on a straight stretch of road, with the curricle closing up fast. Only at the last minute did Theo realize what his friend intended to do. He closed his eyes as the curricle swept past the other, traveled on for two hundred yards or so, then slewed around to block the road.

There was pandemonium as the driver of the coach hauled desperately back, with the two horses out of control, blowing badly, and showing the whites of their eyes. The driver, scared out of his wits, jumped down and set off at a run.

"John, quieten those brutes before they kick the box in," Alistair shouted, as he flung down the reins and set off in pursuit, reaching the man before he had gone many yards, bringing him crashing down, and hitting him flush on the chin.

Theo climbed down in a more seemly fashion, secured the reins to a tree, and made his way to the carriage. As he opened one door, Alistair was already wrenching open the other. The man inside had been thrown forward, and was moaning and holding his head. Alistair dragged him out, tossing him to the ground like a rag doll and shouting to Theo to keep an eye on him.

Charity was sprawled on the floor of the coach, her arms about what looked like a bundle of rags. At first he thought she was unconscious, but as he bent to touch her, she flinched.

"Charity! My God, it *is* you!"

"Alistair?" her voice was a mere thread. "Oh, please help me. It is Harry."

And then she was in his arms, being lifted out into the fresh air, no longer certain where nightmare ended and reality began. He lay her down gently on the grass verge and went back to Harry. By the time he returned, she had pulled herself together and was on her feet, struggling out of her pelisse.

"I'll take him, my lord," she said, wrapping the pelisse closely around Harry while Alistair tugged the sack away from him, with the pathetic little dog still inside. To Charity's heartfelt relief, Harry was already beginning to groan. She held him close and spoke soothingly.

"My head hurts," he complained.

"Yes, dearest, I know," she said huskily, "but we'll soon have you home and in bed."

"Will Papa be there? I 'spect the battle's over by now . . ."

She lifted an anguished glance to Alistair. "I expect it is. I don't know about Papa, but Uncle Alistair is here."

"Oh, good," he sighed and fell asleep.

"Poor darling, his mind is wandering . . . he *will* be all right?"

Alistair examined the cut on the side of Harry's head. "Yes, of course. A touch of concussion, perhaps, but sleep will soon take care of that. He is too heavy for you—give him to me. I'll lay him on the carriage seat until we decide what to do about getting you home."

She surrendered her charge with reluctance, and in so doing their hands touched. She looked into his eyes and what she saw therein made her pulse begin to pound.

"Oh, my dearest girl!" Alistair's voice was raw with

emotion, "I haven't the first idea what all this is about, but
if anything had happened to you—if I had not been where
I was—if Theo had not seen you . . ." He turned aside and
lay Harry gently on the seat, and when he presently came
back to her, he had command of his feelings once more. Just
for a moment he held her close, as if he would never let her
go, and with her head pressed against his coat she could feel
the uneven thud of his heart. He had called her *his dearest
girl!* Presently he loosed her, but kept a firm hold of her hand.

They walked toward Theo, who was leaning nonchalantly
against a tree with his pistol trained on the two men, who
had been hustled together and were being just as keenly
watched by John Gage.

"My commiserations, ma'am," Theo said. "You are not
harmed, I trust?"

Charity shook her head, and winced as it throbbed dully.
"Thank you. Just a trifle shaken. I believe I owe my safe
deliverance to you."

He gave her one of his slow, deliberate smiles. "Pure
chance, ma'am. Happy to be of service."

She told them about Harry's running after the dog. "I
suppose the poor little thing was placed in the shrubbery as
a kind of lure, but why? Why us? One can only be thankful
that Miss Vane was not taken too."

"Melissa was with you?" Alistair asked.

This involved more explanations, which he heard out
without comment.

"Well, Stair, what are we to do with this sullen pair?"

Alistair turned Charity to face him. "I think, my dear,
that you had better go back to keep an eye on Harry. He
might be frightened if he wakes."

She still found it hard to believe that these gentle tones
were meant for her. Everything seemed in such a muddle.
"What are you going to do?" she asked, with a quick glance
of revulsion at the two men.

"That rather depends how much they value their miserable
hides."

Charity went without a backward glance. She found Harry

still sleeping and sat quietly beside him, feeling suddenly too exhausted to think. Eventually, Alistair reappeared.

"If you will not mind traveling in this carriage, John Gage will drive you home, and Theo will come with you to see you safely indoors and handle any explanations, should my father wish to hear them."

"And you?" she asked, suddenly apprehensive.

"A little unfinished business," he said, his face giving nothing away.

He had discovered something. She knew it with absolute certainty. "Don't," she implored him. "Whatever you may have found out, we are safe now. What does it matter who was responsible?"

"Hush," he said. "You'll wake Harry."

"I still think I should come with you," Theo said.

Alistair put a hand on his shoulder. "You're a good fellow, but I shall be all right. And I need to know that Charity and Harry are in safe hands."

The horses were rested and eager to be off again. Alistair drove fast, and was soon turning in between high gateposts. A short drive curved around to the front of a square manor house. There was an elderly gardener hoeing a flowerbed nearby. He glanced up incuriously, and Alistair summoned him to hold the horses.

He took the steps in two strides and pulled the bell, hearing somewhere in the distance a hollow clanging. Presently a manservant appeared. He seemed reluctant to admit the stranger and asked who he should say.

"I'll announce myself," Alistair said, brushing past him. "Just lead the way."

"I suppose I should be honored," drawled Sir Rupert from halfway up the stair. "Do come up, Ashbourne, now that you are in, and let me know what I may do for you."

"Oh, I think you know why I am here. You were expecting someone, though not me, I think."

Something in the tone of his voice made Sir Rupert regard him, eyes narrowed. Then he inclined his head and led the way into a large, richly furnished saloon on the first floor.

"Do I take it that certain matters . . . did not go according to plan? The lady got cold feet, perhaps?"

"Lady?" Alistair pounced on the word.

"Ah! that was careless of me." Sir Rupert's smooth manner was belied by a faint tick in his cheek.

"Such mistakes are apt to prove fatal. Do you mean to tell me the lady's name?" But even as he spoke, Alistair knew. He had a mental picture of Melissa talking intently with Sir Rupert at Lady Tufnell's ball, under the trees in the Park, and how many other times, he knew not. Melissa had been in the Park with Charity and Harry that very afternoon, but had escaped their fate . . .

"I see you have made the connection," said the suave, finicky voice. "It is really quite simple. Your bride to be, my dear Ashbourne, wanted everything, and those two stood in the way of her overweening ambition. Had Miss Wynyate not won the duke's favor, she might possibly have bided her time . . ."

Alistair could hardly trust himself to speak. "Did she come to you, or did you offer your services?"

"A little of both, I suppose. But there is a side to Melissa with which you are perhaps unfamiliar, encouraged, no doubt, in her youth by that wild brother of hers—demure on the surface, but underneath . . . well, I have always suspected, you know, that she must have been the kind of child who took pleasure in pulling the wings off flies."

"Enough!" Alistair would listen no more. "You will not save yourself by destroying Melissa's character. She will have to answer to me later for her part. But it was still you who planned and carried out the abduction of Miss Wynyate and my nephew, and it is you I now call to account."

"How melodramatic!" Sir Rupert was now pale, his forced smile at odds with the faint flicker of fear in his eyes. "And what is it to be—swords or pistols?"

"Either will suit my purpose, Darian. The choice is yours."

Sir Rupert's bow was infinitely polite. He walked across to a large cupboard and returned with a pair of fine dueling swords. "These, I think. They belonged to my father, and

I have often longed to try them in earnest." There was a hint of bravura in his smile. "We have crossed blades twice, you and I, and both times you have bested me. I have a fancy my luck is due for a change."

"Not if I can help it," Alistair said grimly.

In silence they pushed back the furniture, removed their coats and boots, and rolled up their sleeves. Sir Rupert asked with scrupulous politeness whether the fading afternoon light from the window was sufficient for their needs and received an abrupt nod. Finally, he offered Alistair the first choice of weapon, his teeth gleaming white, ". . . since they are mine. I would not have you think I took the least advantage."

Alistair withdrew the nearest sword from its sheath and found it beautifully balanced. He nodded curtly. They faced each other in silence and with only the briefest of salutes, the blades engaged, steel clashing on steel. Sir Rupert was fast, pressing hard in hope of a quick penetration of Alistair's guard, but his reactions were equally swift and only once, as he caught the blade high, forte on forte, did the point run along his arm, grazing it slightly. Again, Sir Rupert's teeth glinted white, but Alistair was not deterred.

Neither could remember when the animosity between them had sprung up—only that it had always been there, an instinctive clash of temperament fostered over the years by veiled insult and counterinsult which found expression now in action. Gradually, Alistair began to press his advantage, and Darian's thrusts became wilder; beads of sweat stood out on lip and forehead as he parried again and again.

"Did you mean to kill Charity and Harry?"

A gasping laugh was the only reply. His blade broke through the other's guard, lunged through his shirt, drawing blood, and withdrew. He repeated the question.

"What—do you think?" Sir Rupert's chest heaved with the effort. The swords clashed together, held, and disengaged. He knew he was being spared deliberately until he had answered to satisfaction. "But not until after your wedding," he panted, his only remaining triumph now to do as much damage as possible to the noble lord's pride. "M-Melissa worked it all out—hoped the shock might kill

your father!'' He made a last wild thrust in carte, which was
instantly parried in half-circle. His sword went spinning
away, and he staggered back against the table, the tip of
Alistair's blade resting against his throat.

"So much for luck!" he gasped, his heart feeling that it
would burst, the pain in his side a throbbing agony. He saw
Alistair's grim face through a mist of sweat and fear.
"Well . . . what are . . . you waiting for? For God's sake
man, end it!"

Alistair blinked the sweat from his own eyes as he stared
into the white face, stark with terror, saw the torn shirt
steadily oozing blood. For an instant he hesitated, then flung
his weapon aside and reached for his coat and boots.

"You aren't worth killing!" he said. "Just stay out of my
way in future."

19

The duke's household was in a state of shock.

Hamlyn had, in all innocence, delivered into his master's hands the letter given to him by Miss Wynyate, and was on the point of leaving the room when a sound like the bellowing of an enraged bull fell upon his ears.

The duke demanded an explanation, and upon learning that the letter informing him that she could no longer tolerate the gossip concerning her status in his household and that she had decided to take Harry and go away for a short while to consider her position, had been given to the butler by Charity herself on her way out for a drive with Miss Vane, his hurt found expression in a rage so awesome that even Parsons shrank into the background.

It was at the height of this peroration that a much shaken Hamlyn was summoned to the front door, where he found Mr. Trowbridge supporting Miss Wynyate, with John Gage just behind, carrying the unconscious Harry.

By the time Lord Alistair arrived, the doctor had been and gone, and both Harry and the duke had been put to bed, the latter under sedation having been shocked into near collapse by Theo's brief account of what had happened, and saved only by the doctor's reassurances that no lasting harm had been done and that Harry would make an excellent recovery.

Charity had refused to be sedated, and Alistair found her presently in the little saloon. She was sitting staring into the fire, and looked dejected, defenseless—and utterly weary. His distress found voice and instantly she was on her feet and running to him.

"Oh, my lord, you are safe!" And in the relief of seeing him still in one piece, she burst into tears.

His own weariness forgotten, Alistair's arms closed around her, crushing her to him. And then his lips claimed hers. Charity thought her heart would overflow with sheer joy, for this time there were no doubts; the fierce ardor of his kiss was proof enough.

"You love me!" she exclaimed huskily, betraying her wonder. "You really *do* love me!"

"My poor darling, of course I love you! I have been in love with you since that visit to the country, but I was too stubborn to acknowledge it then. You pricked my conscience, made me look at my own selfishness, and I wasn't sure I liked that. Also, I was jealous—of Fitz in the beginning, and then of, would you believe it, of my father. There seemed to be a bond between you that I resented."

"And there was Melissa," she said quietly.

"True. It was seeing the two of you together that suddenly made me recognize where my heart lay, but I could say nothing to you—I was committed to Melissa, and there seemed no way to resolve the situation with honor. Had I but guessed the half of what she was plotting . . ."

"Oh, please! I don't even want to think of that now!"

"No more do I." And later, "What a lot of time we have wasted," he murmured when she lay cradled against his chest, his arms fast about her. "But all that is at an end. From now on, I shall never let you out of my sight again—not ever!"

This had brought a tremulous laugh. "Not ever, my lord?" she echoed. "Might that not pose a few problems?"

For answer he kissed her again in a most thorough and satisfactory manner, and had continued to do so until she was dizzy with the intoxication of it, and relief dwindled agreeably into the gentle idiocy of love talk.

Much later, however, he did reveal the full extent of Melissa's treachery, and Sir Rupert's role in its enactment, and Charity shuddered to think how close she and Harry had come to death.

"Even so, I'm glad you didn't kill Sir Rupert," she said. Then, hesitantly, "And Miss Vane?"

"Melissa need not concern you," he said abruptly. "When I have done with her, I doubt London will see the Vanes for many a long day."

Mrs. Fitzallan came to see Charity, full of the wild speculation that was rife among the gossips following the notice that had appeared in the *Gazette* stating that the marriage between Lord Alistair Ashbourne and the Honorable Melissa Vane would not take place—by mutual consent. The announcement had been followed by the speedy departure from town of the Vanes.

"Such wickedness!" she exclaimed when Charity gave her a carefully expurgated version of what had happened, relating it as a mischievous ploy which had gone wrong, without any hint of its true horror. "Fancy trying to hurt you and little Harry in that way. One wonders how she could have hoped to succeed. But at least it has enabled Lord Alistair to release himself from her clutches!" She beamed at Charity. "Oh, my dear, you can have no idea how happy I am for you! And you may depend upon my absolute discretion—I shan't breathe a word. Let us hope a fresh scandal will soon emerge to take peoples' interest. Appropos of that, Fitz tells me that there are all kinds of rumors about Sir Rupert Darian in the clubs at present—he has been quite ill, it seems, and has gone abroad to recuperate. Such an odd man."

Charity wondered if Mrs. Fitzallan might be hinting at a connection, but she skillfully steered the conversation toward Mary, and tales of her latest beau soon occupied her mother's thoughts to the exclusion of everything else.

Harry was very soon himself again, and his natural exuberance did as much as anything to aid the duke's recovery. This was steady, but although he undoubtedly welcomed the news that Charity was to become his daughter-in-law, his brusque manner seemed to lack something of its former fire. Charity, who had once had more cause than most to fear his tongue, told Alistair sadly that he reminded her of an impotent old stag waiting for his time to die.

"Don't you believe it, dearest," he said. "Old stag or not, he will come about, you'll see. Meanwhile, I have a little unfinished business, and as you were in at the beginning of it, I think you should be there to witness its completion."

He took her hand and led her along to the large saloon where she had first met his grace—a whole lifetime ago, or so it seemed. The duke was sitting in the same chair, giving her an immediate sense of *déjà vu*.

"Sir," Alistair said with more trepidation than he had expected to feel. "I have a confession to make."

"Have you indeed?" The shaggy brows drew together, showing something of the old style. "Well, get on with it. It ain't like you to dither about."

"No," his son admitted wryly. "The fact is that since the first day Charity came here, I have been keeping something from you, and perhaps now is as good a time as any to rectify matters." He took a letter from his pocket and placed it in his father's hand. Charity recognized it at once and her heart leapt. "It is Ned's last letter, Father," he said quietly. "I didn't destroy it as you thought—I couldn't bring myself to do so. Instead, I burnt one of the other papers."

The duke sat immobile, staring at it. Charity willed him to say something, but he made no move. After a moment Alistair signaled to her that they should leave. "What you choose to do with it," he concluded, "is up to you."

It was late summer at Ashbourne Grange, and the events of May, if not forgotten, were at least beginning to fade from Charity's mind. It was impossible to dwell on them when there was so much happiness all around her.

As soon as Harry and his grace were fit to travel, they had all repaired to Ashbourne Grange, and she and Alistair had been married quietly in the village church, with only the family, Mrs. Bennett and the household staff, and Theo and Fitz to witness their union.

The sound of childish laughter drew her attention to the far edge of the trees. Alistair and Harry were coming back

from the river with their fishing tackle. Harry saw his grandfather sitting on the terrace, where he spent most days when
the weather was fine. They had never found out whether he
read Ned's letter, but Charity was privately convinced that
he had. She watched now as, after a word to his uncle, Harry
ran across the lawn and up the steps, where he could be heard
explaining to the duke how he had almost caught a trout
t-h-a-t big!''

Charity, with Emily in her arms, laughed and went to meet
her husband. Upon seeing her uncle, Emily made strenuous
efforts to be released, and when she was set down, set off
at a determined stagger to fling herself upon him. She was
already growing into a lively, precocious child—the very
image of her mother with her mass of bright golden curls.

''Uh!'' she demanded, tugging at the leg of his pantaloons.
And as he swung her up, she planted a kiss on his cheek.
Oh, yes, thought Charity, just like Arianne. ''She will break
hearts, that one,'' she observed with a smile.

''Incorrigible child,'' murmured Alistair in mock protest.
''I hope our own offspring, when they arrive, will prove
more conformable.'' And with his other arm possessively
about Charity's waist, they turned and walked up toward the
terrace.

Charity was smiling to herself at his words. Perhaps, she
thought, I will tell him tonight.

ROMANTIC ENCOUNTERS